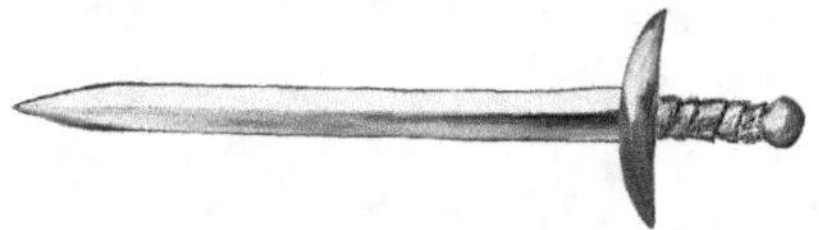

"I _failed_ you. We _all_ failed you... Failed the _Realm..._"
Adam's words were choked out.
"Failed _Genevieve._"

Damien's heart, still exhilarated from his run across the country and his reclamation of Farivera, stilled from its wild beat. He had known. In some part of himself he had *always* known what he was coming home to find.

"Tomas Elsevier has her hostage, does he?"

Adam nodded without raising his head. "Her and..."

"Jason."

Adam nodded again, eyes tightly shut, and with tears still leaking out. The Royal Guards he had brought with him down to the docks looked uncomfortably at this collapse of the stoically sarcastic man who had trained most of them. They were knights all and were not so far away from their days as squires under Adam's sharp eye.

"And the city is under siege?" Damien asked. He hadn't noticed any such thing as he ran down the surface of the rivers. But... he wasn't sure he *would* have, immersed in his magick as he had been.

"What need?" Adam whispered bitterly. "Without any Alsterling to hold it, what were we to do but follow Tomas' orders? With him holding..."

Damien's arms went around Adam.
"We'll fix it, Adam. Somehow... we'll fix it.""

THE UNCAPTIVE KING

Book Five of the Chronicles of Ilseador

(the Prydeen Prophecy Cycle)

MANGALA MCNAMARA

Also available in eBook and hardcover editions.
McNamara, Mangala
The UnCaptive King/ by Mangala McNamara Indiana: Rising Dragon Books, 2024
250 pages, 2 maps
(McNamara, Mangala. Chronicles of Ilseador; bk. 5)
Summary: Damien figured out how to escape Azella the Unpitying just as he realized his Realm and Queen are in mortal danger. Now he must try to return to Ilseador in time to save everyone from the demon Azella is sending to destroy them all.
ISBN 978-1-960160-65-2 (pbk)
1. Kings and rulers - Fiction. 2. Wizards and Magic - Fiction
ISBN 978-1-960160-66-9 (hc); ISBN 978-1-960160-64-5 (eBook)

ISBN: 978-1-960160-65-2
First Print Edition: November 2024
10 9 8 7 6 5 4 3 2 1

For my mother, who made all the worlds of religion, philosophy, fairytale, legend, magick, miracle, and wonder seem like a series of open doors just waiting to be explored and incorporated. She never stopped seeking for deeper truths and more real realities.

And for Piers Anthony, who inspired and encouraged me to write the stories that I needed to.

A note to sensitive souls:

Damien has come face to face with what it means to be tempted by a true mistress of the craft of Evil Wizardry... and now he has to figure out how to heal and move forwards.

Proceed with caution...

CONTENTS

And for your delectation:
An excerpt from Book One of the Chronicles of Ilseador:
The Rebel Duchess

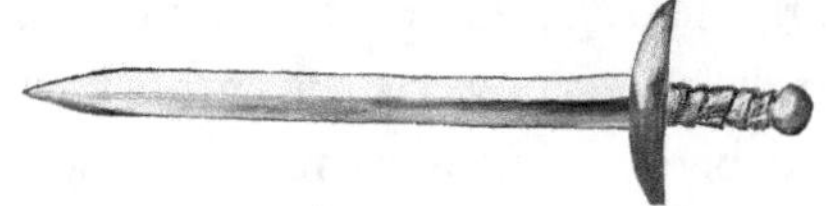

PROLOGUE

a reminder of what has gone before

DAMIEN ALSTERLING HAD COME TO the throne of Ilseador unprepared to rule.

And worse, *he* had known it, although no one *else* seemed to.

His friends and advisors, who had made the throne secure for him, seemed to think he was doing fine. His wife, Genevieve – the former Rebel Duchess – had taught him some of the finer points of governing that his grandfather and predecessor, the Evil Wizard tyrant Reginald the Ruthless, had kept from him, but she swore he had a talent and gift for the skills.

She reminded Damien constantly that the Monarch's Sword – the ancient blade that Chose the Realm's Heirs – had 'spoken' for him. And it was true, when he unsheathed it for the purpose of proving his right to the throne of Ilseador, the Sword would blaze up with a light like a coruscating rainbow in a dazzling display that half-blinded anyone watching.

*(Thank all the Gods at once that it didn't do that when he practiced with it. The thing was too important and precious to leave lying around and Damien could hardly carry **two** swords around everywhere. Nor would he be effective at being his own last measure of defense if he tried.)*

But Genevieve had ruled the sparsely populated mountain province of Elaarwen, where blood-feuds and avalanches were a bigger problem than the logistics of trade and finance. Ilseador's capitol city of Emeralsee was one of the larger cities in the known world. Elaarwen had been an ideal place to protect the nucleus of the Rebellion that had defied his grandfather's tyrannical rule, and his beautiful, soul-bonded bride was a capable strategist and general.

She was not, however, deeply versed in the complexities of multi-layered courts and sewage systems.

And even if she did know all those fine distinctions and details, Genevieve's skill at war had immediately been needed. Ilseador had five Lost Provinces to reclaim, after all – pieces of the Realm that had seceded to the allegiance of the neighboring lands, claiming asylum from Reginald. Damien would as soon have waited on that – were it not the will of both the people and the Land Itself, to which he was magickally Bound – that those places be won back.

Had he his choice, he would have kept Genevieve and her greater – although still incomplete – knowledge of governance by his side, both because he loved her and because he also needed an Heir.

He was the last – they had then thought – of the Alsterling line, after all. And now that they once again possessed the long-lost Monarch's Blade, it seemed unlikely that anyone but an Alsterling could actually claim the throne.

In his queen's absence, Damien learned to govern mostly by using his prodigious memory and rapid ability to assimilate new information. He read everything – every report, every message, every update casually sent in to the Royal Archives – and fit it all together in his own mind, finding patterns where others saw only chaos.

It was a method of desperation – he could only hope to outflank the pieces of information that were always, always, *always* missing from the whole.

And it was utterly exhausting, even without his other fearful obsessions:

First, that the magick which the Realm of Ilseador lent to him so profusely would fail him when he needed it most – in the attack of some other Evil Wizard, say. Damien had no one to teach him, after all. No way to learn how best to use what he had other than the secretive journals left behind by his grandfather.

And second… that he would *become* like his grandfather should he do more than lightly peruse those journals. Or perhaps even if he didn't.

Reading the journals – even as he feared them – became another obsession as Damien struggled to understand what had caused his grandfather – once a loving father and husband – to become evil… And how he might avoid that fate himself.

By five years in – and after ten traumatic, tragic miscarriages in the same length of time – Genevieve was near to dying and Damien with her, dragged down by their soul-bond.

Exhausted as he was, he would almost have been glad to give it all up – save for Genevieve and his sense of responsibility to the Realm.

In desperation, they turned to the prophecy which his grandfather's apprentice – Lord Prydeen – had made with his dying breath: that Genevieve could bear living children for Damien if only her first was sired by his Champion, Sir Jason Solway.

Eventually, Jason – and his long-time lover, Sir Adam Loveress, Captain of the Royal Guards – agreed to do that. They were the royal pair's closest friends and Damien's closest advisors and loved the king and queen both dearly.

The two knights had actually half-raised Damien, having discovered the orphaned prince hiding out in the Royal Library some four years after his parents had been executed in King Reginald's Throneroom at His Majesty's whim and word. Their loyalty was unimpeachable – secretly giving the king and queen a child was just one more sacrifice in a long line of such that they had suffered in their quest to see Damien to the throne.

Jason also, reluctantly, agreed to be temporarily Named Heir to the throne and a coronation was planned. In gratitude, Damien altered long-held Ilseadoran tradition to allow Jason and Adam to be wed.

In the ensuing months – as they all awaited Genevieve's recovery from her latest miscarriage such that she might risk another pregnancy – further complications arose. In order to protect the sickly queen from a too-early pregnancy, forced upon them by the unthinking demands of the soul-bond, Jason took Damien as a lover.

And then... just as Genevieve reached a point of health where they were all willing to take the risk... and in the immediate wake of the coronation-and-wedding...

... a terrible ice-storm smashed its way across the Realm, trapping most of the country's nobility in Emeralsee.

To handle the emergency, Damien taught his sworn vassals – the entire nobility of the Realm – to cast a barebones *compulsion* spell to send the people of the lands they were each Bound to under cover before the storm hit. And whilst they did that, he himself battled the storm directly.

Directly and – ultimately – futilely, though he managed to mute some of its fury on the farther western provinces. It hit Emeralsee hard, coating everything with several inches of ice and sealing everyone in the vast city indoors.

And worse... Damien had been able to determine that the terrible storm had been both *sent* and *called*.

Sent, presumably by mages from Deltheran, their neighbor to the west, where Genevieve had been 'negotiating' with Queen Estelle for the return of the Lost Province of Elendria. 'Negotiating' with the Ilseadoran army at her back and her reputation as a warrior and a strategist at the fore. It was the third such 'negotiation' – and the other two Lost Provinces had each come home without swords being unsheathed.

Deltheran was weeks' ride away, but the storm had been *called* to Emeralsee by a mage on what appeared to be an entire *fleet* of pirate-ships hiding behind the Cape that sheltered Emeralsee Bay.

A mage... or rather a sorceress.

Azella the Unpitying, she named herself when she caught Damien using his magick to aid his ice-trapped people.

And she said he would come away with her when she bade him and nevermind his duties to wife and land and the unborn child who was just bare days from conception.

It all came true, despite Damien's efforts to prevent it.

The pirates came in, nearly a thousand of them, ready to ravage. And with the aid of the sorceress and the *salamanders* she controlled, it seemed likely that Damien and the small force of nobles and knights he had with him in his castle wouldn't be able to stop them. An attack by Fire Elementals like salamanders and a Powerful, trained, and unscrupulous Evil Wizard were most of his darkest fears coming true.

However...

Azella offered Damien a bargain.

She would withdraw, taking with her the salamanders and her magick – though the pirates would remain.

If only he went away with her, back to her evil lair.

Damien didn't hesitate.

He gave the Monarch's Blade to his wife – it had 'spoken' for both Genevieve and Jason by then, Jason having been proven his command of the castle to their most experienced general – Duke Tomas Elsevier of Siovale, his trusted friend and his second sworn vassal after Genevieve herself.

And he gave over himself to the evil sorceress.

Who lived up to her word and withdrew, abandoning her pirate-allies.

The soul-bond allowed Damien and Genevieve to stay in contact, so he was aware that the pirates had withdrawn and Emeralsee and his Realm overall were slowly beginning to recover... until Azella pinched off the soul-bond and Damien's Binding to Ilseador both. *(Temporarily, at least with respect to his Binding to the Realm, it turned out, though it was months before he had been sure.)*

Azella took Damien back to her keep – on a stone promontory that had been artificially raised by magick on the very cusp of the border between Ilsedaor and its southern neighbor, Sindalla. And there she kept him, held high above and away from the living stone that would have let him re-connect to his Realm, tempting him with her body and offering him her love...

...and finally trading him knowledge for the opportunity to persuade him to stay.

Because the Evil Sorceress was, apparently, *lonely*.

Her goal was to convince Damien to fulfill his other remaining deep-seated fear and become an Evil Wizard himself, thence to extend his lifetime through foul means to be her eternal mate and partner. She wished, therefore, not to *break* him, but to *suborn* him, and she was willing to teach him all those things he had never learned in his solitary quest to learn about magick.

Damien was not such a fool as to believe that the insecure and ambitious sorceress would not turn upon him if she suspected him of even approaching her own Power. But he desperately needed the knowledge she had access to and embarked on his own plan to keep her... *entertained* until he had what he needed to defend the Realm, despite how the thought of dishonoring his marriage vows disgusted him.

But quite honestly, with his Binding to Ilseador pinched off, Damien really didn't have the Power to fight Azella.

The sorceress spent the Winter months teasing and teaching Damien. When he proved resistant to her own wiles, she sent one of her lackeys – an all-too-beautiful slave-boy named Mikhail – to him.

The boy had been bred for the use of Evil Wizards, Damien discovered to his horror. Mikhail's beauty and intelligence and well-designed sex appeal were difficult enough, but his curiosity and hopefulness were Damien's downfall. Even given direct and horrible evidence that the boy's seeming openness almost masked his... nearly-innocent evil and ambition to emulate his mistress, even then, Damien found himself falling for Mikhail.

He had no one else really close to being a friend in that dire place, after all, and his warm heart was desperately craving human contact. Nor had the line between *friends* and *lovers* ever been all that distinct for the king, dating back to when his advisors – Jason and Adam and a noblewoman named Ciriis Celavell – had decided to make sure their young prince would never be vulnerable to the wiles of the corrupt nobles of his grandfather's Court.

By the end of Winter, Damien – with his prodigious reading and memory – had managed to make his way through all of Azella's storehouse of wisdom in the ways of Elemental mages. It was largely wisdom which she had herself disdained, given that her own Power was that of a Siphon – she absorbed Power from all the things around her. This was usually a harmless thing to do, given that all living things emanated magick, but her natural abilities merely aided and abetted her in removing an overabundance of Power through death and torture.

Damien was an Elemental mage himself, with a strong affinity for Earth – but no particular barrier to being able to use all five of the magickal 'Elements.' *(Though at first, Azella refused to believe he could do that, having never heard of an Elemental mage with such breadth.)*

His bargain with the sorceress having expired – and his connection to the Realm, if not Genevienve, restored – Damien was ready to depart when Azella taunted him with the reminder that *she* could summon *demons*. All his vaunted Elemental magick – even supplemented with that of Ilseador, now that he again had that access – would do him no good if the sorceress could send demons against him.

And so, he had stayed to learn what he could of demons.

It had eventually become apparent that Azella would never really grant him access to her spells for demon-summoning. This, after all, was the base and center for her Power over the rest of the world, insofar as she chose to exert it.

Nevertheless, Damien kept studying, hoping to do as he had always done and find the missing parts of the pattern by noting the shape of the holes in what he *did* know.

And he explored her keep while he did so, meeting the slave-girl Denisa – bred for this, as had been Mikhail – whom Azella planned to use as a demon-sacrifice, and the numerous boys whom Azella also kept. Like Mikhail, the older boys – and even Denisa – thought only of becoming Evil Wizards themselves, should they have the opportunity to do so. The ambitions of the younger lads seemed less sharply formed.

Azella forbade him to see the younger boys after learning that the king had been speaking subversively to all of her slaves. She merely seemed amused at the idea that he could turn any of the older ones against her.

Damien was appalled to discover that even Denisa preferred her fate of living in comfort until 'the Mistress' required her death than to consider fleeing into the unsure world for freedom. Not that any of them were free to try – Azella controlled them all by the magick of their true-names.

Nonetheless, the king did his best to persuade them – or at least Denisa, and perhaps Mikhail – to change their minds. If he could only be sure that he would not be releasing a plague of young Evil Wizards upon his Realm and his neighbors, the king would have freed them from Azella himself.

For he had discovered what had been thought impossible – the way to defeat the Power of one's true-name being held by another.

Between that and the lack of progress in his studies in regards to demon-summoning, it was enough to make a man despair.

But as the day approached when Azella was planning to sacrifice Denisa, Damien realized that the *pull* of Ilseador was suddenly growing stronger. And not merely *stronger*, but that *pull* was making him recognize the shape of the *missing piece* that his strategist-wife had recognized was hiding some relevant and critical part of the ice-storm-and-pirate invasion of the previous Autumn.

And that missing piece was...

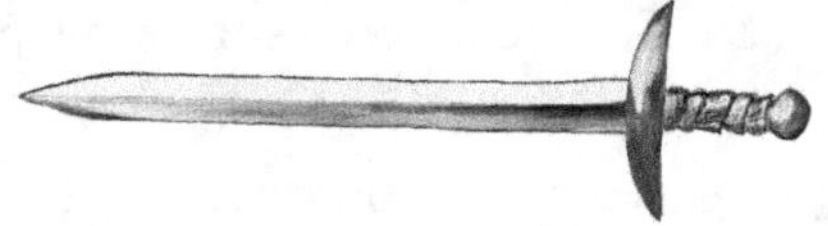

Chapter ONE

It's All in the Name

"*S*IOVALE*!*"

Damien surged up out of his comfortable spot on the bed, spilling Mikhail from his shoulder as he came to his feet in one smooth motion. The boy woke looking confused, then scrambled away as he saw the look of rage on the captive king's face. Unfortunately for him, there was only so far he could go, without coming up against the sorceress...

Azella woke with a great deal less drama at Damien's shout.

"You didn't just make *common cause* with Estelle in Deltheren. You plotted with *Tomas Elsevier.*" Damien's voice was now quiet with deadly fury.

The pale sorceress looked at him calmly, not bothering to so much as lift her head from the pillow.

"Duke Elsevier wanted Ilseador. *I* wanted *you.*" She smiled. "Queen Estelle wanted to rid herself of Elendria's special status and *your* irritating attempts to retrieve the province to your Realm. At least one of us got what she wanted." She stretched comfortably. "Oh, and I suppose Evan got his Megan. Though not his son or his crown. But after all, the crown could only go to *one* of my allies. And while my Master had made the initial contacts with the pirates and

Elseviers both, Duke Tomas seems like he'll be more useful to me in the future."

"Damien," Mikhail said fearfully, shrinking away, "You are *glowing.*"

The Sorcerer-King glared at the sorceress and her slave-boy both, then stormed away to the washroom to dress. His clothes – the single set that she had permitted him and that he had handwashed earlier this evening, as he did every night, then hung up to drip – were entirely dry and even neatly pressed in an instant. It wasn't even a spell – just the wisp of a thought – to set the clothing straight, now that his mind wasn't clouded and he had no reason to hide his Power.

On his return to the bedchamber, Damien picked up the pot-metal sword from where he had last left it, leaning scabbarded in a corner. He half-drew it, just so Azella would see the changes as they happened. Damien was an Earth mage first and foremost, and metal was Solid and therefore of Earth, even were it not extracted from rocks.

It would not match the Monarch's Blade, but he had a sword of sharpest, strongest steel now.

Azella tried to hide how impressed she was, but Damien was enough of an empath to know *that* as well. She narrowed her eyes as he stepped to the door.

"Where do you think you're going?"

The Sorcerer-King of Ilseador didn't bother to answer her.

He was *done* with this subterfuge.

Done with this keep.

Done with Azella the Unpitying.

But... perhaps... not *done* with Mikhail.

Damien looked at the beautiful boy, cowering naked in the bed.

"You may come with me if you so choose, Mikhail."

The boy's bright blue eyes flickered to his Mistress.

"Mikhail," Azella said. She had come up to a seated position, but still looked casual. "Use his name the way I taught you. Command him to kneel."

The boy looked fearfully from her to Damien, then pleadingly at the man. "Damien, I must obey her."

The King held out his hand. "Take my hand and I will protect you."

Mikhail's expression was skeptical. "You can't even protect *yourself* if I use your name."

Damien snorted. "That was a bluff. Try me."

Azella was beginning to look impatient. "Mikhail. *Dandelion.* Order him to come back here and make love to you. So I can watch." She gave Damien a long-lashed lascivious look. *"Again."*

Mikhail had wilted entirely at her use of what must be his true-name.

Damien gave her a disgusted look.

"Damien," the boy said pleadingly... but with fear and Power behind the name. "Do as she says. For both our sakes."

The Power found no grip on the Sorcerer-King.

He held out his hand once more as both youth and seeming-maiden gaped at him.

"Mikhail," he said again. "Take my hand."

Unbelievingly... *almost* unwillingly... the boy did so, crawling across the wide bed and off.

Damien smiled reassuringly at him. At least, he hoped it was reassuring, given that he was most certainly still *glowing* and had just terrified Mikhail by breaking what both the boy and his evil Mistress thought was one of the most fundamental rules of magick.

The dark-skinned lad looked... maybe not *reassured,* but perhaps... hopeful?

"How?" he asked as he put his hand in the older man's. "How did you break the Power of a true-name given away willingly?"

And, with a fearful glance at the sorceress. "Can you do it for *me?*"

Damien pulled him close, and was briefly overwhelmed by the astonishing beauty and native sensuality of the bred-youth. He settled for giving the boy a brotherly kiss on the forehead – he'd taken enough liberties with his marriage vows, whether or not it had been in the good cause of learning what weas needed to protect his wife and land.

The Sorcerer-King was aware that Azella the Unpitying was waiting to hear his answer as well. Doubtless it was only for the sake of hearing how Damien had done this that she had permitted Mikhail to seek his protection.

Not that it would do her any good.

"You must break it for yourself. By finding a name that is *more* true."

Mikhail frowned, but Azella looked thoughtful.

"Has there ever been a name that *felt* more like it described you? Accept it as your own, and you are free of the one given you at your birth," the King tried to explain.

Damien had struggled with this. His name described him very well, he felt. He *was* a 'Damien' all the way down to his toes... and it wasn't any *less* him, for all that he'd finally accepted that he truly *was* 'The Sorcerer-King of Ilseador, Defender of the Realm, Father of Giendra Marlerite Stellarine Alsterling.'

And if that was a ridiculously long name to encapsulate his inner self... it was no one else's business.

The boy was hesitant. "My wet-nurse called me *Jemmy*. The trainers called me *Jerry*. Those were both *almost* right..."

He seemed to want to say something, but his weirdly brilliant blue eyes were focused on the sorceress.

"You can say it aloud," Damien told him gently. "As you know, unless you *give* it to her – or anyone else – it gives them no Power over you just to know it." He gave Azella a withering smile. "Else our 'sweet lady' would not have needed *you* to try to control me."

"Jeremy," the beautiful youth breathed, and... *something*... seemed to come into him as if he suddenly took a breath of air for the first time.

His first breath of *freedom,* Damien realized.

The King released Jeremy from his arms and stepped back.

"What you do is up to you now, Jeremy. You may come with me and I will protect you. But I will tolerate no breath of evil in my Realm. This keep..." He looked at the still-silent Azella. "This keep lies at the very pale of my demesne, neither clearly mine nor Sindalla's. I am quite certain that both this lady and her Master before her have been quite careful to perform their evil wizardries well above the living stone that is still part of Farivera and thereby avoid attracting my attention – and that of my predecessors."

The sorceress looked at him languidly.

"The location was convenient," she admitted. "Though the Siovalese Dukes have been importuning us for long years and even ceded Farivera to us for our own uses."

That... was disturbing, but perhaps not unexpected. Now, anyways.

Damien would not allow his heart to break over this. He had trusted Tomas... Dear Gods, Duchess Sildra was Zachary Miramar's elder *sister.* And how *many* of the Elsevier children had ended up staying on in the capitol after the wedding as pages and squires and even ladies-in-waiting to Genevieve?

"Come, Jeremy," he said. "It's time I was going."

Jeremy looked at her fearfully still. "Mistr– Lady, you will let me go with no outcry?"

Azella smiled, and it was *not* a gentle expression.

"Neither of you will be leaving, my *Dandelion.*"

The boy cringed, and trembled, though the name clearly had less Power over him than before. Accepting a new name was not instantaneous, as Damien well-knew... and in his own case he had not needed to entirely give up his old one, merely make it Powerless over him.

"You may *try,* of course," she added. "Doubtless breaking you to my will shall be entertaining. I have a demon-Summoning to prepare for after all. And in the end, *Jeremy,* you will *give* this name to me as well."

The boy began to tremble and looked pleadingly at Damien again.

The Sorcerer-King of Ilseador (etc.) held out his hand again. "My offer is still open."

"A normal length life," Jeremy asked, quaveringly. "And to grow old?"

Damien nodded. "But free. To make your own choices. To bring joy to others. To find love."

"It's all lies," Azella told the boy. "As you'll see for yourself when I break *him* as well. His great love? His soul-bonded *wife?* He has taken other lovers *of his own free choice.* And he was willing to throw her over entirely for *me.*"

Jeremy's eyes went to Damien in confusion.

The Sorcerer-King nodded. He couldn't deny the truth of her words, after all. Though he might argue that *free choice* had never been a part of his life in that or any other matter.

"Though all of it – *all–*" and he let his gaze rest, coolly, on the naked sorceress to make it clear that whatever *personal* charms she had had never interested him, "–has been to protect her and my Realm. Had Azella been willing to give up Evil Wizardry to marry me, I would have given up all I hold dear to know that I had ended the threat she poses. And I would have given her all the love that was mine to bestow and never looked at another again."

He let his smile grow. "Fortunately, she delayed and denied me until it was no longer necessary for me to make such a sacrifice."

The first flicker of uncertainty crossed the sorceress' blue-grey eyes.

"You won't make it out of the keep," she said again. "And even if you do, there is nowhere I cannot find you – both." She cast a dark glance at Jeremy, who cowered before her.

But she'd expressed just the slightest hint of uncertainty in whether she could hold onto him... *them.*

Damien snorted. "Lady, if I do not roust *you* out of this fell place and claim this *margin* for Ilseador, be grateful."

He turned towards the door, and felt a desperate hand grasp at his own.

The path out of the keep would have been shorter if Damien had not diverted to try to find Denisa and the younger boys – but they were not where he expected them, and he had not the time to waste. Now that the pieces of the puzzle had fallen together, now that he *knew* that Tomas of Siovale was Genevieve's missing piece, the Realm was urgently calling him home.

The massive black doors at the entrance to the seldom-used entrance hall opened at his touch, and he stepped out onto the windswept rock of the high promontory. Jeremy still trailed hesitantly behind, still clinging to Damien's hand. They had paused to get the clothes the boy had used during arms-practice, so he was no longer naked. But it was far warmer inside the keep and Jeremy shivered in the gusts of a wind that spoke to Damien only of freedom.

A howl of sylphs sang over his head, nearly lifting Damien up to celebrate that freedom as the Sorcerer-King raised an arm to them.

Almost there... this promontory was nominally part of Farivera, but it was still an unnatural outcropping. It had been birthed of the ancient sorcerer's need for a hidden space between the edges of Realms that traditionally had Bound and Crowned sovereigns that should otherwise have been able to *feel* what might have gone wrong. Ilseador had lost touch with Sindalla some time ago – decades, if not centuries. Last Damien had heard, the country had reverted to being inhabited only by warring tribes; perhaps the Sindallese no longer had the kind of protection that such a Monarch could provide.

Nor would his own Ilseador, if he abdicated in favor of an elected Council, Damien realized at last, despite his own wishes and prior attempts to yield up his secular power. A King or Queen who was Bound to the Realm but had no temporal power over its population would quickly become less able to serve the needs of the Realm... And given how very *much* magickal Talent lay hidden – and perhaps recently revealed – in the noble families of Ilseador, it only begged for another King Reginald the Ruthless to emerge. Another tyrant Evil Wizard, either home-grown or invading.

There must be some middle ground. Some happy place of perfect balance where the Will of the People kept the monarch from excesses and tyranny... but where the Strength of the Monarch served as sword and shield for the people.

And for the land – the plants and animals, the rocks and the life that was too small to be seen.

This was not the time to sort it out.

"Jeremy," he turned to the boy, still clinging so tightly to his hand. "We part ways here."

The boy's bright blue eyes – so incongruous in comparison to that mahogany skin and below those tight, golden-yellow braids – looked at him in fear and confusion. "What have I done wrong?"

Damien smiled at him, but his attention was with his Realm, and it was pulling him far, far away. "Nothing at all, lad. And you are most welcome to follow me. But I need to go faster than you can."

"I can go fast," Jeremy quavered. "I'm strong."

"The Realm will sustain me," Damien explained. "It can't do the same for you. Not... as fast as I need to go, anyways. If you stay in my footsteps, you'll be safe from Azella. The Realm knows I want you protected."

"What is this *Realm* you keep talking about?" Jeremy demanded, not releasing his hand.

Damien knew it was a delaying tactic.

He needed to go... to *move*... That internal Fire that gave him his insatiable curiosity, that made him pace... that was going to feed him on this harrowing journey.

But he had promised Jeremy freedom and protection both and he could take a little time to soothe the boy's fears. Or to try to, anyways.

"The Realm is the Soul of my Land. The Aether of Life that evolves from all that Which Is and has consciousness, from the soil and rocks to the birds, the trees, the humans... the other-than-humans. It Chose me to be its Guide and Guardian. Its Healer. As It Chose my ancestor so long ago, when humans became such a Powerful force in the world. And the Realm has husbanded my Line through all these centuries and millennia. Right now... it knows that the Line is threatened, and I m*ust go.*"

Damien's eyes were being dragged to the north... he wrenched them back to look at the confused youth.

"Stay in my footsteps," he said again. "You will have everything you need. But I must reclaim Farivera – and Siovale – and I cannot do that the whiles I take you with me. I cannot run as fast while bringing you."

Now Jeremy looked entirely alarmed.

"So, you really will *leave* me? To the Mistress' not-so-tender mercies? You promised to *protect* me! And... and... how can you run so *far?* Damien," he looked askance at the King's feet. "You did not even put on your boots! You are barefoot!"

The Sorcerer-King of Ilseador simply didn't have time for this. His bare feet itched with the need to run, to Heal the breach between Farivera and the rest of the Realm that still oozed magick and misery... and to *go home* to Emeralsee. There was... *something* there that threatened his unborn daughter's life and well-being.

His daughter's... and possibly also Genevieve and Jason's? Were they not the other possible Heirs to the Realm? Not that the baby and Genevieve were exactly separable at this point in time...

"In my footsteps you will be perfectly safe. The Realm knows I have claimed you for Ilseador." Damien wriggled his fingers out of the boy's tight grasp and handed him the newmade sword. "You know how to use this well enough to protect yourself from non-magickal dangers. I'd stay to guide you myself, but I *must go*. I must go *now.*"

And The Sorcerer-King of Ilseador, Defender of the Realm, Father of Giendra Marlerite Stellarine Alsterling, began to run. Barefoot along that unnatural outcropping of rock as it bent to the west, dipping down to meet the Fariveran plain from which it had been drawn up so long ago.

Jeremy stood watching, arms wrapped around himself. He was not a runner, having spent all his life in enclosed spaces, so perhaps he did not understand the more-than-human speed with which the King ran.

But if he had wondered how he would identify Damien's footsteps to follow him in promised safety he could do so no longer: every place where the King's foot had stepped, be it the smoothest of solid rock, burgeoned with grass and wildflowers, spreading to merge into one long trail even as the boy watched... a ribbon of green disappearing into the distance and the gathering twilight...

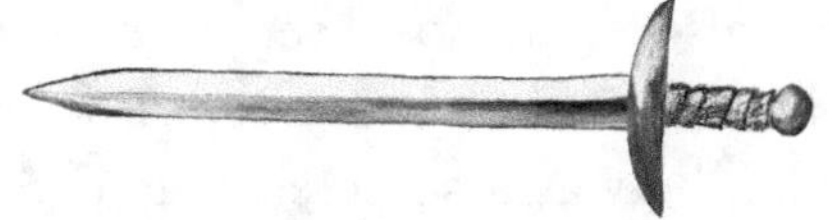

Chapter TWO

The Long Way Home

D AMIEN HAD NEVER GIVEN HIMSELF up to the Realm in quite this way before.

He felt filled with Life, with Energy, with... Connection. He'd thought he was connected to every life in the Realm before – but those connections had almost always been made in the Castle, which focused all the magick, concentrating it through the Throne-room and the Throne into a single, white-hot point. In time of need, it could be focused even *more* tightly, using Damien as a conduit, into the Sword.

Which Alsterling ancestor had been the architect of all of that he had yet to discover.

It was effective – almost *too* effective, as he had reason to know, the Realm through the Throne having tried to devour him more than once in its desperate yearning to have him join with it more fully. Only just as desperate efforts by his soul-bonded wife had been able to save him from being so devoured.

Damien had no idea how his grandfather and earlier ancestors had managed, there not being a soul-bonded King or Queen of Ilseador recorded for some two hundred years before him. But Queen

Marian, his great-great-grandmother and his predecessor-but-one, had not had the mage-Talent to be a sorceress, though the Sword had spoken for her and – through whatever will or stubbornness – she had remained in Emeralsee as a ghost ever since.

And the Sword had never spoken at all for Damien's grandfather, King Reginald, though he was a sorcerer. Reginald had never been Bound to the Realm, though he had managed to tap into a great deal of Its Power.

Compared to using the Throne and the Sword, contacting the Realm through his bare feet was an entirely different experience for Damien.

It was – *buoying,* not *suffocating.* With every stride, he felt *rejuvenated.*

And... *Farivera* seemed to rejoice as he ran over it.

Was it Tomas, or his father, Duke Hector Elsevier, who had ceded the County to the Evil Wizards in their dark keep at the southernmost edge of the Realm? Or even earlier?

Farivera soaked up the contact with Damien and gave him back its... *love* was the only word he could think of that fit. It had missed him ... or not *him* exactly, but the Bound member of his Line. It had never been the right of the Elsevier family to give it away. The Alsterlings *belonged* to Farivera – to the *Realm.*

Damien was dimly aware that Spring followed in his footsteps. The ground was waking as he ran over it. He was almost oblivious to the humans in the land; by comparison to the plant and animal and soil life they were almost inconsequential, sparse and disconnected.

The rest of the Realm beckoned him home, but Farivera needed him so badly *right now...*

At some point, Damien became aware that he was climbing, but the Realm beckoned him on and through the mountain-pass that led into Siovale proper. The air was thinner, cooler. It was like going backwards in the year, to an earlier phase of Spring. Warmer air followed him, trees and grass wakened at his passing.

And then he was heading down again, racing along beside laughing streams and feeling the very rocks leap to full awareness at his touch.

He had never been so *happy,* so *complete...*

The plains of Siovale beckoned him, the foothills giving way to the broad open grasslands with their neat farms. The Eldalla River called to him, suggesting he run beside it for its ecstatic joining with the Emerald; the combined river, that emptied into Emeralsee Bay was still called the Emerald, but it was just as much the Eldalla... and just as much Ravencreek coming in from near his grandparents' holding, or the Rock River that meandered across the plains of Reyensweir.

It was only humans that made these distinctions, these names.

The Realm was one.

The broad expanse of plains *one*.

The waters sourcing from different areas... but still, essentially and crucially *One*.

Damien avoided the roads made by humans. He needed the feel of the land. He *was* the Land.

Humans – they were less sparse than in Farivera, but still more thin on the ground than any other form of life. He knew he was heading home to Emeralsee, where the greatest concentration of humans was, but even there, the other forms of life so far outnumbered and out*massed* them that he was hardput to identify humans. Easier to follow the rivers than to try to sort out humans from among all the other Life.

He was on the west bank of the Eldalla, however, and could not follow along the banks to head east towards the rivermouth in the Bay.

It wasn't a problem. The rivers were as much a part of the Realm as the land. Damien ran lightly along the surface of the waters. He knew somehow that he could have run along the river*bed* just as easily, but some wisp of awareness that his people – his *human* people – were marking his passage, and needed very much to *see him,* kept him atop the water instead.

And suddenly he was in the Bay.

The Sorcerer-King of Ilseador, Defender of the Realm (and Father of Giendra Marlerite Stellarine Alsterling) came to a halt, standing on the surface of the waters of the Emeralsee Bay.

Somehow, he had thought the docks would still be empty. The pirates had burned a number of storm-ravaged ships that had been moored there... and the icing over of the Bay had surely foundered many more.

But the piers were busy now, ships sailing in and out of the mouth of the Bay.

And the docks were filled with day-laborers, sailors, fishwives...

Eyes, ogling him from all directions.

Nothing he wasn't used to, for all that it had been months since he'd had crowds to stare.

Damien waved genially, and strolled off the waters.

It *almost* came off without a hitch. Except that as soon as he touched the manmade structure of a pier, the support of the Realm disappeared and he found himself floundering in the chill, salty water, soaked from head to toe. Rescued by confused dockworkers, none of whom recognized their king.

Apparently, a full beard really *was* an effective disguise for a man.

They wrapped him in blankets and listened to his tale, looking at each other dubiously. On the one hand, this fluffy-bearded fellow looked nothing like their neatly barbered young king. On the other, they'd just seen him walk across the water of the Bay, and everyone knew the King had strange powers.

The *rats* of Emeralsee, it might be noted, had no doubts, and came up to greet him and fill his mind with their complaints and joys. There being none but the King who might seem so pleased to be surrounded by a carpet of the magickally golden-furred, green-eyed rodents that shouldered the humans out of the way... and who would sit there seeming to listen to the rats and nodding thoughtfully on occasion... Someone finally decided to send word to the Castle.

"Damien!" It was Sir Adam Loveress – Damien's tall former Captain of the Royal Guards and current Champion – who came to him there at last and, without any regard for proprieties – or rats – strode forwards and lifted his king and friend and former protegée and... former other things... up into a fierce embrace.

"I'm home, my Champion," Damien said gently. "But... you might want to set me down. There's a... rather lot of people watching."

To his surprise, Adam set him down, standing, then fell to his knees weeping before the King.

"Adam, what's wrong?" Damien reached down to try to get the Champion to rise, but ended up kneeling before him. Adam was a good four inches taller than was the king himself, and he had the musculature of a man who had been practicing the sword daily since childhood vigorously enough and with such skill as to be named King's Champion.

"I *failed* you. We *all* failed you... Failed the *Realm...*" Adam's words were choked out. "Failed *Genevieve.*"

Damien's heart, still exhilarated from his run across the country and his reclamation of Farivera, stilled from its wild beat. He had known. In some part of himself he had *always* known what he was coming home to find.

"Tomas Elsevier has her hostage, does he?"

Adam nodded without raising his head. "Her and..."

"Jason."

Adam nodded again, eyes tightly shut, and with tears still leaking out. The Royal Guards he had brought with him down to the docks looked uncomfortably at this collapse of the stoically sarcastic man who had trained most of them. They were knights all and were not so far away from their days as squires under Adam's sharp eye.

Adam and Jason had been a pair nearly as long as some of those young men had been alive.

And though they surely all knew that the Queen was pregnant... they wouldn't know the child had been sired by Jason and that therefore Adam would see the babe as his own child. Adam and Jason hadn't yet been wedded a half-year...

"And the city is under siege?" Damien asked. He hadn't noticed any such thing as he ran down the surface of the rivers. But... he wasn't sure he *would* have, immersed in his magick as he had been.

"What need?" Adam whispered bitterly. "Without any Alsterling to hold it, what were we to do but follow Tomas' orders? With him holding..."

Damien's arms went around Adam. "We'll fix it, Adam. Somehow... we'll fix it."

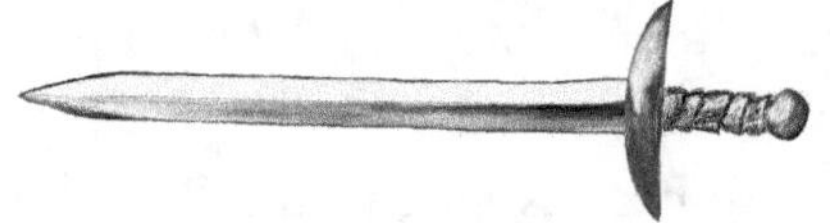

Chapter THREE

A Crisis of Conscience

"IT'S NOT YOUR FAULT," DAMIEN said firmly. "Not *any* of your faults. The Elseviers have been conspiring with the evil wizard at the far end of Farivera for a long time. They *gave over* the County to the wizard."

He'd had to deal with one weeping, guilt-ridden friend and subordinate after another and had finally rounded everyone up in the Throne-room. It was the only place large enough to hold the crowd.

Most of them still wouldn't look him in the eye.

With a sigh, Damien walked up onto the dais and – as Adam suddenly noticed what he was doing and voiced a wordless cry of protest – sat down on the Throne. He and the Realm had come to a different understanding.

"Yes, Sir Loveress?" Damien asked, raising one eyebrow.

"You said... without Genevieve..." Adam's eyes narrowed. "You've changed."

Damien gave him a wry look and nodded, then let the Power of the Realm come up into him from the Throne. The spell he cast was one of Aether – a Healing for all the broken, guilty hearts in this room. Including, he had to admit, his own.

"If there is blame to be awarded," the Sorcerer-King of Ilseador addressed the crowd of Royal Guards, both Secret and not; squires and pages; friends and advisors; Castle Guards and Castle servants.

"*If* there is blame to be awarded," he emphasized, "then the lion's share must surely fall to *me*.

"*I* forgave Duke Tomas his part in the Rebellion, which was of his own free choice, and *I* forgave him his part in his half-brother's usurpation, which was magickally compelled. *I* Bound him to his lands – as I have done all my vassals – and to the good of his people and Siovale.

"*Not* to *me*."

Damien nodded ironically to Adam. "I was warned – later – that this might not have the results I hoped for. But I would *still* rather see each of you the master of your own conscience, those of you who have your own holdings, or look to inherit them."

He nodded at Sir Tim, Adam, a handful among the pages and squires.

"Now. We *are* going to solve this. We *are* going to get the Queen and the Crown Prince back. We *are* going to set to rest this newest rebellion. I need you to do what each of you can do best to help us reach those objectives. Whether it is studying," he nodded at the pages and squires, "guarding," his Royal and Castle Guards, "or ensuring that the rest of us are fit to do our jobs," the Castle servants.

"We do neither the Queen nor Prince Jason any good by wailing and bemoaning and assigning blame. I tell you again, it is on *my* heart and conscience.

"See that you do not seek to usurp *my* privilege and *my* obligation."

The King nodded sharply.

"Sir Loveress, Sir Ancellius, Lady Aryllis, Lord David, Madame Elista, Lady Alanna, Miss Marianna, Lord Aaron... and Lady Elaina, Lord Roger, and Lady Esmerelda. I will see all of you in the Council Chamber in an hour. Lady Aryllis, please let the Royal Councilors know that I will meet with them after that, briefly, before dinner."

Damien stood and strode out of the Throne-room, heading for his own chambers.

Adam fell into step beside him. A pair of Royal Guards preceded them and another pair trailed. Damien supposed it was unlikely that he would be able to reduce the presence of Guards around his person for the foreseeable future given the events of the last six months.

"You really think we can get them back?" Adam asked, his voice ragged with exhaustion and grief as he followed the King into the royal suite and sealed the heavy door behind them, automatically adding in the magickal latches against eavesdropping that Damien had placed there years ago.

Damien didn't answer right away. "What day is today?" he asked instead.

Adam frowned. "Why?"

The King gave him a dry look. "Humor me."

"It's two days before the Vernal Equinox," Adam answered, looking baffled and irritated on top of everything else.

Damien laughed aloud. "Yes, Adam. We're going to get our loves – and our *baby* – back."

"What did that have to do with the date?" Damien's amusement was certainly not shared.

The King stepped close to his second-oldest friend – the secret empath who had recognized the half-feral child hiding in the library and turned him into a king – and put his arms around the older, taller man in a reassuring embrace.

"Because I just *ran* across half the Realm barefoot. In *two days*. Without *noticing.*"

Adam seemed to notice Damien's lack of footwear for the first time and his face grew aghast. The habit of looking after the younger man was still strong, even after all these years and it was surely only his own exhaustion and heartache that had kept him oblivious to those bare feet for so long.

"Last I knew, you could barely *stand*. What do you mean you *ran...*" His voice trailed off, and he stared at his king as the words sank in. "Dear Gods, Damien, what happened to you this Winter?"

"I grew up." The dark-haired man sighed. "And... I grew into myself. In more ways than one."

Finally.

"Nice to see you, too, Grandmother," Damien told the ghost of Queen Marian.

This lad has been doing a more than fair job of coping since my other grandchildren were tricked away. But he needs about three days in bed. And he's not the only one.

"That's actually my top priority," Damien answered. "People don't think straight when they're this tired."

Adam had slumped into a chair. "I don't know how you manage all this. And I've *watched* you cope with all of this. I've *helped* you cope with all of this."

"I have some extra resources," his King replied dryly.

I kept telling him that. He wouldn't listen.

Adam flashed a look of irritation in the ghost's direction. "I didn't have *time* to sort out a new way to do everything."

Damien blinked in surprise. "You can see Queen Marian? And hear her?"

"To my sorrow, yes," Adam replied sardonically, but at least that sounded a bit more like himself.

The ghost Queen rolled her eyes. *He's my grandchild by marriage now.*

Adam snorted.

Damien laughed and headed into his bedchamber to wash up and change into something more regal – or at least less suggestive. Azella's choices for him were not, perhaps, the best for maintaining the respect of his subjects.

And possibly to shave. He still wasn't sure why the sorceress had permitted him neither scissors nor shaving supplies, and she had limited his contact with others as much as possible, which had meant no barber. She hadn't seemed to like his beard at first... perhaps it had been the novelty, compared to her *khareem* of beardless slave-boys.

There might be some value in keeping the full, curling, fluffy beard for awhile at least. He'd grown out the small, trim one a couple years ago in hopes of looking older than the twenty-four years he'd had when he was crowned. Old men and women hadn't been inclined to take him seriously despite the crown on his head. The trim little beard had helped, but this luxuriant tangle would surely do even more in that way – and it was going to take time he didn't have to transform it into something more elegant.

Time... and probably a skilled barber. And possibly a consultation with his wife, who should have at least some say. Genevieve had grown up around her bushy-bearded Elaarwen men, but she was used to his trim little beard. Or, um, Jason's smooth-shaven cheeks.

Damien decided not to think about that.

Much better to think about how much he wanted to kiss his beautiful wife. And more than *kiss* her. More than kiss her in as many places and ways as...

This was also not a productive line of thinking, Damien realized as his... *heart* began throbbing with his need for her. His heart and... *other* parts. It was only Azella's pinching off of his soul-bond to Genevieve that had made it possible for him to be parted from her for so long...

Two days until the Vernal Equinox. The dark of the moon would be about a week later. That gave him nine days before Azella was likely to strike in retribution.

The Sorcerer-King had always assumed the pale sorceress would retaliate against his departure. Simply letting him go would make her look weak before underlings and rivals both, after all, and she was neither so Powerful, nor so secure in that Power, that she dared permit such. He guessed that he'd simply moved too swiftly – literally – for her to respond so far.

And now... Azella might be distracted and using up her resources to try to reclaim Jeremy. If the boy had the sense to stay on the trail Damien had left for him, the Realm should protect him without any further intervention by its Bound and Crowned King. Azella probably wouldn't even be able to identify *where* on that trail he was, unless she could somehow get physical eyes on him... or unless she had the Gift of the Seeing Eye, as did Jason.

Or unless she had an underling whose Seeing Eye she could use... as he had himself done with Jason.

Even if the pale sorceress did have access to the Seeing Eye... the trail Damien had left for Jeremy wound back and forth all over Farivera. He hadn't sped over *every* acre of Fariveran soil, but he'd come close and the new growth outwards from the path was filling in the parts he hadn't touched. The Sorcerer-King doubted that, even if *all* her remaining slave-boys had the Seeing Eye, Azella could survey the thousands and thousands of acres that the green growing plants in his path had now covered in Farivera.

Yes, Damien *hoped* she was wasting her resources searching for Jeremy – he'd hoped to free Denisa and at least the younger boys in part to add to her confusion and dismay... as well as for the hope that they would be worth it in their ownselves, if given the choice. But he'd be a poor chess player indeed if he hadn't anticipated other possibilities.

The Sorcerer-King *knew* Azella wouldn't come after *him*, personally, until she had her greatest Powers available.

Which meant the night of moon dark.

Which meant she'd be sending a demon.

Or more than one, though he knew she'd only been preparing to summon a single demon.

Damien wished he could feel Genevieve through the soul-bond, but their connection was still pinched tightly closed.

He wanted to tell her that he was home and well. He wanted to know how she was doing... and the baby... and Jason.

He wanted to tell her that in nine days he would come for her.

Damien emerged from his washroom, clean and dressed, to see Adam and Queen Marian bickering amiably. Adam looked and sounded much more like his usual self, if one ignored the tightness of his posture, the dark circles under his eyes, and the several-day stubble of beard.

The sight of the two of them amused Damien. The ancient ghost-Queen had become visible and audible to Jason just before the wedding and his installation as Crown Prince and Duke of Emeralsee when his heritage as an Alsterling was revealed so dramatically. Adam had been the only one left of Damien's closest advisors – now that Ciriis was gone – to be left half-out of the conversations.

And perhaps now the wicked old woman would cease her suggestive comments if Adam could hear them also.

*What, and give up the chance to make you **both** blush?*

He'd forgotten that she had some ability to read his unspoken thoughts.

Mischievously, Damien made himself think wistfully of the four months he had spent with *only* an evil sorceress attempting to listen in to his thoughts... rather than a well-meaning old busy-body with too much time on her ghostly hands...

Well, I never!

But the ghost-Queen's smile at him was genuine and not at all offended. Relieved, rather.

"So, Adam," the King began casually, "Where's my Sword?"

Adam's face fell again.

"So, it's in Tomas' hands?" Damien surmised.

"As best we can tell. Genevieve took it with her. We think."

Damien raised an eyebrow. "There's quite a story there, I think. But it's almost time to meet everyone. Did I pick the right group to get all the pieces?"

Adam sighed. "You did. I don't know how, but you did."

"I just looked for the guiltiest-looking faces," the dark-haired man told him. "And a few others for support, like David. Not that I think any of you have a reason to feel guilty," he added quickly. "But it was the group most likely to think they did. Which means they – you – know more about what happened than the rest."

He gave Adam a wry smile. "*You* taught me to be observant, Adam."

His Champion and former... *mentor* nodded heavily. "So, I did. Praise all the Gods it was just a matter of pointing out how much you were missing by only keeping your nose in a book." He snorted slightly.

Damien offered the taller man a hand to heave himself out of the chair and pulled him into another tight embrace. "I always felt you were the one who should have the Heir's coronet, Adam. You've done well. And we'll get them back. I promise."

Adam still felt strung tighter than bowstrings, but Damien could feel some slight release in his friend's body. He didn't believe, yet, but he was willing to *try* to believe. Or to hope, anyways.

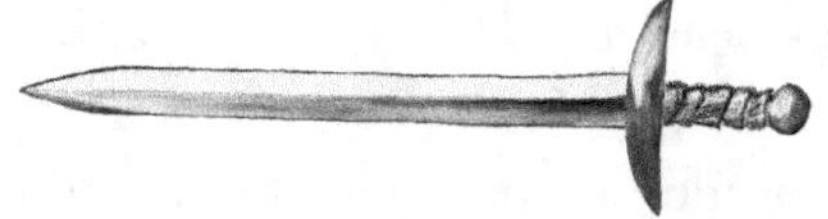

Chapter FOUR

A Council of Crisis

THE SMALL COUNCIL THE KING had called to catch him up on the kidnapping of his wife and his Heir had all settled in by the time he arrived with Adam. Most of them struggled to their feet with those guilty expressions. Notably, Lord David did not, leaning back instead with an ironic look on his face.

Damien decided to turn things on their ear and ask a different question that he did truly want the answer to than the ones that they were expecting. "David, have you heard anything with regards to Megan?"

The foreign merchant-prince, who had made Ilseador his home for the sake of his love for Lady Megan Solway, gave him an appreciative look, both for the question and for how the King was using it. "No. But I have the fleet out searching."

The Metreedi merchant fleet, obviously, not Ilseador's ice-damaged navy.

They both knew how unlikely it was that Megan would be found. Everyone knew that the pirates had their own secret islands where they kept their non-combatants... but keeping that archipelago secret was the one thing that *every* pirate agreed upon. Captured buccaneers had been known to commit suicide before giving up even a clue.

"I noticed a lot of merchantmen in the harbor," Damien nodded. "You've been as good as your word about bringing in resources to help the Realm recover, I take it."

David bowed his head, but Damien went on before he could say anything else.

"I thank you for doing so even while dealing with Megan's kidnapping and helping your children," he nodded at Elaina, Roger, and Esmerelda, "We'll talk about those recovery efforts more later. I want you to join the Royal Council."

David looked startled and pleased, but Damien was already looking around at the rest of the room. "But for now I want to hear about what happened to Genevieve and Jason."

"Who is *also* my stepson," David murmured pointedly. Elaina gave her father a furtive look and the younger two just looked scared, but Damien nodded.

"I'm sure he appreciates knowing that you think of him so, David," the King told him. "Certainly, *I* would rather have you for a father than Evan Eldridge Alsterling."

"Or as a father-in-*law*," Adam agreed quietly.

David and the Champion exchanged ironic nods. Apparently, they had come to their own understanding in the months the King had been gone.

"So," Damien leaned forward on his elbows, propping his chin on his folded hands. "What happened? Genevieve told me the pirates had withdrawn the day after I left... and then the sorceress pinched off our soul-bond to where nothing else could come through."

Adam winced at that thought, but it was Lady Aryllis, his Spymistress and therefore a person who knew every last detail as well as the big picture, who answered.

"We got the city defrosted with the help of the Army – mostly by chipping the ice away bit by bit, some by starting coal-fires in the streets to melt more. As soon as possible, the various nobles started leaving to go home and see to their provinces. That was a couple of days after you... left. Tomas Elsevier sent Duchess Sildra and little Gemma and Gary home to coordinate the assistance Siovale was to send to Reyensweir, but he and the older four children all stayed."

Interesting in and of itself. Mark was Tomas' Heir and surely old enough to stand in for his father. And even Arabella was old enough to be of use in administering Siovale in the Duke's absence.

Not that Duchess Sildra should *need* such assistance, but training Mark to take his father's place – *and* Arabella, whose place it would be to be his Heir if anything happened to Mark – should surely have taken priority in an emergency than integrating them into the ranks of the Secret Cadre of Royal Guards?

Aryllis looked torn. "Tomas... was very useful. We had so much to *do* in those first few days. *Weeks.* Damage reports kept coming in from everyone in the path of the storm, most of the ships in the harbor were foundered... And Emeralsee seems to have been hit the worst."

Damien nodded. "I expected that."

Even if the storm hadn't hit his own duchy the hardest, the concentration of humans here would mean that more *people* would need help here than elsewhere.

"You did well with all of that," he assured her. "The sorceress also pinched off my connection to the Realm. I didn't get it back until ten days ago. I've been assisting magickally where I could since then, but by that point there didn't seem to be much in the way of storm-recovery to see to. Just the normal end of Winter stuff."

He'd had to fight the Realm last Fall in order to get its help to hold off any part of the ice-storm and the devastation it had wreaked. The Realm hadn't cared that the storm was magick-born; ice-storms were natural phenomena and simply something else to be expected and accepted.

For the recovery, Genevieve – and perhaps Jason or even Adam – had used their own, less-personal connections with the Realm to do what they could for the humans, but the largest part of the Soul of his Realm had been in Winter-sleep. When he again made contact with it, just as the Realm itself was waking fully, it had not needed anything more of him for the other-Life – all that was not human – than it normally did.

Aryllis gave him a smile nearly as tired as Adam's, and by instinct Damien extended a thread of awareness to her. Yes. She was pregnant again. And he guessed she wasn't yet aware of it – certainly *Tim* wasn't, or her husband would be hovering much more protectively. Aryllis' only other pregnancy had proven nearly fatal to the slender, willowy woman. He would have to talk to her – to *them* – privately to see if she wanted to try again or terminate this pregnancy. The King knew it had to be an unintentional one – his dear friends had been so very careful...

On the other hand, his own grown Power could almost certainly make sure Aryllis and the child – another boy – survived the birth. If they were willing to take the risk.

And that assumed he himself would survive the coming confrontation to offer Tim and Aryllis the option. Nothing could be certain when anticipating the arrival of a demon.

"Did Tomas stay through the Winter?" Damien asked.

"No," Adam answered. "He and Genevieve kept ratcheting around the strategic situation with Deltheren. We still haven't had word from Queen Estelle," he added in an aside. "Eventually, though, Tomas claimed he was throwing up his hands and the Queen's 'missing piece' was just going to have to stay 'missing,' as far as he was concerned. And he headed back to Siovale. At that point, we all thought he'd been staying as much to make sure his children settled in as he was to be helpful."

Damien turned to those who should know about that. "And did they settle in? The young Elseviers, I mean."

Lady Alanna and Lord Aaron exchanged a glance. "We thought Mark and 'Bella were happy here, Your Majesty," she began, but the King cut her off with a wave.

"Just Damien for now, Alanna. You're all my friends and family as much as anything else, and we have problems to solve that shouldn't stand on ceremony." He smiled at Madame Elista, his Chatelaine, and the younger Solways. And caught an approving look from David Solway.

Alanna nodded, swallowed hard. "Elaina and Marianna spent the most time with Arabella. We thought it was a good thing, that the new recruits were bonding so well."

Aaron leaned back and folded his arms, his expression deeply ironic. "It's a pity the way this is going to turn out. With the way they hid their real plans, I could train that girl and her brother to be excellent deep-cover operatives – to be sent to someone *else's* Court. Queen Estelle's, say."

Damien winced – internally, he hoped. He really didn't want anyone focusing on the eventual, necessary outcome of dealing with this treason. He didn't want to focus on it himself.

"And Lucinda and Denis?" He looked at the youngest pair in the room. "Did you two get to know them at all?"

They looked at their father, and he gathered them close on both sides. "We've talked about this, loves. He's the King, but he's also your Uncle Damien. Your older brother's best friend."

Damien blinked and glanced at Adam, who gave him a wry look and a one-shouldered shrug. Clearly, Lord David had spent the Winter months disentangling the family tree for his children.

"I like the sound of 'Uncle Damien'," the King said with a gentle smile. "And Jason is more than my best friend."

He ignored Adam's quickly-hidden look of alarm. "He's been my teacher since I was just a bit older than you, Roger. I'd spent five years living in the Royal Library and I was more animal than boy at that point. So, he also had to *tame* me. He's the most patient person I know."

Adam snorted to hide his relief at secrets not revealed. "A very well-educated animal. But, yes," he gave his words to the children, "that's essentially the way it was."

Apparently, between their father's reassurance and Adam's – *Adam's?* – the Solway children were willing to speak up in this august group.

"Cindy's even older'n me, Your–" Roger cut himself off as Damien grinned and shook his head.

His eyes grew a bit round as he realized the King had meant every word. "Uncle Damien. We're both starting late, and... we both had some... *things* the others would tease us about. I thought we were friends. I thought..."

He looked down.

Esmerelda picked up the thread. "Elaina and Marianna and 'Bella would come and get the four of us, and we'd get Lord Aaron and their big brother, Mark, and we'd all play games together after Duke Tomas left."

Damien smiled at the miserable-looking young women. "That was kind of you."

"Jason and Adam joined us sometimes," Marianna nodded to her brother. She blushed a little. "Mark was... very sweet. To both of us."

The King nodded. He thought he had a general picture of things now.

"So, when did things fall apart?" he asked.

It was Madame Elista, the Chatelaine of the Castle who answered this. "I'd been getting word that all the Siovale children were... hoarding food in their rooms. It seemed odd, and we don't allow the pages and squires to do that to prevent infestations of rodents and insects. But there's no rule against what your young ladies-in-waiting and gentlemen-of-the-chamber keep in their rooms," she nodded at Alanna and Aaron.

Aaron barked a short laugh. "You don't want to know what's in *my* room, Elista, trust me."

The capable older woman gave the foppish-looking assassin a steady look. "Doubtless. And you'll notice that none of my people go into your room, Aaron. As we agreed when you joined our merry crew."

She re-focused on the King. "I talked to Denis and Lucinda myself, to explain the rule, and to see if there was a reason why they felt the need to do that. They were both abashed, but it seemed... *odd* to me. Siovale has never had any food shortages that I'm aware of, and certainly the children of the Duke should be the last ones to feel it if there were."

The Castle Chatelaine sighed with regret. "I should have noticed that *what* Mark and Arabella were hoarding was the sorts of things that would keep well for travel. Perhaps the fact that what the younger two had kept back was no such thing made it less clear, but..."

Aaron made another derisive sound. "*I* should have noticed, too. Don't blame yourself Elista. *I* saw what 'Bella had in her room. And *I* had no idea what Cindy and Denis were doing."

Alanna and Aryllis both looked directly at the young gentleman-of-the-chamber. Apparently, this was news to them.

"And *what,* milord Aaron, were you doing in Arabella Elsevier's *room?"* Alanna asked more than a trifle sharply.

Damien was amused to see a faint blush stain the self-assured young man's cheeks. Though he'd known Lord Aaron long enough to have reason to believe that there shouldn't be a reason for concern. It was Alanna's place to see that the ladies-in-waiting were properly chaperoned from even the appearance of scandal at all. And the young men, surely, though she wasn't asking if he'd been in *Mark* Elsevier's room... which might be a somewhat more *fraught* question...

"I wasn't *alone* with her, if that's what you're implying, Alanna," Aaron retorted a little defensively. "One of your other ladies was always there. Elaina or Marianna, usually. Or Mark once or twice, but if her own *elder brother* wasn't a sufficient chaperone..."

"Hmmn," Alanna said, but turned away. Damien thought he caught a hint of humor in her eyes, so perhaps she was just teasing the younger man. Alanna wasn't terribly older than most of her charges, but she had fought on battlefields for the Rebellion and that sort of thing tended to mature one.

A new wrinkle. It wasn't hard to see that the assassin had begun to be close friends – with the Duke's clever daughter.

Or perhaps it was more than *'begun'?*... Months after all, of working together, not to mention years of having known both Mark and Arabella both during the Rebellion. Damien was aware that Aaron had sought refuge in Siovale and from the Elseviers after King Reginald had wrought the tragedy that had taken the young man's family.

And Elaina and Marianna – *both?* – obviously had more than marginal feelings for Tomas' eldest son and Named Heir.

The King sighed, trying not to let it sound too heavy, despite how all of this weighed on him. "So... there's no way that at least the older pair didn't know what was to happen."

Marianna wrapped her arms around herself and looked away, and Aaron folded his and retreated into a look of deepest irony. Elaina looked on the verge of tears – holding them back only because of all those years beneath her grandmother's gimlet gaze. Her younger brother and sister were looking scared despite their father's arms around each of them.

Damien's empathic sense was still too weak to pick up more than the gist of general guilt from everyone at the table, but he was more attuned to Adam, and caught the thread of sadness that his baby sister should have such an introduction to the duplicity of Court after managing to shield her from it for so many years... would she ever be as carefree and joyous again?

Sir Tim, however, looked thoughtful. "I'm not sure. It's possible that they knew *some*thing was to happen, but not what. Tomas *may* have merely told them to be ready to grab their younger siblings and flee home. Or... simply flee. Remember, at this point we were looking for a force of unknown strength from Deltheren and an all-too-known Power that had snatched *you,* our incredibly powerful sorcerer-king away. And the Queen – Genevieve – kept insisting there was a 'missing piece' to the strategic situation. Something else *unknown* that was confusing her evaluations."

Tim shook his head. "If Rico were in such a situation... *I'd* probably consider telling him to make that kind of preparation. Or, given the stories he's growing up hearing," he smiled at his wife, "I wouldn't be at all surprised if he'd do it on his own."

Marianna looked marginally less miserable at that, but Aaron's look became, if it were possible, even *more* deeply ironic.

"So... when did they leave?" Damien asked. "And how did it happen that Genevieve and Jason went with them?"

He very, very carefully kept his tone and his gaze light and scanned around the table, not looking at any person longer than an instant.

It had been Adam's task as Champion to serve as Genevieve's personal bodyguard – or Jason's, if *she* was secure – not to take on administrative duties, no matter how good he was at them.

It was Sir Tim's purview to ensure that the Queen and the Crown Prince had adequate Royal Guards.

And Aryllis', or perhaps it was now Alanna's, to ensure that there were sufficient of the Secret Cadre present as well. Even though Mark and Arabella were both new recruits to the Secret Cadre of Royal Guards, they alone should never have been considered sufficient.

As the silence stretched on, and no one would meet his eyes but David, Damien let his brows rise. "Come now. It's not like I'm unaware of how headstrong Genevieve is. Or how easily she can rope Jason into following her lead."

Or me, he thought but did not say.

Definitely 'or you,' grandson, Queen Marian's acerbic voice in both of their heads made Adam glance around in surprise. *I seem to recall a rather insane two-person assault to re-take this Castle from that usurping brother of your treacherous Duke, after all.*

Which succeeded, Damien retorted silently. *Spectacularly.*

*Only because of **my** assistance,* the irascible old ghost-Queen informed him.

And since he couldn't disagree, because it was all true... At his side, Adam snorted very slightly. He might only have heard Queen Marian's side of the conversation – a change from the old way when hers was the half-conversation he could *not* hear – but he had clearly gotten enough to figure out the rest.

"It was about ten days ago," Adam explained reluctantly.

"*Exactly* ten days ago," Aaron muttered, and the Champion sent him a quelling glance.

"I think the first hint we had that something was wrong was that the Elsevier children were missing. *All of them,*" Adam went on. "And after all the fuss you'd made about not wanting them to look like hostages... we all damn well knew that we'd better not let anything happen to them because we'd somehow let them out of our supervision."

He snorted. "They're all kidnapping targets *themselves,* of course, and we've no other ducal children here, after all." Because none of the other dukes and duchesses had children of age to be here... or children at all in the case of four of the remaining six duchies... Emeralsee and Elaarwen included, to Damien's personal sorrow.

"We thought they *must* be in the Castle," Tim explained. "No one had seen any of them – or anyone meeting even their vaguest description pass the gate after all. So, we turned out the entire Royal and Castle Guard."

Aryllis gave Aaron a dry look. "And then it turned out that *some*one had begun showing the new recruits the secret passages. The ones leading out of the castle."

Aaron looked away. "It's our job to get the King and Queen away in case of disaster. I didn't show them anything that would let them sneak around *in*side of the castle." He looked at his King almost pleadingly, a very unexpected look for the self-assured young assassin. "I've known Mark and Arabella for years, milord. My family's holdings are on the border of Siovale and Emeralsee, but my family sent me to Elaarwen – via Siovale – when they feared we'd all be..."

He stopped and bit his lip.

"I know, Aaron," Damien said gently. He knew the dark tales behind every one of his Guards. The story behind how a young nobleman could become a highly-trained assassin... and be so completely, unquestionably, loyal to his King and Queen had been chilling even by comparison to most of the others.

"You felt you knew them enough to trust them. I understand." He gave the younger man a wry smile. "I'm the one who pardoned their father – *twice* – and took him as one of my closest advisors. And one of my dearest friends."

And oh, how a part of him still hoped – *wished* – that Azella's damning words could somehow be proved a lie...

Aaron sagged into himself, his attitude of ironic assurance completely gone. Marianna put an arm around him, and he leaned his head on her shoulder without hesitation. Damien could practically feel Adam's eyebrow go up.

The King nodded. "All right. So, the children were gone. And there was a good chance they were gone from the Castle. What then? They had no horses, I assume."

"We turned out the City Guard," Tim admitted, "but finding four young people in a city the size of Emeralsee... we almost *hoped* they'd left the city, both because it would likely be easier to track them and... for their own protection."

Damien nodded, a little grimly. Siovale's capitol was hardly more than a town. Even Mark would have had little idea what he was getting himself into in the darker parts of Emeralsee.

And to take the younger children... Arabella was seventeen and Lucinda just fourteen. The older sister had been denied a chance to earn her shield and the younger one was newly a squire – Damien had met the girls long enough to know that they had an overblown sense of their own abilities, though a few months in the company of his practical Secret Cadre might have knocked some of that out of 'Bella. Little Denis, at twelve, had one of those sweet faces that would bring money even if he were not the son of the Duke of Siovale.

"And while we were doing all that, the Queen – Genevieve – got it into her head that she knew where they must be going – and why," Alanna said. "She seemed to think they felt their lives were in danger and that *only she* could put that fear to rest. They... still call her 'Aunt Genevieve,' after all."

Damien had seen that. It seemed to be the only lasting positive result of his wife's first marriage. And... the children had started to call *him* 'Uncle Damien'...

"She was getting more and more agitated about it," Alanna was continuing. "Jason seemed to think it was bad for the baby. He tried to persuade her to lie down and rest. I found him a sleeping draught that the Healer said would be fine for a pregnant woman, and he said he'd do his best to get her to swallow it."

Damien sighed. "And when you went into the royal suite to check on them, they were gone." He looked at Tim. "*You* knew where they went."

"It wasn't as clear as all that, Damien," Adam put in before Tim could do more than wince and nod. "They'd put up those damned wards."

The King frowned. "On the royal suite? But we were just up there and when we went in, the wards weren't... up..." He felt his eyes widen and fought to keep his jaw from dropping. "Which one of you is a Spell-Breaker?"

Marianna looked embarrassed. "That would be me."

The King laughed and glanced at Adam. "And Martin is a Healer. A very Talented family you have, my Champion."

He had the feeling Adam had only scratched the surface of his *own* abilities, given that the Realm found him more interesting and sympathetic than the Queen and Prince actually Bound to it.

He wants you to know that you are to let this drop. I disagree. I think you should bring the whole Loveress clan back up here and find out what they all can do. Queen Marian paused, while Adam looked annoyed at this very low fidelity transmission of his intent.

In fact, the ghostly Queen added thoughtfully, *you may **need** to if what I've been picking up out of your surface thoughts is what I think it is...*

Kindly stop trying to glean things that way, Grandmother. I'll give you the whole story later.

Mind you do, boy.

"So, you got in – however much later – when *Marianna* tried the door," Damien said aloud. "And they were gone. You checked the exit we came out of before?"

Tim held out his hands. "Of course. Not that it would have mattered, since the entire City Guard had already been on alert and anyone who saw Her Maj– um, Genevieve would have passed the word. Everyone knows she's carrying the Heir to the Throne... and how much trouble she's had with trying to do that in the past. And neither she nor Jason are exactly easy to keep anonymous."

No, not with her red hair and his unusual height...

Though they'd done it before...

The King's heart clenched at Tim's description, and he caught a sense of anxiety from Adam.

The baby Genevieve carried would never be Heir to his Throne if Lord Prydeen's last-breath prophecy continued to hold true. Despite the Alsterling heritage she carried from both parents... *neither* of whom was Damien.

His daughter and firstborn-to-be, nevertheless, he thought fiercely.

"The Sword..." Damien said carefully, knowing that he was sharing information not known beyond himself and Genevieve before this, "Allows its bearer to walk through *any* of the walls in the Castle. And possibly any stone anywhere. It's how Genevieve and I made it to the pantries to rescue the Castle Guardsmen during Harald's usurpation. We didn't test it after that to see how much more it might do."

He looked apologetically at Adam. "In retrospect... that may have been a mistake."

Adam looked... very growly, presumably at not having been made aware of this before.

Tim sighed. "At least that explains why they weren't any of the places we looked, Adam."

The Champion did not look in the least bit mollified. "*Jason* should have had better sense than this. *Jason* should have at least tried to leave us a message. *Some*where, even if he couldn't talk that reckless woman into sense."

He folded his arms and looked like he could outglower stormclouds.

Aryllis gave him an annoyed look. "She's not *reckless*. She just takes her work *seriously*. If she's the one to do something and the rest of you lot get in the way, she's not going to let that stop her."

Damien started to say something, but Lord David was speaking up again. "Lady Aryllis, that describes the Queen to a T. However, she's also bearing a child that could inherit the throne and ended up taking herself and the Crown Prince into danger when the King himself was out of reach and in deadly peril for all we knew. I've nothing against strong-minded women who pursue their own ideas of what needs to be done. Our own previous Head of House Metreedi, my Aunt Mathildra, for example."

He quirked a wry smile. "She posed as a dancing girl for Emperor Zehangir in order to negotiate with him and managed *not* to become a permanent member of his harem."

Everyone blinked at this, and his children all looked avidly interested. Damien found himself amused by how David was cultivating his children away from the shape and perspective their grandmother and mother had pressed them into, now that he had a free hand. Not that he himself wasn't extremely curious about that tale also. Elaina just seemed thoughtful, but Roger and Esmerelda were eating this up.

"David summed that up well," Damien agreed. "Genevieve should have known better. *And* Jason should have known better. We've known Genevieve to act impetuously in the past – in the perspective of others – but she's never been irrational. She's never been *agitated*. She's simply possessed some piece of information or some insight that wasn't accessible to others. And acted on it, coolly and with planning and preparation."

Like a memory of an eight-year-old with a pair of grey eyes that haunted her dreams... Or a realization that two could sneak into the Castle and free the Castle Guards when a troupe of ten or twenty would be caught.

She'd also never been four months pregnant before.

Adam didn't – *quite* – snort.

Damien ignored him. "Since that *wasn't* what all of you saw, I submit there was something else going on. It sounds... like a *compulsion* spell. Something we've all had rather too much experience with of late."

Yes. He'd taught the nobility of the entire Realm how to lay a *compulsion* spell on their subjects, though hopefully most hadn't realized they were doing more than relaying a warning about the ice-storm. Most of them didn't have the Power to *compel* anyone without the support of others anyways... but it had been a matter of life and mass death and he'd had moments to make the decision...

Not to mention the *compulsion* spells that his grandfather's Apprentice had used to control Tomas Elsevier and his men when he attempted to put Tomas' illegitimate brother, Harald, on the throne. Tomas had been livid when Damien had broken the spell and he'd discovered he had lost two years of his life, including the birth of his youngest child. Livid... but in a coldly calculating way, and he'd thrown away the brother he'd grown up beside with no observable regret, becoming Damien's second major sworn vassal...

Azella... had taught Damien still more about *compulsion* spells. But Tomas...

Siovale had not needed to be warned about the ice-storm. It had all but bypassed the plainsland province to the south, though it had been targeted at Emeralsee – and Damien – and Emeralsee lay *between* Siovale and Reyensweir. And Reyensweir had been nearly as devastated as the King's own city and province. Tomas' inherent magick hadn't been woken or tested in a desperate need to warn his at-risk people the way the other nobles' had.

And the Elsevier children had somehow known to flee, though there had been no detectable signal or message...

This had the marks of Damien's pale sorceress' fingers all over it.

"Ten days ago..." The King stood up abruptly and turned away from the table, forcing himself to stand firmly and fold his arms, not wrap them around himself to ward off the sudden inner chill.

"Damien...?" Adam had clearly picked up on his inner turmoil.

The Sorcerer-King of Ilseador recalled himself. "Ten days ago, I re-connected to the Realm. And infuriated the sorceress by telling her I no longer needed her tutelage. She distracted me with... another field of study that it is turning out will be absolutely essential."

Damien did not think that they were ready to hear about *demons* just yet. Nor did he intend to share what *other* things Azella had done to distract him.

"But this... *feels* like her work," he summarized. "And the timing would make sense."

Tim ran a hand through his hair. "Then does that mean Tomas actually had *nothing* to do with this? You said he was under *compulsions* from Lord Prydeen the last time. Could he be under *compulsions* from this – what was her name?"

"Azella the Unpitying." Damien dropped the name into the room and somehow it created its own wave of silence.

After a moment, Aaron snorted. "Thinks a bit of herself, does she?"

The King turned back and gave him a wry look. "I could wish that an overblown ego is all that it is, but... I know otherwise."

He gripped the tall back of his chair and stared at the table as fiercely as he could, hoping none of them had seen what he guessed had been in his eyes.

Oh, grandson...

He ignored the unwanted, if silent, sympathy and forged on. "She told me that she – and her own Evil Master before her – had been in contact with the Dukes of Siovale for... a long while. I don't know if that means Duke Hector, or even farther back. She told me that they *ceded* Farivera to her Master as a token of their alliance. And that their goal has *always* been to take the Throne of Ilseador."

Damien looked up and met each of their eyes, even the children. "I would not take the word of such a wicked creature alone. She might lie to tie us in knots as soon as tell us a truth that would do the same. But... I will need something very convincing to prove to me she was wrong."

Aryllis frowned. "Tomas acted perfectly normal under Lord Prydeen's spell, Damien. And he did it for two *years* with no one the wiser."

The King nodded. "*I* could detect the *compulsion* spells on him when I spoke to him, the night we retook the Castle. The spells were... *weak* compared to Azella's. And Harald kept poking unintentional holes in them, by mentioning things that had happened while Tomas was enspelled. Like Gary's birth."

Damien couldn't help wincing at that. The idea of *missing out* on the birth and babyhood of his youngest child... Though *his* youngest child was predicted to be an Evil Wizard themselves, if they could believe the rest of Lord Prydeen's prophecy. Presumably having a father absent – or rather literally absent-*minded* – during critical parts of their childhood wouldn't help avoid that destiny.

He shook his head. "I won't know until I see him in person, Aryllis. We can *hope*... but I'll still have to replace him as duke if he's this susceptible to *compulsions*. It's the sort of thing that one doesn't seem to build up a resistance to – each *compulsion* usually makes the next easier to lay."

Yes, and what did that mean for *him*, Damien, when Azella had worked so many *compulsion* spells on him in the last few months? He could tell himself that *he* knew how to ward himself... but then could not Tomas learn? But... did the King want Tomas to?

"When did you hear from Tomas?" Damien asked. "It's three days to his capitol on a fast horse."

"Three days ago," Aryllis told him.

That meant the children – and Genevieve and Jason – had made it to Siovale in no more than four days. They couldn't have done that distance by foot. Which meant there must have been someone waiting for them with horses outside of Emeralsee City. More of that detailed planning.

And... *three days ago*... had been the day when Azella explained how she planned to raise Power for her demon-Summoning. When the Realm had begun to pull at him so Powerfully that he could no longer resist. When it had told him that the Alsterling Line was threatened.

The day he had decided that he knew enough of the Banishing and Unbinding of demons to justify leaving. And now Damien had to hope *that* had been a rational decision and not merely the result of the pull of the Realm on him.

If he had been *wrong*...

Something else must have happened. He vaguely recalled his steps slowing in central Siovale as he passed by Castle Elsevier. Where, he now knew, Genevieve and Jason – and their unborn baby – were located, hostages to the man Damien had once considered one of his most trusted trusted friends.

On some level, he must have been aware that they were there.

But the Realm had drawn him on home, to the Castle and the Throne in Emeralsee that were its beating Heart, despite the fact that it was the danger to Damien's Heirs – the Alsterling Line – that had been his proximal motivation to depart Azella's Keep.

Why?

Was it because the *Realm Itself* somehow knew that Damien could not stand alone against Tomas Elsevier, backed as the latter was by Azella the Unpitying? That Damien would need to be in the center of his own Power, where he had greatest access to the Power of Ilseador Itself?

Was it because, without the Monarch's Sword in his hand to collect and concentrate the Realm's Power for him, the Realm wanted Damien closer to the Castle and Throne... given that they did much the same thing, if not to such a pinpoint focus?

Or... was it because, in Emeralsee, he would not have his captive, *compelled* wife and unborn child – and his dear, um, *friend* – right there in front of him to freeze his brain from thinking things through logically and carefully?

If only he could *feel* Genevieve through the soul-bond.

Damn Azella and her Unpitying heart to the deepest, darkest of hells. Not that she needed Damien's wishes to speed her on her path to that place. If only he hadn't allowed her to taint his own morals and drag him so far along with her...

He tried to pull himself back to the moment.

"What did Tomas' missive say?"

Adam was regarding him with concern. Apparently, he wasn't holding the moment as well as he should in order to reassure his people.

Firmly, the King set aside memories of Jeremy weeping with pain, of offering *himself* up as the sorceress' plaything in trade for mere knowledge, of...

Enough.

"He says," Aryllis answered for them all, pulling out a piece of paper that Damien could see, even at this distance, bore the bold, distinctive scrawl of Tomas Elsevier's own hand. "That the Throne and Crown of Ilseador are his by right of conquest. And that he *might* spare the Queen and the Prince if we throw the gates of the city open and greet him as king when he arrives here in – it says twelve days. Nine now."

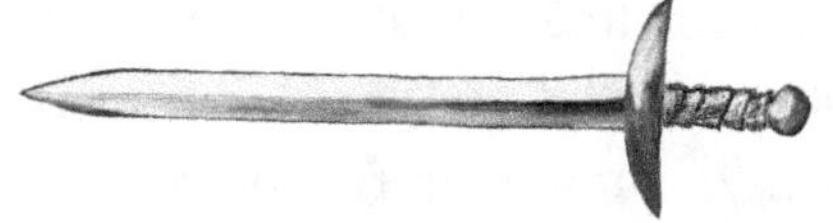

Chapter FIVE

A Look Back... and Ahead

D AMIEN'S SECOND SESSION, THIS TIME with the Royal Council, was less... emotionally harrowing.

Adam, Tim, and David all attended on him there as well, the objective of *this* Council being to catch him up on the administrative state of the Realm. Because, coups and usurpations and invasions aside, there were still roads to be mended and food to be distributed to the stricken provinces – food from crops would not be available until early Summer – and trade-treaties to be reviewed and...

The million, million details involved in running a Realm of humans.

The Lord Exchequer seemed rather displeased to have Lord David join the Council, which simply seemed to amuse the foreign-born merchant-prince.

"I no longer hold any formal position in The Family," David assured the Council. "My interests are entirely aligned with Ilseador. With Megan and my children."

The Lord Exchequer did not look mollified. "And yet you hold significant investments in the Metreedi Family corporation, Lord Solway. And your own brother is Head of House. And when Lady

Megan was kidnapped, the fleets of your merchant ships immediately turned to sweeping the seas for her."

David's eyes flashed, and Damien wondered how much of the difficulty here was reconciling this strong, tough-minded man with Megan's meek husband and Countess Alexa's subdued son-in-law that they'd all known for more than two decades.

The one thing the King could never do was question David's love for his wife and children... to have suppressed himself so much for their sakes...

...which made Damien have to remember what he himself had been willing to do for the protection of Genevieve and their unborn daughter...

Adam was looking at him with concern again.

"–begin to think that your *real* concern is that an *honest* Metreedi accountant might actually look over *your* books, milord Exchequer. How many different sets *are* you keeping these days?" David was finishing.

Damien felt his eyebrows rise as the Lord Exchequer spluttered in furious indignation... but seemed unable to gather himself to refute the accusation. Well, he'd suspected the man of peculation for five years now... and had resigned himself to the thought that all he could do was keep the corruption within bounds. The idea of bringing in a completely external auditor had never occurred to the King and he suddenly felt very young again.

"That is... an interesting suggestion, Lord Solway," Damien cut across the Lord Exchequer's garbled half-protests. "We shall keep that in mind – for a future date. But the Realm has suffered far too much in recent days for such an audit to be Our top priority. Unless the continued financial assistance of the Metreedi Family is dependent on such an audit?"

Lord David looked smugly at the Lord Exchequer, but shook his head to Damien. "Not at this time, Your Majesty. However, if my dear Cousin should become aware of too-grave discrepancies in the accounting... I cannot speak for The Family, as I said. I merely serve as a knowledgeable go-between to prevent unnecessary misunderstandings."

And presumably David would be reporting whatever discrepancies *he* took note of to his *dear Cousin* – whom Damien knew better as the hardheaded Mistress Lenore Metreedi, Head of Metreedi House-Ilseador. In his 'neutral' role as a knowledgeable go-between only, of course.

Damien nodded. "And I believe you gave us to understand that We are not being considered liable for the damage done to Metreedi merchantmen in Emeralsee Harbor by pirates and ice?"

David nodded. "The Family is insured against Acts of Sorcery and Acts of Piracy. And Acts of Nature or the Gods, for that matter. We're all just grateful that none of our cousins lost their lives in the double attack. Ships and cargo can be replaced. Family members cannot."

He looked at the Lord Exchequer again. "And I'm *not* directing the search for Megan. My cousins are looking for her because she is Family by marriage and we don't abandon our own."

"I would that I had a way to help," Damien said honestly. "As Jason's mother, she's *my* family as well as my vassal."

The older man nodded again, but didn't say anything. It would be years before the Emeralsee shipyards would be able to rebuild the ships that had been lost in the attack. And years more before there would be Ilseadoran vessels available for such an endeavor.

Following the first Council, Elaina Solway had begged a moment of His Majesty's time. The tall, blonde young woman, who looked so much like Jason, had begged Damien's leave to abdicate her position as Heir-Presumptive to Brindlewell. Elaina told him that she no longer trusted her own judgment after seeing the mess that Countess Alexa had made of their family. She felt that her recent decision to trust Mark Elsevier only confirmed that she was not the right person to try to rehabilitate the Solway family and Brindlewell when her grandmother finally died and allowed them to begin fixing things there.

Elaina told him that she no longer trusted her own judgment after seeing the mess that Countess Alexa had made of their family. She felt that her recent decision to trust Mark Elsevier only confirmed that she was not the right person to try to rehabilitate the Solway family and Brindlewell when her grandmother finally died and allowed them to begin fixing things there.

Damien had not – yet – granted her request. With her grandmother, Countess Alexa, exiled to the family's seat for the remainder of her days, her mother, Lady Megan, kidnapped, and Jason – once believed to be the Countess' younger son and now revealed as Megan's eldestborn – also held hostage, the King was loathe to rearrange anything further with regards to Brindlewell and the Solway family.

When the Royal Council was done, he kept Lord David back and asked him what he thought about this new wrinkle.

"Elaina's mentioned some of this to me as well," the older man admitted. "She's... taken all of this rather hard. Alexa... didn't foster an environment in which *change* can be considered something positive."

Adam snorted in agreement. "Jason doesn't take *change* particularly well either."

The Champion had stayed at his King's side, of course. Sir Tim Ancellius had as well, as Captain of the Royal Guard, though the latter had stationed himself near to the closed door.

"He took forever to say yes to my proposal of marriage once Damien suggested that he'd make it all work out," Adam added ironically. "And this despite the fact that we've been together nearly as long as you and Megan."

David gave him a wry look. "My point exactly. Elaina... is fragile right now. I think that she may grow stronger... *someday*. But she has a mortal distaste for Brindlewell that I doubt she'll ever get over."

The wry look grew stronger. "I'm not all that fond of the place myself, though perhaps if Alexa were gone... But my dear mother-in-law seems to be one of those types that can thrive on pure bile, so we may have decades yet before that's the case."

From his post by the door, Tim looked curious. "You're not staying *here*, though, are you, David?"

The older man's eyes were far away. "No."

He pulled himself back with another dry glance. "Our dear Lord Exchequer hasn't yet heard, but I cashed in *all* of my investments in The Family. I'm having a ship built – in Dawil, where they have the capacity and it won't impact the rebuilding in Ilseador. It's a small, fast, fighting ship. And I'm going to crew it with the best sailors and fighters I can find. And I *will* get Megan back. No matter what it takes."

"And your brother, the Head of House, was okay with this?" Adam asked sardonically.

David focused on him. "*Veren* didn't get a vote. I'd already given up my say in The Family's councils when I married Megan and became part of your nobility here in Ilseador. That wasn't strictly necessary – we have family members of every social class all around the Merutian Sea, and some retain their stake in The Family and some don't. But with the situation so... unstable in Ilseador, Veren and I agreed that it was better."

Damien raised an eyebrow. "Twenty-five years ago the situation was hardly *unstable*. My grandfather had a solid grip on everything at that point, I rather thought."

David inclined his head. "You'd already lost all the Lost Provinces but Alpinsward by then. Veren and I – and Cousin Lenore, who's now Head of our branch-House in Ilseador–" Damien waved to indicate he was familiar with Mistress Lenore, "–we spent some time touring around.

"We saw the unrest in Alpinsward.

"And we spent a great deal of time in Elaarwen with Duke Aldred and Duchess Giendra. Veren was sure that with adequate support we could make the difference between a successful Rebellion and an unsuccessful one. He was only Heir to the House then, so he had to go back to Dawil and convince Aunt Mathildra and enough of the branch-Heads.

"It didn't really come together until Mathildra passed away, though. When I was able to finally give Aldred the word that House Metreedi was his silent partner... *that* was when he declared Elaarwen in Rebellion."

This was a piece of the history of the Rebellion that Aldred had never seen fit to confide to his young king. And surely *Genevieve* must have been aware of all of this as well. And that Lord David was far more than he appeared. That *Jason* hadn't known, Damien didn't wonder.

David sighed. "When Veren went back home, I stayed. It was easy to see that Brindlewell was ideally located to become either a chokepoint for resources or a confluence.

"I didn't plan on falling in love with Megan.

"I *certainly* didn't count on her falling in love with me.

"To be honest, she was such a timid, sad little creature then, I pitied her more than anything. And... the way she treated Jason... with such *longing* and *despair* and..." He shook his head. "When she took me aside, the night before our wedding, and explained... and told me I could call it all off if I wished, so long as I never told anyone else..."

He looked into Adam's eyes. "I was head over heels by then, of course. But I told her I'd seen no sign that Jason had anything but a kind heart – and I'd known him two years by then. And that if he was my stepson, even if she never wanted anyone to know that, I would still do my best by him. And I did, though I had no idea then how Alexa – *and* Megan – could subvert most of my efforts.

"Eventually I was reduced to simply trying to get them to leave him at Court as much as possible and keep them home in Brindlewell. The Court was poisonous... but it hardly seemed like to be as bad for him as home."

He gave Adam a sad smile. "I was behind the attempt to wed him to Genevieve... and I'd planned to try again after that Summer, but that was the year–"

"That Aldred declared the Rebellion," Adam said. His expression was... tight. And closed. No matter what David had *tried,* Jason had been deeply wounded. "I remember. It was the year I came to Court."

David gave him a reproving look. "I was about to say, young man, that it was the year he met *you.* All I had to do was read his letters home to know you were special. Once I saw the sparkle in his eyes when he spoke of you... and the way *you* looked at *him*... I knew there would never be anyone else for either of you."

"Oh." Adam blinked in surprise. There was an additional sparkle at the rims of his eyes.

Damien looked away as Adam's eyes sought his own. Yes, the pair of them belonged together, just as *he* and *Genevieve* did. And bedamned to this *second soul-bond* she'd discovered with Jason... and the very real reasons they'd had a chance to discover it at all.

"I'm from *Wave,* Adam," David informed his stepson-in-law a little tartly. "The largest city in the world, and it has been for thousands of years. We're far less stuffy than you backwater provincials."

The older man flashed Damien a grin. "Though Emeralsee is definitely catching up."

His face grew sober again. "I thought I'd done the right thing until Jason ended up as Prince Oskar's bodyguard... And now... *Now,* I keep asking myself if trying to shield your relationship from Alexa and Megan was the right thing to do, or whether I should have pressed to send Jason to Elaarwen after all."

Adam and Damien exchanged a glance. In this they were in complete agreement, for all the havoc it would later have made of their lives.

"I think we'd all rather Jason had been protected," Damien said lightly. "Though if he hadn't been here, I might still be hiding in the Royal Library."

And Jason and Genevieve might have discovered their soul-bond before Damien had had a chance to grow up... and they'd have been married... It was one thing for the queen to secretly take Jason as a lover, with Damien's consent, and bear a child no one would ever know was his. It would have been entirely impossible for the king to father a child with the married Duchess of Elaarwen that he claimed as his own Heir.

Not to mention mooning after her... even if Damien's own soul-bond to her did eventually make itself real...

Adam snorted. "Ciriis and I would have gotten you out eventually."

David gave them a relieved smile. "I suppose every parent second-guesses themselves. Sometimes... it's just a much more stark set of options. You'll be figuring that out soon yourself, I imagine."

It had to be entirely Damien's paranoia that David flickered a glance at Adam.

Oh. The foreign-born lordling was only replying to his stepson-in-law's earlier query. "But to answer the question you started with, Adam: Veren didn't get a vote, but he's fully on board. His son and daughter-in-law were both killed by pirates a dozen years ago, leaving my brother to raise his grandson from the age of three.

"His only request, actually, was that I not take young Devin along with me. The boy is about fifteen and absolutely obsessed with fighting pirates."

Tim sighed. "I suppose that would make sense."

Damien avoided everyone's eyes, drawing patterns in the condensation rings from their water glasses on the polished Council table. He wasn't *obsessed* with defeating Evil Wizards... was he? "Your grand-nephew is older than Roger?"

David shrugged. "Veren found Relita early. I found Megan late. And there's some few years' difference in our ages as well. My sisters' sons are closer in age to Roger and Devin." He paused. "I'll take Elaina with me when I go to find Megan *again*. She's an entire other side of her family to learn about after all."

He met Damien's eyes. "I don't think she'll be coming back to Ilseador. I'd take it as a kindness if you'll release her before we go."

The King stilled and looked up. "You'd leave Roger and Esmerelda while you go *pirate hunting?*"

How could David even *consider* leaving behind his grieving children?

"Not any time soon," David assured him. "The ship won't be ready for over a year."

The King frowned. He couldn't *actually* say what he was thinking without offending the man, but perhaps he could try pulling a different string. "But while you're gone – and arguably even while you're here, with Megan and Elaina both out of the picture – Alexa is their liege-lady."

To Damien's surprise, Lord David stretched and grinned. *"She'll* certainly think so. But I checked legal precedent, and since both of them have been enrolled in your training academy, *you* are their liege-lord until they are either dismissed or knighted. Normally that would also be contingent on the payment of their training fees, but since you so kindly put them on the Crown's Privy Purse before all this got... tangled... or *un*tangled...

"You can check it yourself, milord, but Metreedis of our core-House in Wave are all trained in the law from an early age. *I* can't even stand against Alexa's wishes with respect to Roger and Esmerelda by Ilseadoran law, but they are legally now *your* wards, and *you* stand for them *in loco parentis."*

He gave Adam a slightly smug smirk. "With your Heir and his husband sharing that responsibility, as they are also responsible for the Privy Purse. Congratulations, son, and welcome to parenthood."

Adam's face was... a treat. Tim chuckled from his post by the door.

Damien let out a quiet breath of... not-quite relief. So, this was what David had been referring to a moment ago, not anything... *else.*

On the other hand, the idea that he was *personally* responsible for Jason's younger siblings in the same way as a parent... was not exactly a comfortable thought. He'd already been wrestling with the question of whether he – or his beautiful, wonderful wife with her sly and insufficiently-protective father for a model – had it in them to parent their own anticipated offspring.

But at least they would have time to grow into that role and learn what they were doing. Roger and Esmerelda were old enough to call them out on doing it wrong...

...and now that they had a decent comparison with their father being so much more active a parent in their lives, they would definitely know the difference, wouldn't they?

Damien looked up to meet Adam's dismayed expression and... relaxed despite it. Damien might have lost his parents too young to know how to take care of a child, and Genevieve's father had clearly not protected her, and Jason's family was... all messed up.

But *Adam's* was loving and supportive from birth through adulthood. *(Leaving aside the twelve years where he and his parents hadn't spoken – though how much longer than necessary Adam's own hurt and stubbornness had extended that hiatus, Damien had no idea. The Baronetta and her husband had managed to grow past their initial intolerance and begun corresponding with Jason directly...)*

Surely, *Adam* could teach the *rest* of them.

David's eyes softened as he observed Adam's reaction. "If you and Jason hadn't started taking such an interest in Roger and Esme... if I didn't know Marianna was here to help... I wouldn't be able to consider this. But... I *have* to get Elaina out of here before Alexa somehow tears my little girl to pieces, and I *have* to find Megan before it tears *me* to pieces."

There was a sense of desperation at the back of his serene, confident expression. But then, Damien had heard that David had once served as a Captain in the Metreedi fleet and no man who commanded others and stood up to face storms and pirates... and *voluntarily* became embedded in another nation's struggle to free itself from a tyrannical and seemingly immortal sorcerer-king...

No such man could ever be assumed to have shown the entire depths of his soul.

The potential conundrums in parenting *multiple* children and balancing each of their needs against each other – and one's own needs – was something Damien hadn't really thought about before, either. He couldn't fairly say that Elaina – adult or not – didn't need and deserve the care her father hadn't been allowed to give her earlier on. Damien knew how much *he* still needed and missed his own parents, after all.

Adam nodded. "I've been through too much the same with Jason. Including right now."

"Likewise," Damien agreed. "We're honored that you'll trust us with them, David."

David nodded. "Like I said, it's no time soon. In the meantime, I'm here to do what I can to help my older son. And my son-in-law." His smile at Adam was completely unreserved.

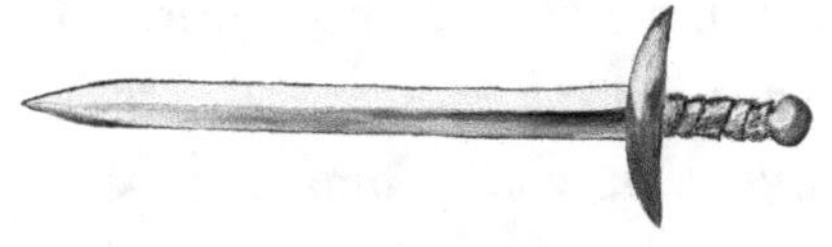

Chapter SIX

A Crisis of Conscience

Y*OU PROMISED TO TELL ME what happened after you were stolen away,* Queen Marian reminded Damien as he tried to settle down to sleep in the huge, empty bed.

The King sighed and looked at the shimmering ghostly presence perched on the side of his bed. *I thought you didn't come into my bedroom, Grandmother.*

She raised an eyebrow. *That's to give you and Genevieve some privacy. She's not here, so there's no need.*

I might need some privacy myself, you know, he suggested.

She snorted. *You've nothing I haven't seen before. And before you suggest it, there's nothing you could **do** that I haven't seen before, either. Though, granted, you have a rather impressive physique for a young man who spends most of his time with his nose in a book.*

"Do you actually want to hear what happened, or are you just going to try to goad me into embarrassment?" Damien sighed aloud.

Neither, actually, the ancient woman responded surprisingly. *You're hurting, grandson, but even when I lived I wasn't much good at giving comfort. Your handsome Champion is hurting, too, and he's not going to get any more rest than he has these last ten nights without some help.*

She leveled her ethereal gaze at him.

Your help, she noted, in case he might be inclined to assume anything else.

The dark-haired king tugged at his sheet. *Grandmother... that is...* **not** *a good idea just now.*

Damien Alsterling, that young man has been your friend and dedicated knight and believed in you longer than you've believed in yourself. Don't you dare be a coward and leave him alone in **his** *time of need!*

Damien got up and found a pair of pants. "You're an unpleasant old woman, did you know that?"

The ancient Queen's ghost came over to him and patted him on the cheek – an incredibly odd sensation. *Whatever it takes to get you moving and doing the right thing, grandson.*

She paused. A speaking pause that he knew she was going to fill in, so he waited patiently.

You're too good for the Throne in some ways, Damien. You've learned to be pragmatic... but sometimes a ruler must be ruthless. Sometimes we don't have the luxury of choosing between right and wrong, but merely between more wrong and less wrong. Sometimes the ends **must** *justify the means. Sometimes a ruler must simply be... expedient.*

Damien raised his chin. "I can't believe that, milady Grandmother. The ends of such a thing are tainted in that case, and that taint will come back to bite us in the end."

Ah, Damien... she sighed sadly, but she didn't argue further as he made his way to the magickal secret passageway between his suite and the windowless one just below.

The passage through the stone of the floor was as unnerving as ever, and it reminded Damien that he could simply have vanished himself to Adam's side as long as he was entering the other man's bedchamber uninvited anyways. Somehow... this seemed less invasive.

Not much less, though.

"Adam?" he called out as he descended the stairs. "Grandmother Marian says you're having trouble sleeping... too."

"Interfering old biddy," Adam's voice grumped in the dark. A tiny dot of light that provided no useful illumination whatsoever gleamed from the wick of a lamp turned all the way down.

"No argument," Damien replied. He switched over to seeing via magick as he stepped off of the narrow, unguarded stair, hoping to use the mild glow of the Castle to see his way over to Adam without tripping.

Abruptly the room was brilliantly lit. *So* brilliantly lit, in fact, that the King's eyes watered and he quickly switched back to normal sight, spots dancing before his eyes.

His own Power was locked down and shielded. The Castle had a mild, warm glow everywhere but in the Throne-room, where the glow became a dazzle.

This... must be Adam. He'd never looked like that to Damien's magick sight before... but it was much closer to the way the Realm had shown Adam to him when he re-connected to It.

"Damien? Are you having trouble with your eyes? I turned up the lamp..."

Adam's hand grasped his arm and drew him over to the bed.

"You came down those damn magickal stairs when you can't even *see?* Damn that interfering old biddy. I was *fine*, I tell you..." Adam complained as he helped Damien sit down.

The dancing spots of color that filled his dazzled vision were starting to shrink. He kept his eyes closed to let them finish recovering.

"*This* wasn't Queen Marian's fault," Damien said, trying to be fair. "I could see just fine as I came down. It's sort of my own fault. You just shine too brightly. I wasn't expecting that."

"Damien..." He'd been hearing that long-suffering tone for almost fifteen years. Half his life. "What are you talking about *now*."

The younger man sighed. "Nevermind. It probably doesn't matter, for now."

"Hmmn." Adam did *skeptical* better than just about anyone else, but he let it go. "So, the old biddy decided to tell you I'm having trouble sleeping."

Damien laughed quietly. "I didn't need *her* to tell me that. I didn't even need my Healing sense to tell me that. Honestly, Adam, I'd have been stunned if you *were* sleeping well. When Azella cut me off from the Realm, and Genevieve, I was too sick to even notice whether or *not* I was sleeping."

He didn't mention that it was a tightly buried core of sheer terror – that he had not even admitted to himself at the time – that had helped him recover before the ship made landfall at the sorceress' Keep. That, and the sense that, even if he could not touch it, he was in Farivera.

Adam and Jason's marriage-bond was nearly identical to a soul-bond from what Damien had been able to determine in the bare couple of days he'd been with them between the wedding and his capture by Azella.

"It's... not that bad," Adam admitted. "I can still *feel* Jason."

"Ah. Good." Damien tried not to sound as hungry and jealous as he *actually* felt over that. "And... Genevieve?"

There was a moment of silence. "I'm sorry, Damien. I can't feel her through him. I can tell Jason is anxious, but it doesn't seem particularly urgent."

The younger man bowed his head. "I hadn't really expected you could."

After a moment Damien added, "I *know* they're okay. I can *sense* them both through the Realm. It's how I knew they were in Siovale. And... the Realm told me they were in danger. But the soul-bond is... effectively gone. Except for tying my life to hers, I assume."

He paused again. "Was... she *okay* when Azella... cut us off?"

Adam sighed and laid down again, pulling a sheet up over his lower body. Apparently, he slept bare, even when he was alone.

"Genevieve was... furious. That's the only word I can use. It confirmed the bond between her and Jason... and me. She gave him a headache, and I got some of it as well."

"That must have been a challenge to explain away," Damien noted, testing to see if his eyes were back to normal yet. They seemed to be.

"I think everyone just assumed it was Jason's usual aversion to confrontation," Adam admitted. "Tomas... doesn't have a particularly high opinion of Jason, I don't think."

Damien put his head in his hands. "This is such a mess. I should have listened to you in the first place. *And* Genevieve."

He felt Adam's hand on his back. The King hadn't bothered to put on a shirt...

Damien tried to think of the contact as *reassuring*. And not... anything else. Anything *more*. This man – his second-oldest friend, former mentor, current advisor, his *Champion* – was hurting. As he was himself.

They each needed a *friend,* not... anything more. The complicated mess that Damien had been turning all four of their lives into last Fall... should be left in last Fall.

Better to wall himself off to deal with current events than cause more damage to people he cared about. No matter what things had seemed to make sense last Fall... before Azella had showed him just how closely he would be willing to walk to the line of Evil Wizardry.

Better to draw clear lines and boundaries and not try to reshape the world the way he wished it could be.

Better for everyone.

"We need people with your kind of idealism to make the world a better place," Adam was saying. "If you leave cynics like me in charge, this wouldn't happen, but neither would things improve the way they are with you. On the whole, your approach is probably the better one."

"You wouldn't say that if you knew what I had to do to get back home." Damien's tone was full of self-loathing. "I can't believe you can say it even *without* knowing. Given the situation."

Adam was silent again.

Then, "Come here." He tugged Damien to lie down beside him. "It wasn't just for *my* sake that the old biddy sent you down here, was it?"

The younger man didn't say anything. What was there to say, after all? Despite his cynicism, there was something pure about Adam.

Not *innocent* – that would be Jason, despite his time with Oskar – but *pure.*

Incorruptible.

The blonde Champion sighed and snugged Damien's back into his chest. "Do you remember how you used to come to me to help with your nightmares?"

Damien whuffed a bit of a laugh. The memories were good ones, for all that they had been born out of a dark place.

"You *trained* me to do that. You came and soothed my nightmares for *years* before I ever came out of the Library."

Adam chuckled. "I suppose I did. You'd wake me up with them from the other side of the Castle. But that *first* night, when you finally were willing to sleep in a room adjoining ours, and you came in to find me when your nightmares started again... I suppose I set myself up for that."

He paused. "Well, and Jason did. *I* was going to get up and come check on you, but *he* didn't want me to move. I don't think it ever occurred to him that *you'd* come find *me* like any of my little brothers."

He chuckled again. "Or that you'd climb into bed with *us* as if you were seven instead of seventeen."

Damien felt himself flushing at the memory that... wasn't quite as sweet and innocent as he'd thought, apparently, and tried to wriggle away. "I'm sorry..."

Adam hugged him a little tighter. "*I* thought it was adorable. That you felt safe with us. With *me.*"

His warm chuckle rumbled once more, as the man who had *always* been Damien's Champion – no matter who held the title – clearly enjoyed his own version of that memory. "Jason was rather more... startled. Especially when you snuggled in *between us,* cuddled up to me and fell right back to sleep."

"Adam..." Damien was horribly embarrassed.

"I think he was relieved that you were wearing clothes. Particularly since neither of *us* was."

Damien felt he was flushing right down to his toes, but Adam's strong, comforting arms held him in place... *safe.*

He didn't actually remember any of it, though he vividly remembered the utter terror of spending his first night in the Castle outside of the Library in years. He remembered telling himself over and over that Adam and Jason were in the next room and he was *perfectly safe...*

And he remembered waking up in their bed, *feeling* safe at last.

"Why didn't you... get me *out* of there...?" he whispered, feeling like he had to say *some*thing.

"Jason wanted to," Adam said dryly. "I wouldn't let him. You needed us."

He paused. "You needed *me*. In the daytime you still seemed terrified of anyone besides Jason – this was before we took you to Lynncrag. But at night, you needed *me*."

There was something very... *pleased* in the Champion's tone.

Damien stopped wriggling to get away.

"Jason wanted to pick you up and put you back on the couch in the other room. *I* knew you'd just have another nightmare." Adam freed a hand and ran his fingers through Damien's hair. "My sweet prince. Tell me what's wrong. What happened to you these last months? You managed to say surprisingly little about it today."

The younger man felt tears starting up. "I let myself put the end before the means, Adam."

"That's remarkably non-specific."

"I don't want to talk about it."

Adam waited. "Did you hurt anyone?"

"No. Yes. I don't know." Damien shuddered. "I don't know if she has the *ability* to feel hurt like that... No, now I'm lying to myself. I..." He shook again.

"'*She*' would be that sorceress. Azella."

Damien nodded.

"The one who gave you a choice between destroying Emeralsee and giving yourself up to her."

Damien nodded again.

"The one who cut you off from the Realm and Genevieve."

Damien's nod was barely a tremor.

"And kept you away from your pregnant wife for over four months."

"No..."

It felt like it was being ripped out of him, but Damien couldn't lie to Adam about this.

"She thought she was. But I could have left at any time. I stayed... I gave her what she wanted... because she had knowledge I needed. I can keep the Realm safe now. I can get Genevieve and Jason back – and I will. But I stayed there because *I* was using *her.*"

He thought about leaving it at that, but decided that was just as fraudulent as letting Adam think he couldn't have come home sooner.

"To learn magick. I... was like a boy who's taught himself to use a sword, Adam. I could swing it around and look pretty, but I didn't have any of the fundamentals, and any properly trained *beginner* could have taken me in a fight. Which is what happened. Not that Azella is a beginner."

After teaching Franz and Rob... and Jeremy... the analogy was an easy one to draw.

He could almost feel Adam's eyebrows going up.

"And now you feel *bad* about it?"

Damien snorted. "I felt bad about it *then,* too. She's... an incredibly horrible person, Adam. But... she's also a victim herself. And she was trapped in the body of a fifteen-year-old by her own Master. She's never had a chance to grow up emotionally."

Adam sighed. "Perhaps you should tell me about it from the beginning. I don't think I'm going to be able to understand it in pieces like this."

Damien scooted away slightly to lay on his back. Adam let him, but kept him safe in the circle of his arms.

The tale... the whole, sordid thing, took less time to relate than Damien would have believed.

Adam was silent for a moment afterwards.

"So. You tried to make this Evil Sorceress fall in love with you. You slept with her and her minion. You traded sex for magickal knowledge. You left this minion making his own way here from the far side of Farivera on some sort of magickal pathway. And you didn't manage to free the other fledgling Evil Wizards from Azella's grip." His Champion paused. "Is that about it?"

"Pretty much." Damien felt dirty.

"I don't see the problem."

"Adam…"

"You were a captive warrior and you used your skills and wisdom to gain an inside view of the enemy, wreaked what havoc you could in your escape, suborned as many of the enemy's forces as you could, and brought vital intelligence back to your own side. That's exactly what you should have done."

Damien… hadn't thought of it in those terms.

"Adam, you don't *understand*. I was ready to give up *everything* – Genevieve, you, Jason, the Realm… the *baby* – and *marry* that creature if she would turn away from this path." Damien still couldn't believe he'd been willing to do it.

Adam kissed his forehead. "You did what you thought best to protect us all. I'm glad it didn't come down to that."

The kiss was as big brotherly as they came, but the younger man still felt himself reacting to it. "I broke my wedding vows…"

Adam snorted. "One, I just went through those vows myself and there's nothing in them about chastity. Two, you told me yourself that you explained to Genevieve what you were likely to have to do *before* that white witch cut off your *soul-bond*. And three, you're in *my* bed right now, so that may not be your most powerful argument."

As if to emphasize, he added a caress that was… not at all big brotherly.

Damien felt a shiver that… wasn't fear or self-loathing. But probably should have been.

"Adam…"

"*You,* my sweet prince," the Champion said ironically, "Can't help empathizing with everyone you meet. Even King Reginald, if anyone completely does *not* deserve your empathy. And I know for a fact that you've been more than half in love with every person you've ever slept with. So, you started empathizing with and falling in love with this sorceress. And you tried to find a way to make everything work out – the way you always do. Which says worlds of good things about the goodness of your heart. Also, about the softness of your head, but I wouldn't change this about you for anything."

"Um." Damien paused, then gave him a quizzical look. "Jason called me his 'sweet prince.' He's the only person who's ever done that. And only when we... um."

"He got that from *me,* then," Adam said to the younger man's surprise. "I've been calling you our 'sweet prince' since we started working to get you out of the Library. Mostly sarcastically, I'll admit, when you were being particularly obstreperous."

Damien wriggled uncomfortably, and Adam gave him a dry look. "*You* were fine. *I* should have realized I'd need to be more patient. As you've pointed out, *I* was the one who knew that I was feeling what *you* were feeling after all."

Not to mention that Adam had been all of eighteen himself at the start.

The tall knight paused before adding, "It... was kind of a relief to find you, actually. I'd... forgotten until you started pointing all this out, but your nightmares had been waking me up for... a long while before that. But you'd done a pretty good job at hiding yourself away and I had fairly limited time to look for you as a squire."

"I'm sorry..." Damien found himself saying again.

"You shouldn't be. None of it was your fault." Adam gave him a serious look. "Neither was any of the mess this Winter. Genevieve and Jason will probably understand better what you went through, from the inside..."

The younger man shook his head. "How could they? They were the victims in their... situations. Not the... the *perpetrators.* The ones *being* used, not the ones *doing* the using." His voice trailed off as he felt sick to his stomach again about what he had done.

Adam's gruff snort shocked him out of another downward spiral.

"I doubt they'll see it that way. I've... had different conversations with them over the years. Even over the last few months. Genevieve thinks *she* was using *Harald* to keep Siovale in the Rebellion–"

"She'll know better *now,* surely," Damien cut in.

Adam eyed him skeptically. "Hmmn. Maybe. It may be like you were saying about her fairy-story of how you two were fated to be together. If it's something she *needs* to believe, it will take more than this to shake her belief in that viewpoint."

The King looked away. "Well, Jason then... I mean, I know he was all inside-out about Oskar..."

Adam rolled his eyes. "Oh, you have *no idea* how 'inside-out.' Good description, actually."

Damien looked back at him with a certain dismay. "What do you mean? I thought... this was all worked out?"

A shadow passed over Adam's face, and his eyes were far away. "I think... there will always be things about that time that he won't share with anyone. Sometimes... I'm glad." Quite an admission.

The Champion focused on his king again. "*You,* on the other hand, really have nothing to apologize for. Or feel guilty over. In fact, it sounds like you offered kindness and mercy – and even *love* – to your captors, no matter how cruelly they treated you."

Damien flushed. "It... wasn't really *cruel...*"

Adam shook his head. "Did you even *listen* to yourself? Just because you weren't in chains and beaten with whips doesn't mean it wasn't *cruel.* And while you say you could have walked out of there any time, we both know that wasn't really true. First, you had a duty to Ilseador – to *us* – to extract every bit of information that you could, and you couldn't leave until that was done.

"You should probably talk to Aaron about what it was like for him to be a deep-cover operative," Adam told him, interrupting himself with the tangent. "There's always going to be some guilt when you embed yourself so thoroughly into a situation that you make real bonds with people. Aaron will understand that, but I'm not sure if we have anyone else here who will quite so well.

"And then second, from what you've told me you really *didn't* have the magickal Power to leave until you re-connected with the Realm, no matter *what* you kept telling yourself."

"All I had to do was step outside that Keep," Damien began to object. "Farivera was right there, waiting."

"But that woman wasn't letting you *get* outside her Keep," Adam pointed out. "You told me that you could see those Air Elementals, but you couldn't contact them."

"I never really tried," Damien muttered, looking away. "Air... doesn't really belong to the Realm. They're beautiful, but it didn't seem worth the effort."

Adam gave him a knowing look. "You *didn't* tell me about most of the *compulsion* spells she had on you, I think. It's entirely unlike you not to keep picking at a thing until you make it work."

"And *there's* another problem," the King knew he was trying to distract Adam. "If Tomas turns out to have been under a *compulsion* spell and *he* should lose his duchy because *he's* now too vulnerable to another one... then *I* should probably abdicate... what?"

Adam was rolling his eyes again. "Genevieve told me that this is *another* 'rabbit-hole' you keep going down. We're not letting you leave, short of death or an Heir we can all agree on. And that is *not* my Jason. And definitely not *me*. We're both older than you, for one thing, and we're neither of us these pure angels that you seem to see us as."

He gave Damien a very serious look.

"*You,* my sweet prince, are the purest heart amongst us all. No, I'm serious," he added as Damien snorted guiltily and turned his head away.

Adam's hand gently turned the King's head back to face him. "It's probably a part of the reason that we're all attracted to you. This sense that you'll always do what you think is right. Not right for *you,* but for *all* of us. I can't think of one other person who would be turning themselves into knots because they *hurt the evil sorceress' feelings* after going through what you did.

"*I* wouldn't. *Genevieve* wouldn't. Even *Jason* wouldn't, and he's the closest one of us to that pure heart of yours."

Damien still couldn't meet his eyes, and after a moment Adam sighed. "But none of this is what you need to hear right now, is it?"

But the King made the mistake – inevitable perhaps – of looking up when Adam touched his lips gently in a light kiss. And then held Damien's head firmly, making it hard to look away from that riveting, loving, understanding golden-hazel gaze.

"I *forgive* you, Damien Alsterling. Or... what did you re-name yourself? 'The Sorcerer-King of Ilseador, Defender of the Realm, and Father of Giendra Marlerite Stellarine Alsterling'."

He rolled his eyes. "Definitely not something anyone is going to guess, though why you'd go to all that effort and then just *hand* it to me..."

Adam's eyes were the very definition of compassion.

"*I* forgive you, too. For giving yourself up to that white witch when we needed you here. For letting yourself think you're unworthy of the love and honor we give you. For not being here while Genevieve went through all that morning sickness and *I* had to deal with keeping her stuck in her room *again.*"

He paused as tears pricked Damien's eyes.

"And I'm going to *tell* you I forgive you in the one way you never argue about."

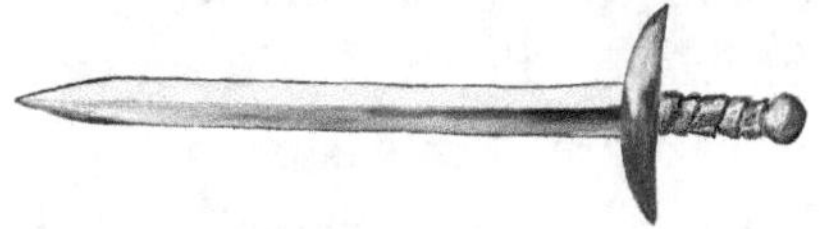

Chapter SEVEN

Demonology 101

"Why didn't you go back to your old rooms?" Damien asked lazily some time later. "Not that I *mind*, of course, but it's kind of gloomy in here..."

Adam had been right of course. He couldn't argue with that kind of... *forgiveness.*

"Jason wanted to stay close to Genevieve. We spent as many nights up there as down here, but this way there were no awkward questions." Adam answered, also sounding just as... relaxed.

The King hesitated. "This is... still a mess, isn't it, Adam?"

"The four of us? Not so much as all that." The Champion chuckled. "Not that I want to tell the world."

He paused. "Well, I do and I don't. I didn't like having to hide how much I loved Jason for all those years. I don't like having to hide how much I love *you*. But... I also wouldn't really want to have to explain all this to... my mother, say."

Adam winced slightly at that thought. "On the other hand... it's not going to get easier to not be... loving... in public. I know *that* from experience."

Damien snorted slightly. "You literally *picked me up* on the docks. I think that cat may be out of the bag... though the story of how you and Jason practically raised me will probably cover most things. Jason and Genevieve... that's a different story."

He snuggled in a bit more. "This is probably the entirely wrong time and place to say this, but... I wish things could have been simpler. I wish I could have just been your 'extra little brother'."

Adam chuckled. "That *does* boggle the mind right now. But I know what you mean. It would be... simpler."

"I'm not regretting anything, though."

Not in this moment anyways. Holding on to that conviction... might be a challenge. He still had to maintain his authority as king, and see that Jason – as his Heir – was also taken seriously.

And this in a Realm where likely the only reason that Jason and Adam's marriage hadn't caused *actual* civil unrest had been the advent of the ice-storm, the pirate-attack, Damiens own kidnapping, and now Tomas of Siovale's insurrection. Whether all of those distraction would serve to make the marriage of two men old news when things finally settled down... only time would tell, though Damien was rather skeptical. There would be other marriages happening to rile everyone up again, after all.

Hopefully he wouldn't spend the rest of his reign doing nothing other than prosecuting those who harmed others simply for daring to be in love...

Which came back to the current issue...

"Nor am I... anymore." Damien knew that it had taken Adam a lot longer to reach that conclusion.

Well... it had and it hadn't, given how ambivalent the King had been feeling, well, just a *little* earlier. And might again, when the whole complicated mess crashed down on him again.

But for just this little, almost-perfect space of time... perhaps Damien could *pretend* he was wholly at peace with it all.

"And... I feel much better now that you're home." Adam paused. "And *here*. In my *arms*. In my *bed*."

If that wasn't just the loveliest thing to hear...

Damien touched the taller man's face gently. "I love you, too."

76

Adam hesitated, then added, "Jason is happy that you're home, too."

Damien smiled. "At this distance you're really only able to send single emotions back and forth, aren't you? So, this was the most effective way to tell him – tell *them* – that I was back. Because there's no one else who would make you feel... *this* way."

The way they were snuggled together he couldn't see Adam's face, but there was an appropriate pause for the raising of eyebrows. "You... knew?"

"It... occurred to me at... some point."

"Hunh."

There was a pause long enough that the King was certain that Adam had fallen into well-deserved slumber. He began to gather himself to slip away, back upstairs to his own suite...

"So, demons." Adam said.

Damien forced himself to relax again.

"That... sounds bad. And you left before you finished what the white *witch* thought you should know."

Somehow it was clear when Adam called her that he wasn't referring to *actual* witches, who were low-Powered Elemental mages for the most part.

There was something about Adam's intonation that made it clear he was censoring his language for his king's tender sensibilities. Since Damien knew quite well the other word his Champion would have used for the sorceress, he found it both amusing and incredibly sweet. Though it was true he wouldn't have used it himself, and not just because of his incredibly mixed emotions regarding Azella.

"It could be," Damien admitted. "It certainly won't be *easy*. But I know the Banishment spells. And I have the full Power of the Realm behind me. It's always most, um, *frisky* in the Spring anyways."

Adam chuckled and kissed the top of his head. "That explains a lot."

He sobered. "But you said she didn't give you access to the books about Summoning demons. How sure are you that the Banishment spells you did find will work?"

Damien tried not to shudder. He needed to reassure Adam, not share his own fears.

"Demons... seem to be something that don't belong in our world. Not all of them are from the same place or are even intentionally malicious to us – though I suppose Azella would only summon ones that are. They all just seem to be... unable to co-exist with our kind of... existence."

"You mean they want to kill us?" He could *feel* Adam's frown.

"No... they're just as... inimical... to the things that you don't normally consider 'alive' – the rocks and water and such – as they are to the things you think of as 'alive'."

"Things *I* 'think of as alive'," Adam echoed slowly. "You... really see the world differently, don't you, Damien?"

The King chuckled... partly to cover his dismay. Usually, he was so careful not to let anyone else see that difference between how he thought and the way everyone else seemed to.

Though Adam had been closer to him and therefore seen more of how Damien's mind worked than most. The tall blonde knight had rarely ever seemed to need to make an *issue* of it before...

"You see more of it yourself than most, Adam. When I re-connected to the Realm, It showed me Genevieve and Jason, and I could see what they'd been doing for It. All of what they were doing was focused on humans, of course, with some small attention to crops and livestock – but it was Winter, after all. But then the Realm showed me *you*."

"*Me?*" Adam sounded incredibly wary. "*I'm* not Bound to the Realm. Or even any piece of it."

"I know. But the Realm believes you take It... or rather *Them*, it's definitely a plural... more seriously than Jason and Genevieve do." Damien hugged Adam's strong, broad chest a little tighter. "Maybe it's because of your connection to Jason. Maybe it's all the conversations we've had over the years and how you've taken the time to learn so much about magick. Maybe it's just... *you*. But somehow the Realm has Chosen and Bound you... and, my friend, my... my *love*, It's woken *your* Gifts all on Its, Their own. You blaze so *brightly*..."

"That's what you meant when you came in earlier," Adam said slowly.

Damien nodded. "I suspect... I suspect that the Sword would even speak for you now."

"No thank you." Adam said firmly. "We are not trying that."

"You'd be the first outside of the Alsterling line."

"*NO.*"

Damien chuckled and kissed Adam's chest. "Always your choice, my friend. But the Alsterlings were Chosen by the Realm, not the other way around. And... as far as you being Bound to the Realm, *I* have no say in that. It likes you," he added somewhat unnecessarily. "You make It feel better."

The younger man paused and added a little shyly, "Almost as much as you make *me* feel better."

Adam snorted. "I'm beginning to think this has nothing to do with *Jason* being Bound and everything to do with *you and me.*"

The King shrugged. He couldn't deny the allegation. "Well, *I* didn't do it."

"You also didn't *lay cobwebs of love* all over everyone, you would have said six months ago."

Damien winced. "I'd forgotten about that. Another thing I'll need to sort out. I think... I think I know how to do that, now. And I *do* need to teach you how to... not blaze so brightly. You'll blind Jason all over again, like at his investiture as Duke, and while people say love *is* supposed to be blind..."

Adam snorted again. "Fine. Later. You were telling me that demons aren't supposed to be part of the world. But that doesn't explain how you know these less-protected Banishment spells will work on them."

"Not part of *our* world. Our... universe." The King paused, trying to decide how much to tell Adam, right now, about all the things that he'd learned.

And not just from Azella's books. Once he'd re-connected to the Realm, once he'd opened himself up to It in that run, it had been as if a faucet had been opened in his mind. He'd had to figure out how to shunt it aside so he could focus on the here and now. Shunt the new *knowledge* aside because there was no stopping or even pausing it.

"Damien?"

The Sorcerer-King kissed his lover's chest one more time and rolled onto his back. "Look, Adam."

With barely a thought he summoned the tetrahedron of Elements to float above them. And explained his insight that the Elements were really States of Being. And the fifth, or 'evolved,' Element, the Aether, that was contained therein.

Adam listened quietly, asking for clarifications here or there.

It was enough to absorb at once. Damien did not try to begin explaining the other things that had been coming to him. About how all the stars were – or might be – 'suns.' About how there were other 'layers' of reality, some of which were accessible and some were not.

It was almost too much for *him*, after all, and he'd had ten days to begin assimilating all of this. Or four months, since he had started learning about Fire Elementals.

Or his whole life, since he'd always somehow seen the world as a puzzle to be solved.

The 'world' was just a lot bigger than he'd realized.

He hoped he could share more of this with Adam – later. It was hard to imagine someone else who would appreciate it so well.

"Demons exist outside of these States of Being, Adam," he explained, pulling them back to the original question. "Some of them – the ones that are not malicious, but seem simply to exist in a different way – they appear to come from a 'universe' where everything is the reverse of ours in some sense. They may look exactly *like* us, but they are inherently destructive to us – and we to them. When they end up here, they are inevitably drawn to their own exact opposite..."

"And if they meet, they are each destroyed," Adam nodded, making the leap. "That would be the source of those legends about meeting your *doppelgänger*. The stories made it seem as if the destruction was later on, through some sort of string of ill-luck, but this makes more sense."

"It would take a string of ill-luck to bring them here," Damien told him. "It's as dangerous for them as us. No one survives the encounter, and it's hard to figure out what's going on in time to find someone who can Banish them safely back to their own... Realm of Existence."

80

"Hmmn," Adam looked thoughtful.

"The type Azella will Summon is different, though," the King went on. "I suspect she doesn't try for the *truly* malicious ones, just the ones that don't see us – creatures of our world – as more than prey. It's like when you go hunting. You don't feel malicious towards the deer."

Adam winced. "I don't hunt, Damien." He paused thoughtfully. "But I see what you mean."

The younger man looked at him in surprise. "Is that why you never taught me? Not that I wanted to *learn...*"

"You're an empath also, aren't you? You should understand." Adam asked. "I... *can't* hunt. It always made me sick to my stomach even to be a part of the chase. And I had to be somewhere else entirely when the kill was made – or livestock slaughtered. Papa... would always take us away to the seashore when the homefarms were doing that."

Though that begged the question of how Adam had managed to fight – and kill – so effectively during the Battle of Siovale.

Damien chuckled. "I think we can guess you get the empathy from your father."

Adam shrugged a little. "That... structure is beautiful, Damien."

His golden-hazel eyes traced the lines of the tetrahedron, floating above them.

"*I* thought so." Damien sighed. "Azella... never seemed to notice. She just saw it as a display of my Power." He paused. "To be fair, I *had* just re-connected with the Realm and told her I didn't need to study anything to reach the conclusion of our 'bargain.' She may have been a little... distracted."

"You try to be *too* fair, Damien."

"Hmmn. So... again, not that I'm complaining, but why didn't *Jason* ever try to teach me to hunt? I know that *he* does."

Adam snorted. "Why hasn't Genevieve? It's extremely difficult to pry you out of this Castle, good milord."

Damien tilted his head as he thought about that. "I suppose... I've been busy the last few years. And before that there was my grandfather..."

Who had never wanted him to go *anywhere...*

To his surprise, Adam shook his head. "No, Damien. It's *you*. Not your grandfather, and not your workload. It's why Jason headed straight out to look for you when Genevieve took you to the grotto. We've had a devil of a time getting you out of the Castle for any reason, so he was sure that if you *were* gone, something was seriously wrong."

Damien frowned. "What are you talking about? I go into the city regularly."

"The last year or so you have," Adam agreed.

"And before I was crowned, my grandfather didn't want me going anywhere. He reamed you and me both out when you took me to Lynncrag," Damien pointed out.

And the old king had made it bluntly clear to Damien that he was aware of Adam and Jason's relationship and that he would not hesitate to use it against them if Damien didn't toe the line.

"He did." Adam agreed again, but added, "But it wasn't like other times I'd seen him do that. King Reginald wasn't *angry*, Damien. He was *frightened*. At the time, I thought he was concerned that you might be lost from his influence or taken to Elaarwen. Now..."

He looked at the King thoughtfully.

Damien twitched under that gaze.

"Now... *what?*" he demanded.

"Now... I wonder if your father's fatal mistake wasn't trying to defect to the Rebellion, but in trying to take *you* away from Emeralsee," Adam replied. "From this Castle, more specifically."

Damien sat up abruptly, and scooted away from his Champion. "What are you talking about?"

His parents' murder was a sore point he had never come to terms with and coped with mainly by skirting around the thoughts. Golden, perfect Prince Eric, tall and loving and capable of soothing away the darkest fears... and his princess-consort, Lady Miria, small and dark and gentle and strong in ways that didn't show on the outside...

Perhaps it wasn't a surprise that he'd clung so hard to the tall, blonde Jason and Adam and tiny, darkly perfect Ciriis... Her cousin, Rosa, would have been even better, all soft and strong where Ciriis was sharp and terrifying.

Adam angled his head to look up at him. "I think the Castle made it clear to King Reginald that *you* were not to leave. Possibly – no, probably – when your family arrived. Didn't you say they were summoned back when you were eight?"

Damien looked at his old friend with a frozen feeling building in his middle.

"Most of my cousins were here, too. Including *Jason,*" he added almost spitefully. "Grandfather wanted everyone under his eye, the better to prevent the Rebellion from nucleating around a true Royal Heir."

Adam snorted. "Duke Aldred – and Genevieve – were all the Royal Heirs they needed. Their provenance is as good as yours, as noted by that damned Sword. Though I suppose if your father *had* managed to carry the Heir's Ring to the Rebellion, that might have been different."

"So... what are you saying?" Damien had started shivering. He wrapped his arms around himself, trying to look more like he was folding them in disagreement... though this *empath* who was also his *lover* and *mentor* was hardly likely to be so easily fooled.

"Most of the others got sent home within a year or less, as I recall," Adam went on. "*Your* family was still here, two years later."

"Father had been named Heir. And with Kandra having run off to join the army when I was six, we were all happy to be close enough to visit with her."

They hadn't stayed because of him. They *hadn't.*

"And why choose your father as Heir?" Adam went on. "Until you were named as Heir, King Reginald never kept any of his children or grandchildren as Heir for more than a few months. Even Oskar, for all that he had the Ring three separate times. *Your* father was Crown Prince from the day he walked into Emeralsee with you until..."

"Until the day his own father had him slaughtered like a pig on the Throneroom floor." Damien knew his voice had gone cold. He was cold all the way through. "I only kept the title because there was no one else *left,* Adam. Father was... *special. Better.* The king who *should* have been crowned."

Adam looked at him with almost aching sympathy. *Empathy.* "None of the other Heirs but you and your father were allowed to keep the Ring, Damien. And there *was* still Jason. Whom you've said you saw in his notes King Reginald was well aware was his legitimate great-grandson. But the Castle didn't want *Jason.*"

"And it wanted *Oskar?*" Damien bit out.

He was shivering uncontrollably now.

Adam *could not* be right.

Because then it would be *Damien's fault* that his parents had been killed.

Maybe even that *Kandy* had.

It didn't matter that he'd been a small child and had had no choice, no *ability* to control even what he ate for dinner.

It would be *his fault...*

Adam gave him an uneasy look. "Jason's Gifts for magick, as you call it, were all latent until you Bound him as Duke of Emeralsee. Oskar... you probably didn't know. He had a touch of magick. Healing magick."

Damien was almost shocked out of his own... shock. "Healing magick? That *monster?* But... but you never find a Healer without *empathy,* and he *couldn't* have been an empath. Not with... with the way he treated people..."

"He... seemed to have his empathy backwards," Adam told the horrified king. "Instead of wanting to fix pain, he thrived on it. And... Jason says he used the Healing to patch up his broken... toys... so that he could... play with them some more."

Damien felt nauseous. "That's... that's just..."

Adam nodded. "I agree. But he had *magick.* And Jason, we now know, has *magick.* And he has Eldridge blood. And *you* have magick. And *your* mother was an Eldridge."

"Queen Eliza's grandmother was an Eldridge," Damien said reluctantly. Oskar's mother. He hated to admit yet another connection to Oskar, even at so many generations removed.

"And both your grandmother, Queen Rena, and Genevieve's great-grandmother, Duchess Shalla, were from Dawil," Adam pointed out. "A land *renowned* for its magick."

"A thousand years ago, maybe," Damien objected. "They have less magick *now* than most of the other Realms around the Merutian Sea."

"Come here." Adam opened his arms to the trembling king. "It's *not your fault* if your grandfather was looking for a way to pass the Throne to a mage-Talented descendant."

Somehow Adam always knew.

Damien fell into that... *forgiving* embrace that had meant safety and understanding since he was fourteen.

But...

"Adam..."

It was easy for *him* to say that. *His* parents – Adam's *clearly very Talented* parents – were home safe in Lynncrag.

Not... not nearly a score of years dead and buried... and slain before his eyes. But with Adam's arms around him it was... easier to *try* to believe.

"At least he wasn't trying to *breed* mage-Talented descendants," Adam pointed out.

Damien didn't stop trembling. "Maybe he was. Why else so many wives?"

But if that were the case, both he and Oskar should have been wedded off at minimum. And hadn't his grandfather been trying to extend his own life? Why bother with worrying about his potential Heirs at all? It wasn't as if he'd shown any signs of a sense of real stewardship of the Realm.

Lord Prydeen had suggested that the Realm had been draining King Reginald. And that, if the old king had been aware of Damien's potential as a mage, Prydeen himself would have been set aside as Apprentice in order for the king to train an heir of his own blood.

Damien had been reading his grandfather's journals. But he had started at the very beginning, more interested in trying to understand how the ambitious and resentful Prince – who was nonetheless a loving husband and father – could have become the evil tyrant that Damien had known him as. The latter years, which might cover these *other* questions were ones he hadn't yet gotten to for the most part.

"Hmmn." Adam switched back to what could only be a safer subject by comparison. "So, you think that you can Banish a demon because they don't *belong* here? And because the *Realm* wants them gone also? Even if the spells that you found are... incomplete?"

A kind way of saying 'useless.'

"Essentially, yes," Damien agreed. "It seems that the demon needs to maintain a sort of... *bubble* of its home-space around itself to remain here. The Banishment spells I found all work off of some variant of popping that bubble or squeezing it out of our world's space. They can't *all* be wrong."

Adam looked skeptical.

"They *feel* right."

"Hmmn. So, what are we supposed to do then? Tomas shows up here – hopefully with Genevieve and Jason. We greet him as required, with bended knee and all... and then you battle this demon that shows up?"

Damien shrugged. "I suppose. Approximately. There's a lot of unknowns, though." He sighed wistfully. "It's *Genevieve* who's the strategist."

Adam shook his head. "And *you're* the one who beats her at chess."

"Occasionally. And in chess there're no unknown variables." Damien sighed. "Adam, it's getting *really* late. I should go up to bed."

"You should stay *here,* with *me.* You can go up in the morning." Adam's arms tightened around his King. "We need each other to get through this. And with only these few days to prepare, we don't dare spend half of each night awake and the rest fighting nightmares."

Damien blinked. That sounded like Adam was inviting him back... "Adam... this is only going to make it harder to go back to normal once we have them safely home."

"My sweet prince," Adam said with deepest irony, "There is no *'going back to normal'* for any of us. We can only go forwards and find a new way to make this... the *four* of us... work."

He lay back down, pulling Damien down next to him. "Now be a good little sorcerer-king and douse the lamp, would you?"

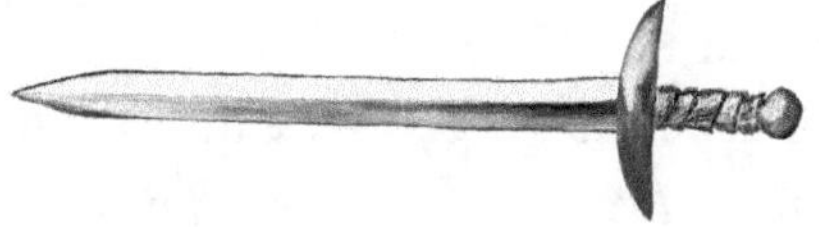

Chapter EIGHT

Trust and Love

THE NEXT FEW DAYS WERE a mad effort to prepare for the arrival of the Siovalese forces. Only with a select few – Adam, Tim, Aryllis, Lord David – did Damien discuss the demon that Azella the Unpitying was likely to send against him.

The rest of his people, including General Direlien, the Commander of the Armies and currently personally in command of the five-thousand person Emeralsee Home Guard, were set to creating a subterfuge. They were to put on a good show for Tomas Elsevier and his men, including giving what looked like an unconditional surrender if necessary. But in reality, the Army and the City Guard were organizing to make it possible to build a resistance movement that would be able to effectively throw off the usurper.

It rankled, of course, but there was a general agreement that all efforts should be made to safely extract the Queen and Crown Prince from Duke Tomas' clutches.

Damien would rather not have told his select few about the demon either, there being nothing they could do about it. However, *some*one needed to be ready to handle things while the King was occupied. It might well fall to Adam and Tim to rescue Genevieve and Jason. On their advice – and not without a great reluctance – Damien finally also brought in General Direlien and Captain Seldebard of the City Guard and explained what else was likely to appear... and what he would have to do about it.

General Direlien gave his king a dark look from under a beetled brow. "It's been *three days* since Your Majesty returned. May I assume it was Sir Loveress who convinced you to share this *invaluable strategic information* with we poor souls who will be on the ground?"

Damien winced while Adam leaned back in his chair with folded arms and a sardonic expression. They were meeting in the small Council chamber and the table was already spread with maps and lists from the general and Captain Seldebard's reports on the progress of preparations in the city.

Lord David sighed. "He's trying to spare us all, General. There being nothing we can do about these demons."

Of all of them, it was David who had gone absolutely white on hearing what was to come. Damien assumed that the foreign merchant-prince had knowledge of how bad demons could be from some other source. None of his native-born Ilseadorans – including, he had to admit, himself – had enough knowledge of the possibilities to feel more than a generalized dread.

But whether Lord David's... concern... came of more than reading a vivid (and potentially sensationalized) account or a father's natural protectiveness, Damien couldn't tell. And he hadn't quite been able to bring himself yet to ask.

The general was shaking his head. "I've played chess with the Queen – and she says you give her a good game, Your Majesty. No more major pieces sacrificed in dramatic gambits, if you please."

Damien met his eyes. "No. I'm done with that."

"Good," Captain Seldebard said with great relief. "Prince Jason was doing what he could, milord, but the people wanted *you*. There was widespread outrage that the nobles–" he nodded somewhat apologetically at Adam, "–had let you go so easily. If it weren't for the Queen being soul-bonded to you and pregnant, I think we might have seen riots. But no one wanted to put her through *that* as well."

Riots? Because he'd given himself up to save the city?

"It wasn't *easily*," Tim noted dryly. "If anyone in this city thinks they can stop our King from doing whatever he damned well feels like, I'd be happy to take them into the Royal Guards. *We* just try to keep up with him."

He reclaimed some of his usual humor as Captain Seldebard gave him an astounded look, perhaps at the idea of commoners in the king's own bodyguard. "Actually Adam – Sir Loveress – did better than the rest of us at that. At least, I got the impression you didn't *mean* to take him down with you to face the Pirate-King, Your Majesty?"

Adam snorted. "No. He didn't. Not that it did either him or Lady Megan any good in the end."

Lord David looked away, and Damien felt his own chest tighten. *He* had come back, but Megan...

"I have to be the one to fight the demon," Damien said after an awkward moment of silence. "*And* the sorceress, if she appears again. But that's because no one else here has the skills and Power. I don't intend to *give myself up.*"

Not anymore.

"And that means we have to get the Queen back alive," the general's heavy-jowled face was thoughtful. "And Prince Jason, if we can."

He nodded at Adam, but Jason was clearly secondary in his opinion.

They – Adam and Damien – had decided to keep the second soul-bond a secret. It would add to the urgency of rescuing Jason as well...

But there was still the succession to plan for. And not just *one* child, but several of them, whose lineage they dared not impugn.

Genevieve had weathered all that had happened to Damien and their soul-bond these last several months. They could only hope she could survive if something dire happened to Jason.

That Adam, with his magickally-induced almost-soul-bond, might *not*... went unspoken.

His Champion kicked the King in the foot under the table without so much as flickering an eyelid at him.

He says to get your head back in the game, grandson, Queen Marian told Damien. *Actually, he was a bit more graphical than that, but there are some phrases I refuse to repeat.*

The King could guess what those might be, given all the years that Adam had been training him as a swordsman.

"So," he said to his general and his captains. "Now that you know what's coming, how does that change your plans?"

They all leaned in over the maps and lists again.

Good boy, Queen Marian approved. *And that's from **both** of us.*

"Now that wasn't so bad, was it?" Adam noted as General Direlien and Captain Seldebard made their way out, still talking to Lord David.

Damien sighed. "No. And the general was right. You were *all* right. They should have been brought in from the beginning. I just don't want to start a general panic."

Tim laughed. "And you think that's not likely to happen if some giant magickal being comes swooping out of the sky to devour people and no one expected it?"

He sobered. "You still haven't given us any details about what you plan to do about this beast, Damien. Except that you don't plan to sacrifice yourself in doing it. Which, by the way, everyone is pleased to hear. At last."

Tim, too was a good friend of long provenance.

The King raised an eyebrow. "And who all is 'everyone'? We're still keeping this close, I thought."

The Captain of his Royal Guards waved a hand. "No one has been spreading word about *demons,* Damien. But the word is out in the streets that the Elseviers have been conspiring with the sorceress for a long while. Aryllis has been putting out counter-rumors that your powers have grown while you were fighting free of the sorceress and that you can face her now. Pretty much everyone is expecting some kind of a mage-battle."

"I thought General Direlien seemed less surprised than I would have expected," the Sorcerer-King noted. "But nothing ever seems to startle him."

He ignored the comment about having *fought* his way free and avoided Adam's eyes.

Though he'd been avoiding Adam's eyes all day. And the last two days, too, while they worked.

"Aryllis says his spies are better than hers for this sort of thing," Tim admitted wryly. "So... what *do* we have to look forward to?"

Damien stood up from his chair to pace. "I'm not actually sure, Tim. I know what I need to do... but it's all untested. And there are a dozen different ways she could have the monster attack – that I can think of off the top of my head – but she could have others. It's why I think we need to follow through on whatever little drama Tomas wants when he arrives. If he wants me to hand him the Crown on bended knee in return for Genevieve and Jason... I'll do it. And it'll be up to you to get them safely away."

"And if he demands you turn *yourself* over to him in return for them?" Tim asked.

Damien turned to face the brave knight whom he had trusted so long. "Then I'll do that. It doesn't *matter,*" he waved off Sir Tim's half-begun objection. "I won't be in Tomas' power, no matter where he wants me to stand. With very few exceptions, I've been impervious to physical attack for the last five years – and so has Genevieve. I set *that* spell up as soon as I figured out how."

Another thing he'd learned from his grandfather's journals. Using anything from those notebooks had made Damien deeply uncomfortable... but to protect Genevieve, he was willing to risk it. Genevieve – and himself, since the soul-bond would literally kill her if anything happened to Damien.

At least he'd been able to figure out ways to use other sources of magick to accomplish the spells than the horrible ones his grandfather had used.

Tim barked a laugh and looked at his own former Captain, getting a sardonic nod from Adam to confirm this news.

"And *now* I find out that my life's work is utterly useless. I suppose I'd rather have it be that way," he added with a sigh. "Wait, you said there have been exceptions? When would those have been?"

"I had to take back the energy that was powering the spell before the ice-storm hit," Damien explained. "I left Genevieve's protections, but I wanted every bit of Power available to fight the storm. And I didn't get mine back up until just before the pirates arrived."

"Was that the only time?" Tim asked intently. "What about when you're tired? Or sick? Or unconscious? Or sleeping?"

Adam snorted again. "That's assuming he actually *sleeps.*"

The King ignored that. Because if he didn't, he'd be blushing... "The spell needs some occasional maintenance, but once I set it up it stays."

"Hmmn," the Captain gave him a thoughtful look. "You said 'exceptions,' though, and you're always careful with your words. So there has to have been at least one other time."

Damien hoped he *wasn't* blushing. "Let's just say your life's work isn't useless at all."

The other times had been when he and Genevieve had pushed the soul-bond – and the Realm's hunger – to its limits. Most notably this last Autumn. He'd simply had no energy to spare when he had bodyguards to do the same work.

"Hmmn," Tim said again, still looking thoughtful, and Damien was forcefully reminded that this very intelligent man was married to his Spymistress. Between them, Tim and Aryllis might well be able to figure it all out. Perhaps it was simply better to stay ahead of the game and bring them into the secret...

...that was a decision they could wait to make. When Genevieve and Jason were available to help make it.

"I have one other thing to mention," the usually ebullient Captain said seriously, his very demeanor immediately focusing both Damien's attention and Adam's.

He looked from King to Champion, then settled his gaze on Damien again.

"Damien, you've made it clear that we did right in acknowledging Adam's right to serve as Regent after we lost Genevieve and Jason both. And that you expect him to serve in that capacity while you're otherwise occupied when Tomas arrives."

"It doesn't make sense to put Genevieve in charge of a strategic situation she's unfamiliar with," Damien agreed.

Tim nodded. "I agree. I doubt there's anyone here who wouldn't."

"So...?" The King didn't see why Tim was bringing it up at all. This seemed like one of the few things they had completely squared away. "I trust Adam's judgment unreservedly. You know that."

"You haven't looked like it the last few days, Damien," Tim said bluntly. "You've seemed to be *avoiding* Adam."

He looked apologetically at his former commander. "Not that it's possible, since he's been shadowing you everywhere, but you've been avoiding looking at him, talking to him... It's at the point where Aryllis says people are starting to wonder. Not that anyone would be *surprised* if you were furious that we all let this happen... or even that you might focus that on Adam, since he was the person left in charge..."

He looked embarrassed. "But you told us all – you even made a *speech* to the *people* – that you *weren't* angry. It's... confusing."

"It's fine, Tim," Adam told him quellingly.

Tim shook his head. "It's not. People could understand if he was angry, Adam. In fact, they might understand *better* if he was. Most of us would be, after all Damien has gone through. All our *King* has gone through recently."

Damien glanced very briefly at Adam... more to make the point that he *would* than to actually look at him.

"I don't dare be angry, Tim," he said softly. "Even if I blamed anyone other than Tomas – or Azella the Unpitying – for this mess, I don't *dare*."

Tim frowned. "No one thinks you're going to turn into your grandfather, Damien."

The King sighed and let go of the chair-back he'd been gripping in order to pace again.

"It's not that. Or... mostly not that. I've... faced that fear and come out the other side for the most part." He still wanted to know how and why King Reginald had changed... but he was coming to the realization that he might never find that out. "It's–"

"Damien..." Adam sighed. "I think you can stop explaining."

He turned and looked where Adam was nodding at the chair he'd just let go. Wisps of smoke were dissipating over it, and Tim's eyes had gone wide. Damien came to take a closer look.

Fingerprints.

He'd left *charred fingerprints*.

Well, at least the chair hadn't burst into *flames*...

"Damn," he said softly, looking at the sooty fingertips he hadn't noticed. "I'm still getting the hang of Fire, I suppose."

Which was not a particularly good sign. Fire was at the opposite end of the spectrum from the Earth he more naturally favored. But it was the evolved State of Being, the Aether, that he would need in dealing with Azella and her demon. He'd have to have all of the Elemental States under control to make this work.

He didn't think he'd been *that* distracted by the conversation.

"Damien, my King," Tim said slowly, "are *you* safe for the rest of us to be around?"

"That's enough, Captain Ancellius," Adam said sharply. "I'll see to His Majesty's safety. You may go."

Tim looked at him sadly. "I had to ask, Adam. And I still need an answer."

"Damien would no more hurt anyone here than–"

"It's all right, Adam," Damien said wearily. "It's a fair question."

He met Tim's eyes. "I'm not angry. Not at Adam, not at you. Not even the sorceress, really. It... makes no sense to be angered at a cat for killing a rat – or even toying with it first. It's simply in the cat's nature and what it was taught to be. Tomas... I'm withholding judgment on Tomas until I know what led to this–"

"Generations of o'erweening ambition," Adam said cynically.

Damien flicked him a glance before returning his gaze to Tim. "Perhaps. I hope not. I hope that whatever *this* is–"

"*Treason*," Adam said pointedly. "Rebellion. Collusion with foreign powers."

"Perhaps," Damien said again. "But we've had enough of that to last us all a lifetime."

He sighed. "And as to your other question… The Realm won't *let* me do harm, Tim. Even if I lose control of my Power, the Realm itself will protect every living creature down to… down to the last snail and guppy."

The Captain relaxed marginally. "Then will you be any *help* against Tomas and his people?"

None of his people were thick-headed, Damien thought with mingled pride and dismay. How could he hope to keep such secrets…?

"Less than you might like," he admitted. "Against the Siovalese anyways. Tomas… has marked himself out to the Realm by putting Genevieve and Jason in danger. I can tell that there are a few others involved, but since *they* aren't Bound the Realm doesn't distinguish them as well. And none of it tells me if any of it is by personal volition or under compulsion – either magickal or… some other."

"Hmmn." Tim shook his head. "It doesn't matter in some ways, Damien. You'll still have to remove the Elsevier family from the rule of Siovale. Even under compulsion, to raise rebellion against the Crown three times in twenty years… Aryllis agrees."

Damien gave him a sharp look. "Why are *you* telling me what she thinks, she's not usually shy about… oh."

He cut himself off. They didn't trust him. Tim didn't want to expose Aryllis to their king's possible ire at the things they'd needed to ask… and to *say*.

The Captain ran a hand through his hair and gave his king the affable smile he was used to. "Well, she'll tell me I was being an overprotective idiot, of course. I'm not sure why she didn't argue more in the first place."

Damien gave him a tentative smile. *He* knew the answer to that, though even Aryllis hadn't seemed to be aware when he'd held that first council three days ago.

"She's pregnant again, Tim. I thought it might be too early for her to tell," he added as Tim's eyes acquired a look of suppressed fear. "I only *looked* because she seemed too tired."

Fear… and ineffable sadness.

"Time for a trip to the Healers, then," the usually-ebullient knight said with resignation. "Not... not our first. They won't make it permanent and there's only so careful you can be without being completely celibate."

Bringing their adored little boy to birth had nearly killed Aryllis.

Damien took a deep breath. "*I* could do that for you, Tim. Or... I have the Power now to help her through it safely. For... both."

Tim looked at him with surprise. Not yet hope... still too new a thought?

"I didn't know what I was doing before," Damien apologized. "Not enough to make the promise."

His old friend nodded slowly. "I'll... talk to her. She... didn't enjoy pregnancy very much either, as I recall." Tim's eyes shimmered. "Thank you, my friend. I'm sorry for ever doubting you."

Damien gave him a wry look. "I'm well aware that much of what I do doesn't look to anyone else like it makes sense. And it's been a trying few months."

Tim laughed, seemingly his usual effervescent self again, though there was still a thoughtful look in his eyes. He shoved his chair back and stood up. "Understatement of the year, my liege."

He strode to the door and bowed himself out.

Damien wandered a bit more... it wasn't directed or energetic enough for pacing... and finally settled himself by leaning his forearm against one of the stone pillars that stood out from the wood-paneling of the room and supported the arches of the ceiling. The stone was cool against his face as he leaned his head against his arm... and clearly, he wasn't the first Earth-mage in the family. The stones of the room – of the entire Castle, he now realized – were fused all the way down to the bedrock, part and parcel again of the living stone from which they had once been carved and a connection to the deepest part of his Realm.

"Ward the room, my King," Adam's voice said from behind him.

"I did as soon as Tim left," the King said absently, his thoughts still entwined with the peaceful, ancient stone. "I didn't think it would preserve either of our dignity to have someone interrupt while you're yelling at me for being an idiot."

Not that he'd had *time* to practice the finer manipulations of his Elemental Powers. Or to learn more about demons. Or...

Adam pulled him off the wall and into a passionate kiss.

"Adam..." he gasped at last, every sense on fire.

"I'm still not sleeping well, you know," the older man said gently. "And somehow I doubt *you're* sleeping at all." He kissed the dark circles under Damien's eyes that the King had been avoiding looking at in the mirror.

Damien tried – unsuccessfully – to step away. "I don't sleep well at night. You know that. And there's been too much to do to sneak in naps during the day as I used to."

"You slept entirely peacefully in *my arms* that first night," Adam told him. "*I'd* sleep better knowing I didn't have to worry about you, too," he added after a moment's pause.

The King looked down. "It wouldn't just be *sleep,* Adam. You know that."

"And *I* told *you* before. We can't go back to some old version of 'normal,' Damien. Genevieve and Jason have a *soul-bond.* They aren't going to be *able* to stay apart entirely."

"I... know." He didn't want to acknowledge it, though. He wanted...

"What we have – you and I – it isn't a soul-bond," Adam went on, "but it's special in its own way. I told you that your nightmares kept waking me up – from across the Castle – when you were a boy. You were *calling* to me, Power to Power, I suppose. If it weren't for Jason..."

Damien huffed a laugh, leaning into Adam's embrace and resting his head on the taller man's chest since his friend didn't seem inclined to let him go... and he really *was* very tired. This had felt like safety, security, *home* since almost as long as he could remember. And the horror of the last months still felt like a sticky shroud... maybe, maybe it was all right to enjoy a hug.

"If it wasn't for Jason, I'd still be in the Royal Library," he pointed out. "No one else has that kind of patience."

He could feel Adam's chuckle all the way down to... no. He wasn't going to think like that.

"No, my sweet prince. I don't think so. *Jason* needed all that patience to lure you out. *I* wouldn't have. Power to Power. You'd been reaching for me already... you'd have come out to *me* in *far* less time than it took *him*."

Damien frowned. "So, you *left* me...?" The embrace suddenly felt confining.

Adam lifted a hand to tilt his face up for another kiss and Damien relaxed again.

"There *was* Jason. I'd been in love with *him* for *years* at that point. And... I wasn't that old myself still, nor... experienced. But I *knew* what he was going through with Oskar and I knew he would need... something more than I could give him. And you... *you* needed an older brother, not a lover."

Damien blushed. "Um..."

The older man chuckled again. "Fine. A mentor. One who saw *his* relationship with you as entirely platonic. No matter how *you* saw *him*. I could *see* I couldn't be that for you. I could *see*, well, *this*, actually."

Another kiss. This one was *deeper* and *longer* and it was all but impossible to deny the fiery ball of desire building inside of him as it went on and on and *on*...

Damien was almost distracted enough not to pick up on the slight extra emphasis Adam had placed on those words.

"You have a touch of Foreseeing?" he managed to fight down his body's urges to ask.

Adam shrugged, trying for nonchalance and almost succeeding. "Flashes. Possibilities. Probably more imagination than anything."

"You never said anything." Damien's tone... might have been accusing if he weren't fighting the rather desperate need to melt into Adam's embrace.

He turned his head to lay it on Adam's shoulder in hopes of making this a little... less hard. Since Adam didn't seem inclined to let him go and Damien wasn't willing to do any of the things that would *make* Adam let him go. Things Adam – or Genevieve – had taught him for the most part, but there were *magick* things he could do as well.

The problem was that any of those things would do some real damage – though he could probably take care enough to ensure it wouldn't be more damage than Adam would suffer in any reasonably vigorous arms-practice session.

Well... that was *part* of his reasons anyways.

"There wasn't anything to really *say*. Jason's method for getting you out made you both stronger. Mine would have made you dependent on *me*. And I was hardly going to mention to *either* of you that I was fantasizing about making love to you when you were fully grown." Adam grimaced. "And I wasn't *fantasizing* exactly."

"Foreseeing..." Damien couldn't help wondering if there was a way to use that in the upcoming conflict.

Yes. *That* was what he was supposed to be thinking about. Dealing with Azella and her demon. Not... sleeping with his Champion.

Foreseeing was notably unreliable, but surely this *had* to give them *some* advantage.

"My sister is much better at it," Adam noted.

"Fontaine? She was going to be a priestess, wasn't she?" Had that been why?

Surprisingly, Adam chuckled again. And he was still holding Damien *very* close, so that *chuckle*... well, it *did* things to him that... he was trying very hard not to think about...

"No, Desirée. Mama, too, actually. They visited again while you were... gone... and it... came up." Adam flushed, unaccountably. "Apparently it's something in our family that arises... when one has children."

Oh. That... did seem strange. Adam wasn't a *father* – Lord David's intent to leave Roger and Esmerelda to his and Jason's – and the King's – care notwithstanding.

"My first flash was... That Day," Adam added quietly. "When... she told you to hide. Jason and I were on duty for decorative value."

They would have been squires still, the matched pair of tall, blonde boys...

That Day... the day his grandfather had had his parents murdered in the Throne-room. Damien's near-perfect recall drew an almost perfect blank on that day. He'd had no idea that Jason and Adam had been there at all. Though he had the vague feeling he'd been told before... it seemed hard to hold onto things about... That Day.

And... thinking about it was definitely effective at squelching... other thoughts. Though he appreciated Adam's embrace even more now; it seemed *comforting* rather than... anything else. His *friend's* arms had loosened a little as well.

"What did you *see?*"

Damien didn't *want* to ask.

Didn't want to *know*.

But... he *had* to ask.

"I saw me training you to use a sword. And you being crowned. And... this." Adam's arms tightened again, and he laid a gentle kiss on Damien's hair. "Me holding you. And then... the *vision* ended and I realized that you had disappeared. And what had happened to... to your parents."

He hesitated for a long moment. "I... we were both pretty traumatized as well. Jason and I. I I don't think I even *felt Jason* for over a year after that."

Trauma indeed for a young empath.

Or... for *two* young empaths, Damien acknowledged.

He'd been numb as well. It had been as if the world had shut off. At first, he'd barely been able to notice that other people existed, since there wasn't anything *there* when he looked at them – no *emotions* but what he could guess from their expressions.

Later... the numbness had worn away and he'd been utterly raw and open to what *anyone* around him was feeling.

The Royal Library had been a safe-ish place to feel like that. Hardly anyone had come in there in those days, scholarship not being well-rewarded under his grandfather's reign. Almost his only 'human' contact had been with the Royal Librarian – his default guardian, Lady Theresa – and her emotions had been as locked down as one might expect for the surviving widow who had turned in her husband as a traitor and who had been 'rewarded' with this post.

Damien also now suspected that there was a sort of empathic shield designed into the Library's walls – the gift of some sensitive ancestor no doubt, and probably originally intended to insulate the scholars working there from distractions.

"That numbness actually helped with training for awhile," Adam noted dryly. "It didn't bother me as much if my opponent got bruised while we were sparring. I couldn't think about That Day, though. Not even to look for you. Not until a couple years later, when your nightmares started seeking me out."

A couple of years... when, presumably, Adam's own trauma had diminished enough to sense what was coming in from the outside again. Damien was tempted to ask if Adam had also experienced a period of intense *over*-sensitivity...

Or perhaps... Oh. That must have been when he first started sensing Damien's nightmares. Though, given that it wasn't until those nightmares were given new fuel, a couple years beyond that *that* he'd managed to *find* Damien...

The younger man didn't want to talk about that. Nothing had ever *happened,* after all, so it was all his own fears. And Adam and Ciriis' appearance in his life had put paid to any worries that anything *would* happen, since it had become abundantly clear that he was no longer half-*forgotten*...

"Sorry..." There seemed little else he *could* say.

Adam kissed the top of his head. "It took a while to distinguish them from my own, honestly. And then... I did what I could to help you directly *in* your dreams. Since I had no idea where you actually were. And then... I enlisted Ciriis to help me find you."

"You never did tell me how you became friends," Damien commented. He'd lost all desire to step away. The conversation was... unsettling, he wouldn't admit to any more than that... but Adam's arms made it feel less so.

Adam sighed. "I sought her out. I *knew* she had ties to the Rebellion, but I couldn't tell her that, of course. She was already a spy – and good at it. Earning her trust... is a very long story. I think it was at least as much because she saw me as a line to Jason and thence to Oskar. Not that Jase and I had much contact with each other at that point."

He swallowed hard, the bulge in his throat moving against Damien's hair, then shook his head with a wry smile. "Jason was perfectly *happy* at that point. It was easy for Ciriis to see why *I* might be willing to turn against the Crown. Though she wasn't all that impressed with what I was suggesting we *do* about the corruption of King Reginald and his Court. *She* was entirely skeptical of looking for an undamaged Alsterling Heir."

Adam chuckled once more, snuggling Damien a little closer. "I was persistent, because you had me about out of my head with nightmares by then, and I *had* to find you. And as a squire I *really* didn't have the free time. *Or* the free-run of the Castle. Not the way a lady-in-waiting to the queens did, anyways."

He tilted Damien's face up again. "You enchanted *her* the moment she saw you, too, my sweet prince."

Damien remembered *that* moment precisely and had his doubts. Ciriis could move more quietly than any noblewoman he'd ever seen – until she trained his Secret Cadre to do it as well. He'd been reading, of course, a piece of his attention alert for the noises that Lady Theresa always made as she bustled in and out. The woman had spent as little time at her royal duties – both the Library and care of himself – as she possibly could. Hardly anyone else had ever come into the Library besides the occasional courting pair – run off by Lady Theresa if she should catch them – and that had increased Damien's education in a different way entirely.

He'd been too underfed to have physically matured enough to be terribly interested... Though he'd just recently had a growth spurt anyways, which had led to the reasons for that renewal of nightmares. Leaving the Library would probably have protected him from his 'guardian,' but Damien had been utterly terrified to do so – he'd quaked and quavered his way through the 'family dinners' that his grandfather periodically had Lady Theresa bring him to. And, to be fair, leaving the Library without a protector would likely have just made him prey to whatever *other* member of the Court happened upon him.

Inside the Library he'd felt safe enough to relax most of the time. And there were books a-plenty to entertain and enlighten him, after all. Lady Theresa made sure he had *some* food every day, and new clothes to replace the outgrown ones when his grandfather summoned him.

So long as Damien had kept his senses alert to the approaching presence of others, he was fine in the Library. He really only needed to keep a close eye out for Lady Theresa herself, since the courting couples and the few others who ventured in really couldn't care less for his existence.

When she was gone – as she most often was, but most especially at night or during Court functions – he could relax and really get into a story, letting his eyes and his *empathy* fill with tales of times and places where the world was a wider place. Even agricultural reports and legal proceedings filled that need to be *elsewhere* – the Library contained the Royal Archives, after all, so there was plenty of fodder for his imagination.

And his sharply-tuned ears were always alert to noises that didn't belong in his space.

He *hadn't* heard Ciriis.

So, when he looked up absently from where he'd been curled up on one of the more comfortable couches, half-trapped beneath a huge volume of fairy-stories, Damien's first impression had been that his *mother* had somehow appeared after all these years and he'd been stunned into stillness. By chance, the gown she was wearing matched one he'd seen Lady Miria wear frequently. Her hair was a very dark brown, not the true black he'd inherited from his mother, and she was probably slightly shorter than his mother had been, but he knew he'd grown in the previous four years.

And he couldn't stop his heart from hoping.

Just as, every time he was summoned to one of those 'family dinners' with his grandfather, there were all those Alsterling uncles and cousins who looked so nearly like his tall, golden-haired father... Though there were fewer of them every time. Prince Oskar had nearly been a younger twin of Damien's father, for all that they'd had different mothers, though the condescending sneer he always wore gave him away every time.

And then Ciriis had turned around from perusing the shelf and the orphaned boy's heart had broken all over again. He'd burst into tears and dashed away, even forgetting his book. Ciriis had looked for him, but *he* knew all the hiding places there were in the Library and she did not.

When she left and Damien finally made it back to his book, it was clear that the mystery woman had flipped through it. He'd felt... almost violated. As if it might have given her a window into his soul without his permission.

Certainly, it had been years before Ciriis had realized that he read more than fairy-stories. Whatever she had thought of him then, an 'enchanting prince' was certainly not it.

"I rather doubt that," he said dryly now. Though he supposed the fierce little woman might have considered him *adorable,* in the sense of puppies and goslings.

Adam shrugged... an action made rather too *interesting* by how closely he was holding Damien and making the King's thoughts focus back in directions he'd decided not to consider. "She knew you were something special. She has some Talent of her own, I think, though I've never been able to figure out what."

"She taught all the Secret Cadre to move as silently as she does, so that can't be it," the King noted. "Adam..."

He wriggled to try to get some more space. They should really be moving on to... Gods, but he was tired. He couldn't recall what was next on his agenda for the day. And *wriggling* against Adam had about the same effects on his ability to think as the taller man's shrugging had a moment earlier.

Nor was it effective in getting Damien free of this increasingly wonderf– *constraining* embrace.

Instead, Adam kissed him again, following his attempts to wriggle away and pressing him back firmly into that stone pillar Damien had been leaning against. It was... almost disturbingly arousing.

"I love you, Damien Alsterling," Adam murmured, and that... only intensified *everything.*

"Adam, are you *projecting* desire at me," he managed to half-ask. His pulse was speeding along like a horse with a burr under its saddle, and he was panting like the rider of that selfsame horse. And, oh *Gods,* but a burr-ridden horse would surely *buck* and that sounded altogether too... um, *interesting* right now. Why not stick with the euphemism that was working?

The taller man chuckled. "I don't think I need to. Are *you?*"

Damien blushed fiercely and shook his head quickly. "Not... not *intentionally* anyways..."

But apparently, he'd been *projecting* his emotional state to Adam *un*intentionally since he was – what? – twelve? So, how could he even tell for sure?

"I love you, too, Adam," he said honestly.

Of course he did. Adam had been taking care of him for the last fifteen years. *Protecting* him and *teaching* him and *kissing* him and… no, that last was only recently… The whole idea was to *stop* this, wasn't it?

"But this… isn't a good idea. I haven't dared look at you where anyone could see… and this will only make it worse…"

Oh, Gods, *that* wasn't what he'd planned to say at all…

Adam kissed him again. "You need *sleep,* Damien. And so do I. We'll neither of us do the Realm any good – or our *other* loves – if we're both exhausted. Or… tangled up inside."

Formal Court-wear didn't leave much skin showing, but Adam was exploring every inch that did.

"This won't *un*tangle me, Adam," Damien tried for a dry tone that failed utterly as he gasped and found himself clinging to his handsome Champion because his own knees were entirely gone to water.

"Won't it?" Adam asked with his usual sharp perception. "It's less me – and Jason and Genevieve – that you're tangled up about than what happened to you in that sorceress' hands. And bed."

How was it that *Adam* could still think and reason abstractly while *doing* these *things* to him?

The tall man snorted. "As if she deserved anything of you. You can choose, Damien. Against the wall or on the Council table."

Oh… oh, maybe Adam wasn't *thinking* all that abstractly. His words were enough to conjure with… There were… reasons he hadn't wanted – or hadn't wanted to want – *this*… weren't there?

It was hard to remember what they might have been with Adam's hands on him like this and his own traitorous imagination expanding upon this idea… Gods, but he was so close just from *thinking* about doing this…

The King blushed furiously again. "We have to sit at that table and make serious plans, Adam!"

"The wall it is, then," Adam told him and began to rotate him to face it.

"You aren't this bold with Jason," Damien half-complained as he... didn't really resist.

"Mmmn. Perhaps I should be."

"I'm not going to be able to hold meetings in here ever again."

Adam chuckled. "It's a big castle, Damien. I think you can find another meeting room to use. Though I might have to knock some sense into you like this again someday. You might just have to get over this little *issue* of yours. Unless you want to start holding Council meetings out in the Great Hall. Or the courtyard."

"Sir Loveress," Damien tried a last effort as his imagination took him on another quick ride and he told himself sternly that he was stronger than this. "Go tell the door-guards I decided to *vanish* myself back to my rooms. For a *nap*."

Adam stepped back at last, and Damien breathed freely. If still much too fast.

"Well," the tall Champion said with a sigh. A *disappointed* sigh? No, it wasn't Damien's concern... "If at least you'll get some sleep, I suppose we're getting *some*where."

He stepped towards the door.

Damien *vanished* himself to his own bedchamber before he could think twice about it.

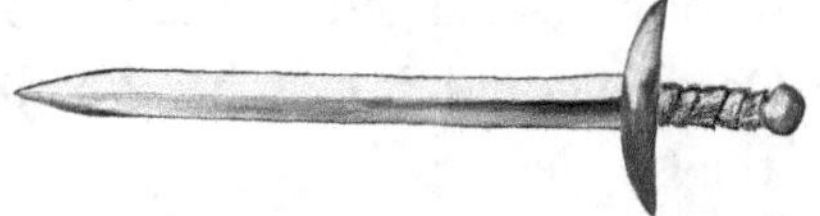

Chapter NINE

Love and Trust

AN HOUR LATER DAMIEN WAS still too tired and restless to sleep.

And too tired and restless to accomplish anything useful.

He'd tried first to ignore how he was feeling. And then tried to do something about it. Which had proved less than useful, given that it wasn't just *release* that he wanted. That he *needed.*

Adam, he knew all too well, had retired to his own chamber below, and was resting about as easily as he was himself.

Damien knew – if he took the time to think about it – precisely where every person in his Castle was with but the slightest thought of them. He could likely do so for every person in the city, or even the province (his sense of the population grew a little hazier past Emeralsee, perhaps in part because fewer of the people out there knew him personally).

While the Seeing Eye wasn't one of *his* gifts, there was a curious porosity to the Castle's walls for its King – thinking about one of his people and orienting on them (because he knew where they were) let him *see* them if he wasn't paying attention not to *look.*

He didn't dare *look* towards the floor of his bedroom.

It hadn't been only for subtlety's sake – for the hope that no one could *tell* how he felt just by watching them – that the King had avoided looking at Adam these past few days. To his magickal sight – which was never wholly disengaged – Adam glowed so brightly and beautifully that Damien couldn't help being half-blinded by him through the walls of the Castle.

And right now, sensitized to Adam as he was...

Likely the Champion was right. Even with his Genevieve returned, they couldn't go back to what had been 'normal.' Not that Damien exactly wanted to, given that 'normal' for him and his wife had included long separations, heartbreaking losses of longed-for unborn children, and finally being near-devoured by the increasingly desperate Realm.

The 'normal' they should have had, though... Tears started in his eyes at the thought.

A room filled with children and laughter.

His wife curled on the couch, her body warm and firm against his side as she taught a little girl with golden-red hair the finer points of chess while he himself ignored a stack of reports to keep the light-haired babe on his lap from fussing and his other arm around her...

Jason in another chair, reading tales to a restless black-haired boy just past toddling, Adam leaning against his husband's legs while cuddling another baby, this one dark-haired and with Damien's own silver-grey eyes, though she seemed more serious than any baby should be.

A sense of a peaceful, settled Realm beyond...

Damien sat bolt upright in bed.

That... was *far* too specific. And *two* babes, simultaneously? Genevieve had felt... weak in the vision. Worse than she had last Fall in some ways. As if she were still at the very beginning of a long recovery.

Damien had no Gift of Foreseeing as far as he knew.

But he knew who *did*.

"I thought that might bring you down here," Adam commented without any particular inflection of surprise when Damien appeared suddenly in his dimly lit bedchamber.

"Imagination or Foreseeing?" the King demanded, standing in a modified parade rest and folding his arms. Posture was all he had going for him here. It was next to impossible to have an appropriately intimidating kingly demeanor with *Adam,* of all people, anyways.

Though putting his shirt back on might have helped.

It might have also helped if the Champion wasn't stretched out atop his own bed, unbooted ankles crossed and with his own shirt off. His fingers were laced loosely across his abdomen, drawing the King's eye to old scars. Adam had earned the title even more than Jason in some ways, having served the Crown in battle since he was knighted.

Better to think about the scars and whence they had come than the way they felt under Damien's hands. Or the hard, powerful muscles beneath those scars. Or what else was hard and powerful and...

Adam shrugged, though the quick sweep of his gaze and his small smile suggested that he was pleased by what *he* saw as well. Or perhaps that was just pleased with his success in luring Damien downstairs.

"I've only ever gotten flashes," the Champion noted casually. "Some of them felt true at the time and have never happened. Some... took so long to come true that I'd almost forgotten they ever occurred." He made a wry face. "Most of them used to involve *you.* It's like Mama and Siri said, a tool for someone raising a child. In our family, at least."

A mess it was, that he'd half-raised Damien. Even *more* of a mess, anyways. Not that Adam was all that much older...

But Damien was briefly distracted. "And you *told* them what you'd *seen?*"

If he'd seen himself *kissing* Damien in the Council chamber as he said he had and told his mother *that*... The King would never be able to face the baronetta baronetta again. He was pathetically grateful that she was Jason's vassal now, and his only at one more remove – not that *that* would make anything easier...

Adam rolled his eyes. "The whole *Realm* knows I helped raise you, Damien." He paused. "But I was... particular about what I chose to share."

Of course. Adam was nothing if not discretion's soul and always had been.

Something else snagged the King's attention. "You said most of your... flashes *'used to'* involve me. What now?"

Adam gave him the most peaceful smile he'd ever seen on this intense man's face. "The children you saw. *Ours.*"

Damien felt as if the air had suddenly been taken from him. He turned and seated himself unsteadily on the edge of the bed.

"There were... *four...*" he said softly, looking at his hands.

It seemed... too much to hope for after all the miscarriages and fear. But he couldn't help twisting to look at Adam hopefully.

"I've *seen* the older girl as a babe alone," Adam volunteered. "And... some snatches of them when they're older." He met Damien's eyes with his own golden-hazel ones seriously. "And the four of us, almost always. *Together.*"

Damien looked away again, almost in shame. "You're going to say I'm making too much of a fuss..."

"No," Adam told him with that gentleness that the squires and pages – and Royal Guards – who had trained on him would never have believed. "You're a man who's just escaped a captivity that had to have reminded you all too closely of some of the hardest parts of your childhood. And anticipating a battle to come. Not to mention that – mental flexibility over the concept of chastity aside – it's one thing to approve of and support Jason and I and another thing entirely to find yourself permanently embedded with us."

Adam paused. "Pun intended. I *was* there in the Throne-room when you told Count Emery that you weren't ready to import triad-marriage to Ilseador. And *this... us...* is a step beyond *that*. And you *are* still the king..."

"Adam..." If there was anything *else* the man could say to make Damien feel like an utter idiot... and now an *intolerant, closeminded, hypocritical* idiot...

"Damien. My sweet prince. Any *one* of these things would be enough to turn you inside-out. *I'd* be worse off," Adam candidly admitted, "if *every single one* of these flashes of precognition didn't have *all four of us* in it. I can still think of ways this isn't reassuring enough, but I'm choosing to believe that I'm *seeing* true and that we'll come out of this whole."

He paused. "I'm choosing to believe that because I've spent fifteen years telling myself it couldn't possibly and I had to *choose*. And that I'd *already* chosen Jason and you had Genevieve."

Another pause. "Twenty-one years, really, though I don't think I knew *why* you supposed to be so special to me the first time I saw you. You *were* a fairly adorable eight-year-old... but you were only eight."

Adam gave him a wry look. "At that point I'd just about gotten Jason to notice me – and it only worked because he was tired of having girls flirting with him all the time and they didn't try when we were together. A very serious student of the sword was Jason at that point."

"So I would've imagined..." Damien shook off this glimpse into his two best friends' life before he had met them.

But Adam had said they would 'come out of this whole.' And what exactly *this* was...

"There's still Deltheran, even after *this* is done," Damien added reluctantly. "And what to do about Tariana and Quillian – or rather their provinces, since I can't combine their duchies when they wed. And... Aldred's child. And... good Gods, *Tomas'* children..."

His stomach cramped abruptly and sharply and he doubled over.

Adam was instantly up, his warm arms wrapped reassuringly around the younger man. "You have to put all of that aside, my sweet prince. One problem at a time, remember."

"I remember..."

His first attempt to *live* outside of the Library – when his nightmares had driven him to Adam in the middle of the night, sleepwalking apparently – had been a disaster. And after Adam and Ciriis had taken him to Lynncrag and Adam's family had accepted him and his own had rejected him... And then they'd come back to find Jason in such dire straits... And then his grandfather had told him not to try to leave ever again...

It had taken them nearly two *more* years to convince Damien to accept rooms of his own outside the Library and actually *sleep* in them.

And the overstimulation of too many people, smells, movement... he'd fled back to the Royal Library regularly.

And each time, Adam and Jason had patiently extracted him again, breaking down the huge pile of problems into ones he could think his way through, one at a time.

Though there had been a fair number of times Adam had simply hauled him off and dumped him in the nearest horse-trough to shock his system out of a widening and descending spiral of terror. Adam hadn't mentioned – until it had happened again when he'd first encountered Azella in astral form, just before she stole him away – just *how* he had known what to do, or *when*.

By that point Damien had become comfortable with his *receptive empathy,* as every Healer needed. Until Adam explained, he hadn't known he also had *projective empathy*.

One problem at a time.

It wasn't any of the ones that he'd named that came tumbling out of his lips, though it had been the thought of Tomas' children being declared traitors – and what that would mean – that had undone him.

"There's still a *person* inside her, Adam. A hurt young girl. Somehow – and I never was able to figure out *how,* or just *who* she was born to – Azella's family sold her into slavery. Her *royal* family. And the Evil Wizard who bought her... he was more than her master. He was her *savior.* She knows the fate of most of those sold as slaves to Evil Wizards... *Power-slaves* they call themselves... and she knows exactly what fate she missed. Gods, Adam, she does those things to them *herself.*"

Adam was silent for a moment.

"You were – no, you *are* – more than 'slightly' in love with her, aren't you." It wasn't really a question. "I suppose you could hardly live practically in her pockets for all that time and not have humanized her in your eyes..."

Damien felt his gorge rise. "Yes. And no. I... didn't tell you what she did to, to her *minions* when *I* wouldn't toe her line. Or how she killed the ancient Evil Wizard who was her master – by stealing his name, just as Lord Prydeen did with my grandfather. The Evil Wizard who *loved* her. And whom *she* loved."

Adam rubbed his back... not at all soothingly it turned out. And this time the arousal that went with the touch was an entirely welcome distraction from having to remember the *things* Azella had done. And condoned.

"No, you didn't. But I can guess at some of it. We... tried to keep you away from most of what went on in the Court here..."

Damien huffed a laugh, sitting up straighter. As if it were possible to have remained *that* naïve in King Reginald's Court. Even with the double-dozen protectors he'd eventually had, such innocence could only have been deadly.

"I knew enough to stay farther away from the dungeons and Lord Prydeen's and my grandfather's 'workshops' so that I *didn't* have to know anymore. I think... Ciriis told my Guardswomen not to give me the details about what he did to them, but some things were impossible to hide when..." He blushed. "It seems so *wrong* to tell *you* about all of this."

"Oh?" Adam asked. "Why?"

The King leaned his head back. Adam's shoulder was there, supporting him as always.

"You... somehow managed to stay out of it all. Just one lover in your life – until I messed that up. I wouldn't want to talk to Genevieve about this either," he admitted.

Adam chuckled as his hands smoothed around Damien's belly. "Is *that* what you think? I'll admit I managed to stay out of Prydeen's and Oskar's and King Reginald's clutches. Though I suspect staying out of Oskar's was more a matter of dumb luck and that he'd have liked to have the 'matched set' as much as the squire-master did when he assigned us ceremonial duty together, despite Jase being older. But I didn't 'save myself' for Jason."

Damien blinked in surprise. "You didn't? But I thought... weren't you a pair even before Oskar...?"

Adam shook his head, and his scratchy cheek buffed the King's bare shoulder. Damien had scrabbled out time to get his own beard tamed, but Adam seemed to have given up shaving entirely for some reason.

"No. I'd... told him how I felt just before he was knighted and we were... just starting to explore that possibility. We'd managed maybe a dozen kisses. A couple of times it went just a *little* beyond kisses."

His tone was wistful. "Remember the attitudes Alexa raised him with. He was fighting his own beliefs about How Men Should Behave, so it... wasn't exactly smooth sailing.

"And then he was assigned as Prince Oskar's 'bodyguard.' And then... he forgot all about me." Adam sighed, gustily, and Damien shivered with the warmth of it across his ear... and neck... Surely this was the wrong reaction to have when listening to this tale... "I'd waited some seven years to tell him, then when I finally bared my heart to him... and then he went and fell in love with your uncle. About whom I'd heard nothing good."

"I don't think 'hearing anything good' was possible with Oskar," Damien muttered. Though that wasn't strictly true. *Jason* had told him... and presumably told Adam as well... his positive memories of the otherwise-unlamented late Crown Prince.

Adam chuckled, though. "No, probably not. Though I... wasn't entirely rational about the whole thing. I'd... had other offers. I took one of them up, hoping to make Jason jealous. It hadn't occurred to me that while *I* knew what *he* was feeling, it didn't go the other way. He never noticed."

There was a pause, while Damien was eaten alive with curiosity, but he would rather his tongue be pulled out with hot tongs than ask...

"It was Sir Edmund," Adam said finally. His tone was wry. "Before you literally explode."

Damien ducked his head. He *hadn't* said anything... but Adam had *felt* his question.

He focused on the answer he had *not* asked for and felt a spurt of shock. "Sir *Edmund?* But wasn't he–"

A warm kiss on his bent neck that turned into a *nibble* nearly made Damien forget everything else.

"The one who replaced Jason as Prince Oskar's 'bodyguard'? Yes." Adam snorted when he was done – for the moment – with Damien's neck. "I don't know what the prince had against me, but I got the distinct impression that *I* was why Edmund was chosen. Not that *he* seemed to mind."

"Um..." Damien didn't like to think about the horror that Adam had told him a few days ago; that Prince Oskar had possessed Healing magick and some weird backwards empathy that made him enjoy others' pain. "You're a Powerful projective empath, Adam. He probably figured that out and realized he couldn't hurt *you* without getting it back. You said he thrived on feeling other people's pain... but you'd have been making him feel it in his ownself."

Adam froze. "Then... he couldn't actually have hurt *you* either."

And Jason need not have gone back to Prince Oskar for the brief time that had so physically damaged him.

Although by the time the cruel prince had realized that mishandling his young nephew would bite him back, Damien might have been permanently traumatized anyways. Those books in the Rpoyal Library that had clued Damien in to his own *empathy* had given him the basics for how to build a fairly successful shield that had likely obscured his uncle's ability to detect Damien's Talents.

It had been Oskar's increasingly overt *interest* in the younger prince that had been why Adam and Ciriis had decided to take Damien to Lynncrag in the first place, after all.

Damien sighed and gave up a shred of Jason's confidences. "Jason told me that it was that second time that made him quit imagining Oskar as some magickal prince charming. Let him see the real beast behind the pretty face."

Adam was still abnormally still, but had relaxed marginally. "He... did seem more willing to be a diversion than I would have expected. All things considered." There was a feeling of his body sagging a bit. "I thought he was happy with *me*."

"Um," Damien said again. "I was – I *am* perfectly happy with Genevieve. It didn't stop certain... fantasies from... erm... cropping up. Even though I had absolutely nothing to base them on."

He could feel Adam's sudden surprise. "That's right. All those lovers of yours... they were all *women*."

"Again, not my idea," Damien muttered. Not that he regretted any of them.

"But... you fantasized about Jason..." Adam murmured. Into his *neck*... "And... *me?*"

The King flushed. It was awkward to admit to this. To how *much* of *this* there was to admit.

He'd told Adam this much before anyways. When Adam had inadvertently gotten stuck listening to Jason, well... *jumping* him seemed a bit overly dramatic, though entirely accurate. It certainly hadn't been *Damien's* idea... though he hadn't tried as hard as he might to have gotten away.

Much easier to say was...

"*You* were mostly terrifying. I never seemed to meet your expectations at anything. And... you kept dumping me in the horse-trough. But... you made me feel safer. I've just spent the last several months wishing one of you would come rescue me. Or Genevieve, but with the pregnancy that seemed unlikely."

"I'm glad we didn't," Adam said unexpectedly. "You needed to know you don't need a rescuer."

Damien had... actually decided on that himself.

He let his mind wander back to the problem of Azella.

"She reads *romance* novels, Adam," he sighed. "And when she 'consorts' with demons... she means that *literally.*"

Adam choked a bit on that.

"Damien, love, this woman isn't 'save-able.' Romance novels or not. The only question to me is whether you can get her out of *Farivera.*"

Damien shivered and Adam's arms went tight around him again, but it wasn't a physical chill. "It's... possible. I won't know until I face her on the field of battle."

"For which you need to properly *sleep,*" Adam pointed out. "I doubt you slept much at all while you were in her clutches."

"Not well," Damien had to admit.

Adam laid back down and tugged the King to lie beside him. "You'll sleep here, with me, until we get our *other* loves back."

Small question that it wouldn't just be *sleep.* Nor did he want it to be, if he were honest with himself. Thoughts of *walls* and *tables* mingled in helter-skelter fashion with snippets of things Azella had said and done and all his other worries and the silken texture of the skin of Adam's lower abdomen...

And the taste of Adam's lips that had *almost* managed to entirely chase away the remembered feel of Azella's.

It wasn't just the physical, however much Damien craved that.

It was the sense of *belonging* that Adam made manifest. He *belonged* to Adam, after all. If the tall knight was *his* Champion, Damien was just as much *Adam's* King.

Azella had treated him as a possession... a *thing* she *possessed,* for all that her stated goal had been to convince Damien to become her mate and partner. She had thought so, anyways. In reality, she would never allow anyone near her who might be her equal.

The difference between being a *possession* and *belonging* was... infinitesimal.

And infinite.

The King no longer cared to object to Adam's insistence on sleeping together.

Safe... Adam could keep him *safe* better than anyone else in the world. And he really was... very... tired...

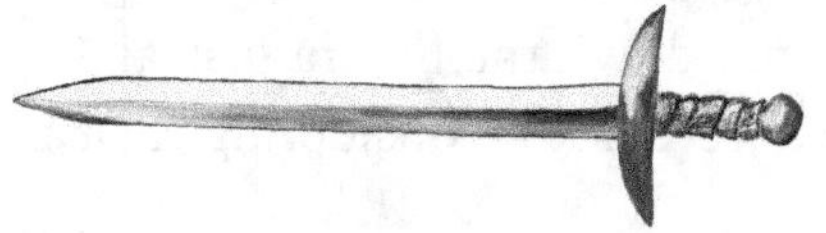

Chapter TEN

Pre-Battle Jitters

THE SIOVALESE FORCES HAD BEEN sighted the day before the deadline, making camp along the Emerald River, close to where Ravenscreek joined the larger waterway. They were a half-day's ride from the city wall, all of them mounted. Siovale was famous for its mounted warriors... and for breeding most of the warhorses for the rest of the Realm.

The word of what had happened had spread, of course. Reyensweir wasn't much farther than Siovale, and Cedarwen wasn't much farther than that. Most of Damien's other vassals were either too far away to arrive in time or would wait to see which way the wind blew, but those two he could count on to come. As well as most of his vassals – now Jason's, technically, he supposed – in Emeralsee itself.

Damien had sent riders to tell everyone to stand down.

Genevieve and Jason's lives were hostage to making a very good show of handing over the city to Tomas Elsevier and the more people who were involved, the more difficult this could become. Damien hoped to resolve the situation with as little loss of life as possible – on either side. The Siovalese, after all, were still his people, regardless what they might think about the matter.

The early Spring he had brought to Farivera had spread as a rumor through the Realm, as well as the stories of seeing him running through Siovale, flowers and fresh growth rising from his footprints. And then how he'd run down the Emerald straight into the harbor.

If Tomas' people were not reconsidering their allegiance, he'd be surprised.

Duke Quillian had accepted his king's message and sent back word that he would do as he thought best. This, apparently meant massing his own troops, such as they were, just west of the provincial border. Baron Raphael of Cedarwen had done the same. Close enough to be called on, Damien assumed they were thinking.

Close enough to cause trouble... or be demon-fodder... was the King's own thought.

Damien had warded the city of Emeralsee as best he could... and the closer outlying farmers and noble vassals had been warned and given the option of coming into the city. Some had taken him up on that. Others had fled for farther locations. The population of the city had been given what warning they could and Damien had offered to evacuate as many children and families as he could; his cousin, Baron Eldridge, and Adam's parents had offered to take any who would leave, even if they all had to camp outside in the pastures.

Surprisingly few had taken him up on it.

Aryllis had been persuaded to take Rico to their new holding of Elmirscroft.

"I'd ask all the Secret Cadre to leave," Damien told her bluntly when his Spymistress – and long-ago lover – had answered the royal summons to appear in his office. "We're going to win this, but there will be an in-between stage when things may go... badly. Tomas knows who you all are and has no illusions about just how effective you can be. If he didn't know before, Arabella and Mark will have enlightened him."

Not to mention what effective levers any of them might be on Damien's own actions.

The pale woman, still girlishly slender despite her maturity and motherhood, looked him straight in the eye. "You're also preparing not to win. And for me to be the nucleus of a new resistance movement."

They were alone in his office. Tim had begged him to have a word with his wife, and the King had agreed on the contingency that the Captain absent himself from the discussion.

Damien inclined his head.

"I am."

The words hung there for a moment.

"Dammit, Damien, you told us all you were *done* with this sacrificing yourself." Aryllis looked furious.

"I am," he said again, but this time elaborated; Aryllis knew him in ways even her husband didn't. She deserved more of an explanation. "I've grown, 'Ryll. Being king doesn't seem too big for me anymore. And I have all the Power of the Realm to fight this demon – and the sorceress sending it. But *Tomas* has *Genevieve*. Our soul-bond still isn't working properly, but if he kills *her*... that's the end of *me* as well."

Her fury faded. "Then we have Jason."

Damien winced slightly. "Maybe. I wanted to wait to talk to them before telling you this... but *you* at least should know. Jason and Genevieve are *also* soul-bonded. We don't know how it happened..."

There were still some things he wouldn't tell her. Someday maybe. If it seemed safer than not...

Aryllis looked... shocked. He didn't blame her. "So, if Genevieve dies, we lose our King *and* our Heir? May I at least *hope* that this came about *after* he was crowned? Because otherwise that was a really *stupid* idea."

The King spread his hands. "Whom else could I have named Heir, Aryllis?"

She frowned, but didn't argue. "So. Adam, then, for our king. If it all goes to hell."

"Actually..." Damien sighed. "It seems that the marriage ceremony creates something very similar to a soul-bond. Just... one you've chosen, rather than had imposed on you. It's not as 'tight,' but it probably explains why so many people who weren't soul-bonded don't last terribly long after their spouse dies."

He gave her a somewhat sickly smile. "You'll notice it's usually people who have something very important to live for... like my father-in-law. Genevieve was all of eight when her mother died, I believe."

Aryllis was the palest woman he had ever met. Her hair was a fine, platinum-blonde, her eyes were a pale grey, and her skin – especially this early in the Spring – was now almost as white as the papers on his desk. He hadn't guessed how much paler she could get.

"You're asking me to support Adam – after Jason is dead. And after *Tim* is gone. And you're assuming that *I* can hold on... because of Rico."

Clever woman. Actually, he had hoped she would go only so far as that first part and not realize just how much he was asking of her. It would be too much for most women – for most *people*.

But Aryllis was one of the strongest people Damien had ever known.

She had been his third lover – after Ciriis and Lena – but when she had come to his bed at Ciriis' instigation, she had seemed to be the most delicate, fragile fairy princess of a woman he had ever seen. Damien had feared to touch her, lest she break further.

Instead, he had discovered that – despite what his grandfather had done to her – Aryllis was far from broken. The pale noblewoman had positively *burned* with a desire to see King Reginald and his foul Court brought low and a new, healthy regime set in its place.

She had taken on whatever tasks were needed to protect the young prince with an almost religious zeal – from learning to defend him physically to keeping him safe from the temptations of the Court 'ladies' by giving him no reason to have a wandering eye.

Truth be told, while Aryllis had been a skilled lover, she had more than slightly intimidated Damien at the time with her fierce and quiet intensity. He'd managed to tease a more playful side out of her on rare occasions and ever-cheerful Lena had somehow become her closest friend.

When the ebullient Sir Tim had courted her and then won Aryllis' hand, there had followed a tense period between him and Damien, given the history. But within weeks after Aryllis had accepted Tim's ring and pledge, the young knight had sought out his prince and asked his forgiveness. Aryllis had explained everything, he said, including that it had been Damien who had helped her find a healthier way to get past her need for vengeance and learn to trust and love.

While all of Damien's Ladies besides Lena and Ciriis had eventually married members of his *official* Royal Guards – and he'd had to go through similar conversations with most of the men as he had with Tim, and for similar reasons – there was something special between Tim and Aryllis. To ask that she take on the role of holding Ilseador together *after* losing Tim was... cruel.

But necessary.

And Damien could not tell her it was for *his* sake as well.

Because the idea of *Aryllis* dying in the coming insanity was... almost as devastating to him as the thought of losing Genevieve. Or Adam. Or Jason. He couldn't protect any of *them*.

Nor Tim, who as Captain of his Royal Guard would be offended even to have it suggested that he should take his wife and son and flee.

But Aryllis... and Lena, whose sweet self had been the only woman he had ever even halfway considered as an actual mate during those years he had been pining – fruitlessly, he'd thought then – for Genevieve.

Aryllis was the only person who *knew* enough and was *strong* enough to hold the country.

She was, perhaps, what Azella the Unpitying might have been like if circumstances had been different for each of them, though Azella was but a distorted mirror-image of Damien's beloved Spymistress. Though it was probably that physical resemblance and core of strength and determination that had let him fall for Azella so quickly.

A pity that the sorceress had not half Aryllis' heart nor wit nor wisdom.

Damien bowed his head in acknowledgement of her realization. "And that you can lead a resistance and prevent a civil war between Aldred and Tomas... and whomever Adam designates as *his* Heir. Because your son doesn't deserve to grow up in a war-torn country the way we all did."

Aryllis had been standing in front of his desk, glaring at him. Now she stumbled for a seat on the chair behind her.

He waited a beat while she processed all of this.

"It's only contingencies, 'Ryll," the King said at last. "I don't plan to *lose*. Not my City. Not my Realm. Not my wife and child. Not my best friends – *any* of them. But it's my job to plan for contingencies."

His Spymistress looked up at him. "Zachary Miramar is Duchess Sildra's younger brother."

Damien nodded.

"And Tariana Eledor's mother was an Elsevier."

Damien nodded again.

Aryllis took a shuddering breath. "At what point, Your Majesty, do I admit that the Realm belongs to... the opposition?"

The King spread his hands. "At the moment, milady, I have no way of knowing how far this conspiracy extends. Duke Quillian is betrothed to Duchess Tariana – and his troops stand just west of the border with Emeralsee. Are they there to help *us* – or Tomas Elsevier? I would have trusted Zachary – and Rosa – with my life or Genevieve's. I *have* trusted them so. And when the sorceress took me away, I entrusted her – and the baby – to Tomas' care."

"Then what do you want me to *do?*" she almost wailed.

Damien leaned forwards. "What you need to, love. Like you always have. Don't let Rico grow up with a tyrant on the Throne – or his mother in a dungeon somewhere. Or executed for treason to a Crown you never swore to. Do what you can. And if you can do no more, take him and flee. To Dawil, to Vindalia, to somewhere else across the sea."

"Damien..." Tears were dripping down her cheeks, crystal shimmers against her pale skin.

He leaned back in his chair, putting on his best air of confident, assured nonchalance. If anyone should be likely to see through it, it would be Aryllis.

But people wanted to see what they *needed*.

Even Aryllis.

"None of it is going to happen, Aryllis. We're going to *win*." He paused. "But take Lena with you to Elmirscroft."

And with that she had to be content.

But she took Rico and Lena to Elmirscroft.

Naturally he couldn't talk any of the *rest* of his Secret Guards into leaving.

Lord David and his cousin, Mistress Lenore, who was Head of Metreedi House in Ilseador, accepted his commission to put as many of the younger pages and squires and younger Metreedi cousins aboard one of their ships to sail just around the Cape until the battle was done. Roger and Esmerelda Solway found themselves meeting cousins they'd never known existed, but Elaina shadowed her father and insisted on staying on as a member of the Secret Cadre.

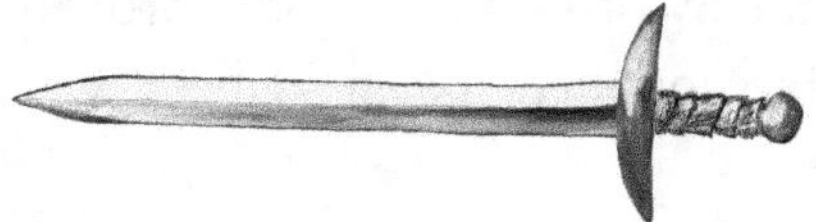

"I still can't *feel* her," Damien said sadly as he lay in bed with Adam, trying to get some rest before what was sure to be a harrowing day.

"You will," Adam told him confidently. "Once the two of you are back in the same place."

"Maybe..." Damien didn't add what he was thinking; that perhaps Jason's soul-bond to his wife had superseded his own. He didn't want to say it aloud because Adam was in very nearly the same situation and it would do no good to worry him as well.

"You think too loudly when you're fretting," Adam told him wryly. "Thank you for trying to spare my feelings, but *my* bond with Jason doesn't seem to have suffered at all."

"Sorry..." the King sighed. "I feel like I should get up and pace... just lying here is... making it hard to settle."

Adam snorted. "If this is the way you try to be romantic with Genevieve, it's clearly the soul-bond alone that's responsible for all those pregnancies she lost."

Damien flushed. "I wasn't suggesting..."

Adam leaned over and kissed him. "I know, love. You're having a terrible attack of pre-battle nerves and looking for excuses to fret. This... is really the first time you've been through this, isn't it."

"What are you talking about?"

"Anticipating a battle. You haven't done that before."

Damien frowned. "What about the pirates? And when I went with Genevieve to re-take the Castle?"

Adam rolled his eyes. "In the one case you were anticipating giving yourself up in order to save the rest of us – *I* could see it, *Jason* could see it, *Genevieve* could see it... And in the other... you weren't quite yourself, having just found the Sword and all. This is different."

It was.

They had a strategy and were planning to fight to *win*.

If they lost, it would be because he had screwed up.

"Is not having the Sword going to be a problem?" Adam asked a little hesitantly. He sounded like he'd been wanting to ask that question for awhile.

Damien shook his head. "No. It's handy, but I don't need it anymore. The Realm knows where I am now, with or without the Sword."

Adam frowned. "When the pirates came, you had wanted to lure the sorceress into the Throne-room. Would you have been able to defeat her if we had?"

The King shook his head again. "I didn't know what I was doing then. I would have had better access to the Realm's Power if I was sitting on the Throne, and been better able to direct it holding the Sword. Unfortunately, I didn't know what I could *do* with all that Power. And I also had to spend a fair amount of effort preventing the Realm from eating me alive, and that was... distracting."

"I imagine," Adam muttered. "And there's no way Tomas can wield the thing and confuse the issue. At least we know *that.*"

"No. It doesn't do anything but make pretty lights for potential Heirs to the Throne and nothing at all for anyone else," Damien agreed.

Besides the Monarch, that was. In *Damien's* hands and with a real threat to his life facing him, according to legend it could make him virtually invincible. Not that they'd ever put that to the test; he'd never counted on the Sword to provide him with what his training and personal effort had already given him.

But just as with setting the spell to make himself magickally impervious, it was – or might be – another layer of protection.

Or it would if he had it in hand.

He shifted restlessly. "Let me up, Adam. I need to pace."

"You need to *sleep*," his Champion corrected him.

"Well, *that's* not happening. At least I can get up and not prevent *you* from sleeping."

Adam rolled his eyes. "Because *I'm* going to get any rest with you ratcheting around."

"I'll go upstairs."

"And then I'll spend my time *worrying* that you're not getting any *sleep*."

"Adam..."

"There's other ways than pacing to take your mind off of tomorrow, Damien. *Better* ones."

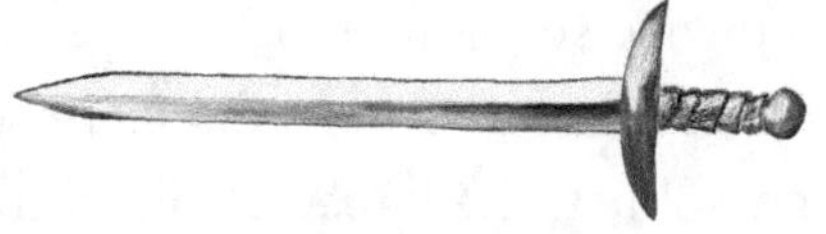

Chapter ELEVEN

Not-So-Cordial Greetings

THE CITY GATES WERE THROWN wide.

Damien sat his tall palfrey, Sunset, below the arch of the gate that led along the River Road. He wore the Crown and his scarlet-and-miniver royal cloak over the Alsterling colors of turquoise-and-gold. The long cloak draped down on both sides of his elegant bay mare nearly to the ground.

His twelve Royal Guards were ranged around him, with Tim as Knight-Commander properly at his left. Adam had claimed his rightful place as Champion on Damien's right, regardless of all arguments that as the only remaining Heir to the Throne he should be somewhere safer. It was hardly to have been expected that he could keep himself away when they expected Jason to appear.

General Direlien and his General Staff awaited in the parade-ground on the Emeralsee plains that had been established when it became obvious that the city had long since overflowed the walls. The city had grown past the parade-ground at least a century before the present date and showed no signs of stopping. Perhaps in another century or two Emeralsee could challenge Manjipur or even Wave in size.

Seeing it all reminded Damien that he needed to do something about the city's sewer system. He had found sewage flowing into Emeralsee Bay when the ice-storm had locked everything down...

The Army was to genuflect as Tomas Elsevier rode past them.

A number of the soldiers had reacted in outrage, which was heartwarming to Damien, but he had completely agreed with the general to keep those men and women far from the scene. Reluctance was fine and to be expected.

But outright refusal...

Tomas might feel a need to make an *example*...

"Doing all right?" Adam asked. He was rubbing absently at the chin he had finally shaved this morning.

Damien gave him a short nod.

Tomas had sent word ahead that he would meet them at the gates just past noon.

From what Damien understood about demons, it was unlikely that they would face *that* assault until at least sunset, if not full dark. The disparity in times meant that the Siovalese force would likely be well-established in his Castle by then... and Damien himself might be placed in the dungeons.

Not that that would discommode him more than briefly, but every moment that he had to use to extract himself from some sort of confinement might mean lives lost.

Adam's Foreseeing suggested they would win and the four of them would be fine. But Adam had admitted he hadn't *seen* any of their other friends, though that was likely because the visions focused on his children. *Their* children.

Damien had a different speculation. He suspected that the future was much less settled than common belief might make it out to be. Adam's visions might represent the most likely future – or the future he would most prefer. But any detail they could not anticipate might throw a wrench into the works and change everything, like ripples in a pond... or an irrigation trench suddenly unblocked to allow the water to flow in a different direction.

There were too many houses here in the outer city. Too many people who had refused to leave in anticipation of these potentially dire events. And it was worse in the inner city within the walls. The King suspected that his people were still too used to his grandfather's rule; the likely advent of a demonic attack should at least have generated *some* concern.

Adam had told him that it wasn't that. It was that they trusted their Sorcerer-King to protect them.

That... did nothing useful for his peace of mind.

The Siovalese forces were approaching.

Tomas Elsevier was very confident of himself. He rode at the head of a column of his people, dressed in mail and light plate, but with his head bare of any protection and his warriors all behind him.

Duchess Sildra rode beside him, with their oldest children, Mark and Arabella, right behind. A single file of his men-at-arms guarded them on each side, and the four-wide column stretched back farther than the eye could see.

They were, after all, meeting in the center of the main street of the city that led up to the old walls and gates. The upper stories of half-timbered houses, the white-wash on their lower levels splashed with Spring time mud despite the cobbles, loomed over the invading force.

There was simply no *room* for proper military formations.

The invaders stopped some fifty feet back from the gates, reining in their splendid mounts. Clearly Siovale kept the best of their breeding for home use.

"Ho, Damien Alsterling," the Duke of Siovale hailed him. "Grandson and Heir of the Wizard-Tyrant Reginald the Ruthless."

Not a bad appellation for his grandfather, Damien had to admit. It was what he called the old man in his own mind, after all.

"Tomas Elsevier," the King acknowledged. "Oathbreaker twice over."

The Duke snorted, and let his fine steed paw the ground. "I've broken no oaths to *you*, weak king, for you never *demanded* any of me save that I be a good steward of my lands. And King Reginald broke *his* oaths to all of us long before the Rebellion was founded."

"And what of the ceding of Farivera to the Evil Wizard whose keep lies at the farthest southern point of this Realm?" Damien challenged him.

"For that you would have to ask my father," Tomas retorted. "Cease this stalling. You were to greet me as king, and with the city-gates thrown wide. I see the latter, but not the former. Kneel to me, Damien Alsterling. Give over your Crown and your cloak."

"My Queen and my Heir, first, Tomas," Damien replied.

"You think to dictate terms, Damien?" the traitorous Duke sneered. "I hold your soul-bonded – and therefore your life – in my hand."

Damien spread his hands. "I'm simply following the rules you set out for this meeting, Tomas. If you want me to trade my Crown for their safety, then you'll release them. You may understand that I have little faith in your given word just now."

Tomas glowered at him, but gestured behind him.

A ripple in the ranks, slowly percolating forwards.

Genevieve appeared, and Damien feasted his eyes on her. Jason was just behind, and he looked almost as eagerly at his oldest friend.

Jason met his gaze briefly and warmly before looking for Adam.

Genevieve's beautiful blue-green eyes wandered aimlessly, showing no particular interest in anyone or anything.

"Damien. Something's wrong." Tim said softly.

The King nodded. "I know. I wasn't expecting any less. It *is* them, though. And I have to fulfill my side of the bargain. Get them to safety, please. As we discussed."

He swung down off of his horse, twitching his cloak to get it to slide smoothly off of Sunset's rump. The reins he handed off to Sir Tim.

Damien took a deep breath, then walked to the center of the untenanted roadway and knelt on the cobblestones. He took off his crown and held it in his hands.

"Yours to come and take it, Tomas Elsevier, once the Queen and Prince Jason are freed."

Tomas gestured at his people again. Genevieve and Jason emerged beside himself and Sildra.

"Go back to your people if you would, Jason Solway," the Duke told him, "But give me the Heir's Ring before you do."

Jason gave the older man a tired look. "We've been through this before, Tomas. It won't come off. It hasn't since the investiture."

"Try again."

Not bothering to argue, Jason held out his left hand for the Duke of Siovale to tug at.

"Mark," the Duchess, silent until now, instructed. "Cut off his finger."

To his credit, the young man recoiled. "Mother, no!"

Damien was hardput to stay humbly kneeling upon the ground. He met Jason's eyes with a small smile and a shake of the head, and his friend relaxed. He heard a fuss behind him and guessed that Adam was being restrained by someone.

Duchess Sildra looked at her son. "You can't wear the Ring until it's off of him, Mark."

"You promised Sir Jason wouldn't be harmed, Father," the young man appealed.

The Duchess turned to her daughter. "*You* do it, 'Bella. Show them that the secondborn can have more guts than the first."

The girl looked uncertainly between her parents.

Duke Tomas looked at his wife, then his son, then Jason... and finally back to his daughter. "Get it off of him, Arabella, and it's yours."

"'Bella, *no*..." Mark said softly, his eyes horrified.

The look the young woman gave her older brother was undecipherable, but she met her mother's gaze and urged her horse forwards.

"*'Bella, NO!*"

Even Damien had to look up in surprise at that. It was Lord Aaron's voice. The Secret Cadre had been stashed around the area in case help was needed to get Jason and Genevieve out of the way quickly.

The young assassin had broken cover and was flinging himself towards the Siovalese party. Marianna Loveress was darting after, trying to stop him.

Jason's expression was alarmed again, going rapidly between his young sister-in-law and where more scuffling noises to Damien's rear indicated that Adam was trying to reach his baby sister... Except should he succeed, it would be the King's Champion breaking the truce they needed to get Jason and Genevieve back...

*"Don't do it, Arabella, you're **better** than that–!"*

The Siovalese men-at-arms were no slouches. They didn't even need their lord's word. One had moved instantly, his sword flashing from its sheathe to defend a seeming assault on his liege-lord's family.

It was, perhaps, a miracle that Aaron dodged the blade, automatically flinging up a hand to ward it off. He *hadn't* been attacking, or there would have been a blade in that hand and he might have stood a chance.

Blood spattered everywhere, and the young man's hand came to rest in front of the kneeling king. Damien would have leapt to his feet – it was just barely possible he could fix this if he moved very quickly – but every Siovalese blade was drawn and pointed and he didn't dare.

Instead, he closed his eyes in remorse and sent his Healing magick to seal over Aaron's wrist, saving the young man's life... but making it impossible to even consider attempting to reattach the hand.

Marianna wrapped herself around Lord Aaron, her eyes filled with tears as she glared at the Siovalese men-at-arms and particularly the one whose sword dripped with Aaron's blood. A couple of other ladies-in-waiting emerged to help her pull the young man back out of the way, and the men-at-arms allowed them to pass. Elegantly gowned noblewomen hardly seemed a threat, after all; no matter how Tomas might have instructed his people, some things were too deeply engrained.

Aaron, of course, was deeply in shock and seemed almost unaware of his surroundings.

Mark Elsevier looked... ill. He tried to look away from the severed hand, but his gaze kept being drawn back. Desperately, he raised his eyes slightly... and met Damien's. He cringed, but didn't drop his gaze.

The King smiled very slightly. There might be some hope for Mark Elsevier yet.

But not, it seemed for his sister.

Despite the dramatic interruption, Arabella seemed ready to follow her mother's direction. She had a knife in one hand and Jason's hand in her other. The edge of her blade seemed unable to find purchase, however, no matter how she tried.

"Try the wrist," Duchess Sildra said impatiently, but that was no more effective.

Jason gave Damien a relieved look.

I'm so sorry, Aaron, the King thought. But it had never occurred to him that the young man would need such a protection. And it wasn't exactly trivial to set it up. Protecting *all* of his people this way would be... impossible.

"It probably wouldn't do you any good, anyways," Damien said mildly to the Duke of Siovale's baffled daughter. "Rosa said she had a devil of a time trying to get it to stay on. It's meant to be on an Alsterling's finger."

Duchess Sildra glared at him and seemed ready to say something else. But her husband was more irritated that his grand entrance was becoming poorly staged theater, if not a farce.

"Away with you then, Jason Solway," the Duke declared. "Take your indecent self away from my family. Leave the horse, though. Even a Siovalese gelding is too good for the likes of *you.*"

Another casual gesture from Tomas and all the Siovalese swords were sheathed.

Damien saw Jason wince. He'd heard too much of that before. How had they never realized what a bigot and traitor and... just plain *evil* the duke was?

Without a word, Jason dismounted in one smooth motion and walked, slowly, unmenacingly, out of Damien's field of view. To Adam's stirrup, he assumed, where they would be exchanging a handclasp and a look, perhaps.

There was still Genevieve to be reclaimed, so there wasn't yet time for the more heartfelt reunion both men craved.

"And my Queen." Damien said calmly, almost as if nothing else had happened.

Duchess Sildra gave him a malicious look. "She can go if she likes. Do you want to return to the man who *abandoned* you, sister-in-law dear?"

Genevieve's eyes were glazed. "No."

Damien's heart caught.

He took a breath.

Another.

It must be a *compulsion* spell.

He could fix this – break the spell and free her.

But he needed to be *closer* to her to be able to break it.

He looked at the Duke. "My Queen for my Crown, Tomas."

The Duke grinned a little savagely. "Don't you know that bearing women will do as they please, Damien? Or no, I don't suppose *you* would. Sending her off every time she got with child to ride and fight. You don't deserve her. *Or* her child. But then... it's *her* child and not *yours,* isn't it?"

The King looked up at him with narrowed eyes. "What are you talking about, traitor?"

"Oh, come now, *Damien,*" Duchess Sildra said silkily. "Five years and ten miscarriages and not a one that made it past the third month? And suddenly she's carrying it well?"

Damien closed his eyes and bent his head. Outrage... outrage was what he needed. It wasn't something he knew how to do well, though.

In a single smooth gesture, he rose.

"You're telling me my *soul-bonded Queen* is carrying a cuckoo's child?"

"Not just *any* cuckoo," Duchess Sildra crowed. "Your former Champion is the sire!"

It was unlikely that there was any eye there that didn't swivel instantly to Jason. Even Damien half-turned.

Apparently, self-control had its limits.

Jason looked up from the fairly passionate kiss that Adam had leaned down from his horse to bestow upon him to see himself the object of everyone's attention. And blushed.

Adam met his King's eye smugly... The resonance that was still between the two of them wasn't *quite* enough to convey Adam's actual words, but Damien could practically hear that sardonic voice saying that he'd expected some sort of accusation of that nature and had made his own plan to make it look as silly as possible.

Damien bit out a short bark of laughter. "On the one hand you accuse Prince Jason of not fitting your idea of *manliness* and the next you claim he's capable of siring a *cuckoo's chick* with my *soul-bonded Queen*. I think you need to make your minds up."

He looked at Genevieve. "Are you coming, Genevieve?"

She wavered slightly in her saddle, her eyes still glazed and seeming unaware of her surroundings. "No..."

Damien's heart was breaking into pieces.

He looked coldly up at the traitorous duke.

"No Queen. No Crown."

And to the shocked stares of everyone on *both* sides of the road, he jammed the thing back on his own head, marched back to his horse and mounted, flaring his cloak so it settled properly back into place.

It was the work of half a thought to create a spell of Air that amplified his voice to carry and fill the ears of everyone for at least two miles in all directions.

"You have come in bad faith, Tomas, Traitor of Siovale. I will meet you – or whatever Champion you set forth – in the parade-grounds west of the city at sunset. There you will give me my Queen – will she, nill she – my Sword, and yourself and your conspirators to be dealt with as traitors must always be dealt with."

Sunset – his Elaarwen-bred mare – wasn't quite of the caliber of the Siovalese horses, but she was happy to rear up and turn on her tail for Damien. He rode her under the city-gate, then turned again and waited until all of his mounted people had made it in. There were small side-gates – people sized, rather than for horses or conveyances. The Secret Cadre would make it in through those.

Jason was riding behind Adam, his long legs dangling too far down, his arms clasped tightly around Adam's middle for the practical purpose of keeping him astride as much as for the joy of holding his husband. His expression, before they reined up behind their King, was torn between utter relief and devastation – *he* hadn't been separated this far from his soul-bonded since the bond had set in.

"Get thee hence, False Duke." Damien said and raised a hand – purely for the drama of the moment – and the city-gates flew closed with a resounding clang.

He could *feel* the stunned silence on both sides of the gate.

He could *feel* – but through the Realm, not their mangled soul-bond – Genevieve's bright form departing.

He could *feel* Aaron's pain and blood-loss... and the beginnings of grief and black despair...

"Make sure they leave and do no damage to the outer-city as they do," Damien told Captain Seldebard of the City Guard. "I've done what I can to get them out past most of the residential neighborhoods. Have you finished evacuating that area?"

The City Guard Captain nodded. "All but the few hold-outs – there's always some, milord."

Damien nodded. "They've been made aware of the risks and offered help. There's nothing more we can do. When the General's messenger arrives, make sure he is sent up to the Castle immediately. Keep a horse here to carry him."

"Aye, milord..." Captain Seldebard hesitate. "Your Majesty... the Queen... and the unborn prince or princess..."

"I'm not abandoning my wife and child, Captain," Damien assured him. "No matter what it looks like. Just choosing better ground. *You* know what else I'm awaiting. And why the parade-ground is where we want to have them."

"Aye, sir." The captain looked rather less than reassured, but he at least seemed to accept that something was being done. "We... It's just that we're all very *fond* of the Queen."

Damien gave him a wry look.

"So am I, Captain, so am I."

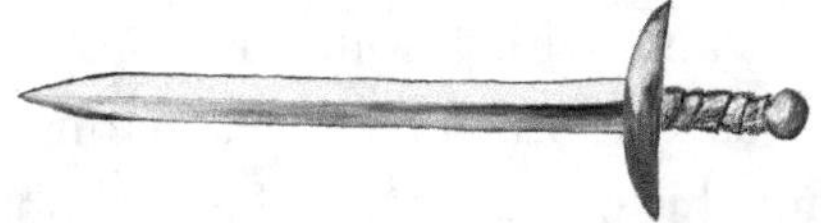

Chapter TWELVE

Dealing with Disappointment

"Go, be with each other," Damien waved at his Heir and his Champion as they all stood in the courtyard of the Castle and stablehands bustled around them, leading the horses away. "I have to talk to Tim and wait for word from General Direlien and see what I can do for Aaron when he finally makes it in here and..."

"Damien." Jason had stepped in and wrapped his arms around him. His voice was very quiet. "We need to talk."

The King shook his head, tried to step away. "I can't right now, Jason. I just... can't."

It was only mid-afternoon. There were hours yet. He had to find some way to calm down and prepare his mind for what would happen this evening.

To cope with the fact that he had somehow come out of this meeting free and still king, but without Genevieve. None of the scenarios he had kept himself awake with over the last week had ended this way.

It was... it was too much and he needed to sort himself out before Adam felt the need to dump him in another horse-trough – which he was *fairly* certain counted as something close to treason if the Royal Crown and Royal Cloak went in with him.

He couldn't – *couldn't* – cope with anything else. And certainly not the welter of confused and confusing emotions and yearnings and wants and needs that came with Jason. Or… his reactions to Jason. Or… or maybe that was just his *empathy* resonating with Adams and none of that was really his own… if only he could be so lucky…

These were supposed to be his Genevieve's arms around him. Not… not *Jason's*. Except… Jason's arms around him *were* helping, just as Jason had *always* had the patience and time and wisdom to be able to help Damien…

A *rock*, the man was, quite nearly as much as…

Damien's eyes searched, automatically, for the person he had come to rely upon above all others these last few days… no. These last five *years*. And for the ten before those.

Adam was standing a dozen feet and Tim was hovering close, looking concerned. The pair of them appeared to be having a whispered, hurried conference about something. Security for King and Heir, no doubt, since half the Royal Guard had gone back to help the Secret Cadre retrieve Aaron.

Castle Guard were stationed about reassuringly… and now Lord David had joined Tim and Adam…

"Jason, let me go. I have *work* to do…"

"Take him upstairs and get him settled," Tim was concluding. "David and I have everything here under control for the time being."

Jason loosed his grip on his King and turned to embrace the older man roughly.

"We missed you, son." Lord David told the knight. "Take care of your King. We'll talk later."

"The children?" Jason asked, his voice rough. "My… my sisters and brother? I heard some disturbing things in Siovale…"

"They're on a Metreedi ship with their cousins and the younger pages and squires," Lord David answered. "On the other side of the Cape. Probably learning to climb the shrouds and dive off the side like proper Metreedi children." He paused, his smile dimming. "Except for Elaina. She's still here, filling her duty with the other ladies-in-waiting. She's missed you."

Jason just nodded.

Adam had waited a couple of steps away out of respect for the slightly awkward family reunion, but now he took hold of both Jason and Damien's shoulders. "Upstairs, Damien. We can walk or do it your way. But it's this or the horse-tro–"

They were in the tower before Adam could finish.

"–ugh." He grunted, realizing where they were. "Jason, take that crown off of him."

He lifted the heavy scarlet-and-miniver cloak off of Damien's shoulders and handed it to Jason as well.

Damien could feel himself shivering with reaction – the heavy cloak and crown had weighed him down enough to prevent the shivering. "I'll be fine. I'll just go upstairs to my own suite. You two need some time alone together..."

Adam looked at his newly-returned husband with a relieved smile. "We do. And we will. *Later.* You've given us back our forever, my sweet prince. And right now, *you* need *us.*"

He kindly left off the part about how they *all* needed *Damien* to pull *himself* together so that he could do the next thing.

But he was abruptly sandwiched between them, and he was able to put his arms around Adam's neck and bury his face in the taller man's chest and cry instead of shiver.

"She was supposed to be *with* us now, Adam," Damien almost whimpered. "I *left* her there."

"You did what you had to," Adam said gently. And after a pause. "I didn't think you'd be able to. But you got us Jason back. *Whole.* You never even told *me* you'd added that protective spell to Jason as well."

He sounded profoundly relieved, though he could hardly be as relieved as *Damien* had been that someone – had it been Tim? – had managed to stop *Adam* from rushing out.

Discreetly working the spell that tied Jason's own newly freed magick into powering the protection spell had been something he'd done in one of the dark spaces of lying awake while they all waited for the storm to blow itself out – it had seemed a *necessary* thing to do to protect Genevieve in the wake of the second soul-bond, and he'd mentioned it passingly to Jason before Azella had taken him away.

But he'd done given no such protections to Adam, in part because he'd need to fuel it himself, rather than from the minor magicks that seemed to be his... friend's to claim. *Empathy* wasn't the right sort of thing to do this at all, and at the time that had been all that had been available to work with.

In retrospect, however, it was clear Damien needed to protect Adam as well. His heart had nearly stuttered to a stop when his Champion had managed to hold onto him when he vanished himself down to meet Azella and the pirate-king... Jason's father. And if he hadn't known heard Adam being restrained *today*...

Now *Jason* shivered momentarily. "Poor Aaron..."

And that set Damien off shivering again. He *should* have been able to stop that from happening. He *should* have been able to reattach Aaron's hand. He *should*...

He squeezed his eyes tight shut and tried to curl up on himself.

"You're not a *God*, Damien," Adam said sharply.

But that didn't help. He knew *that*.

"He's only getting worse, Jase. It's – well – I guess the bathtub or..."

"Hmmn."

"Help me start stripping these clothes off of him. He'd better not be wearing this outfit for what he has to do later, but–"

"What *is* going to happen later? It... sounded like he challenged Tomas to single combat... but shouldn't that be *your* place?"

A disgusted noise. "Yes. And if he thinks I'm going to let him..."

A low laugh. "I missed you, love."

A soft pause. "I missed you, too, Jase. More than I can say."

"So... he's naked. What do you want to do with him, Adam." It didn't sound like a question. And... Jason's voice was resigned.

Damien tried to pull himself together. "No. I'm fine. Really." He tried to laugh. "Cold, though."

He was laying on their bed. He pulled himself into a sitting position.

"He has that emotional spiral mostly contained. I don't suppose we need to dunk him." Adam wrapped a blanket around the King, then sat down next to him and began rubbing his back, but otherwise ignored him.

"You were gone three *weeks,* Jase. *He* was gone four *months.* He's not recovered yet, for all that he thinks he is. And this evening he's planning to battle the sorceress who spent all that time turning him inside-out and her pet demons."

Jason sat down heavily on the other side of the King. *"Demons?"*

"Hopefully just the one," Damien managed. "I can handle more if there's more, I think, but... one should be plenty."

Adam snorted. *"One* should be more than enough. *None* would be just about perfect."

Damien shook his head. Which had the side-effect of exacerbating the headache that was beginning to bloom behind his eyes. "Perfect... was never an option. I just... I just want to find our way to that future you saw for us, Adam."

"What's this?" Jason... sounded like himself, thank all the Gods at once. Curious, a little tired... not fearful or broken or... inside-out.

"Nothing," Adam said quickly. "Just... my imagination."

If that was how he wanted it.

"Beautiful imagination," Damien muttered, his attention on fighting the headache. *"Four* children. One for each of us to hold."

"But we'll each love them all," Adam said firmly.

The shivering was subsiding. And those words somehow soothed away that headache, too. He leaned into Adam's shoulder.

"Doing better, love?" Adam said sympathetically.

Damien winced at Jason's start. A new headache threatened... "I am... but it feels like you both... aren't."

"Hmmn," Adam said noncommittally.

"I'll just go upstairs so you can talk."

"If we're talking, then you should be here, too. *And* Genevieve."

"Adam... I need *clothes,* too. To *fight* in. And a *sword.*"

And headache powders or... something. He couldn't Heal this for himself, but he maybe could have another Healer summoned.

Because fighting demons – or dukes – with a headache sounded like a terrible idea.

Jason made a noise of objection at that. "When was the last time you trained with a sword that wasn't the Monarch's Blade?"

That... struck the King as funny for some reason... and next he was having laughing hysterics instead of... the other things. If Jason could only see that useless hunk of pot-metal Azella had saddled him with...

"I'm sorry," he gasped when he could, as Adam went off, muttering about horse-troughs, to fill their bathtub. "I haven't even asked what happened to *you...*"

Jason eyed his uncontrollably giggling monarch with some consternation. "Nothing particularly terrible. It was clear there was some kind of spell on Genevieve... but I couldn't *leave* her and there was no time to get help. I knew once she disappeared into the walls, I'd lose her... The spell wore off just as Siovale's men surrounded us. Too many of them."

"And you actually didn't try to fight anyways, Jase?" Adam said dryly as he came back into the room. "I seem to recall you offering to fight the entire *garrison* he brought with him the last time."

"Genevieve is pregnant," Jason said defensively.

"She was then, too," Damien pointed out, having mostly subdued the hysterics, though he still felt dreadfully off-balance. Lightheaded, though not headachy. He wasn't sure it was an improvement. "And there was a sorcerer right there."

Jason's head dropped. "And she *lost* that baby, Damien. This one... she's doing so much *better...*"

The King reached up and touched his oldest friend's cheek gently. Though, maybe he needed to re-think this 'oldest friend' business, given all that he and Adam had talked about the last nine days.

"And this is *your* baby."

Jason caught his hand and gave him a searching look.

"And she's *your* soul-bonded now," Adam added, settling down on the opposite side of the bed.

Jason's searching look moved to his husband.

"You're... *easier* about this than you were," he noted after a moment. "*Both* of you."

Damien shrugged. Now... he just felt utterly exhausted. Drained, even. "Not... exactly. I'm... learning. Adam's the one who has all of us sorted out."

Jason's eyebrows reached for his hairline as he looked at his husband.

"I thought you *hated* all of... this..." he let his voice trail off, clearly not sure what words to use to describe their situation.

Adam snorted. "I *hated* worrying that I might lose you, Jase. But this," he held up his hand to show off the wedding ring, "*this* says that isn't going to happen. Ever. And... Damien needed me."

The last was said almost helplessly.

Jason actually laughed slightly. "He's *needed* you since he was a boy. And you've always put him first."

"So have you."

Adam's voice was so calm... *too* calm. Could Jason hear that underlying quiver that gave the lie to all of his new husband's bold words of a moment ago? Or was it simply the effect of the remaining *empathic resonance* between himself and Adam that let Damien notice it.

"I suppose so." Jason looked like he'd like to have argued, and had realized he really couldn't. "But you... it wasn't like this before, though."

He frowned a little at the way Adam had laid down beside the King and was petting his hair.

And the way Damien was snuggling into the safety and security of Adam's arms.

He probably *shouldn't,* the King told himself, he'd promised himself that he *wouldn't* further mess with their relationship, no matter what Adam said. But he was so very wrung out with everything that had and hadn't happened and everything that was yet to happen.

He... *needed* Adam more than he could remember doing since he was seventeen and terrified of any space that wasn't his Library.

"He's *older* now," Adam said dryly. "*You* seemed to have noticed that a bit yourself."

Jason flushed a bit guiltily. "Adam..."

"I don't love *you* any less, Jase. But we're having a baby with Damien and Genevieve. And you're *soul-bonded* to her. This isn't going away... and I don't want it to. We *have* to have our own unique way of making this work."

"I'm sorry to make this so hard," Damien put in after a moment of awkward silence.

"Not your fault," both of them told him simultaneously, then looked at each other. Jason's face was all surprise, Adam's almost smug.

"I wanted children, Jase," Adam reminded. "A big, happy family, like the one I grew up in."

"Like my grandparents' home in Ravenscroft," Damien added wistfully. He was starting to feel drifty. "Tell him about all the children, Adam... Four isn't so many, but we're starting late..."

"Genevieve may disagree," his Champion pointed out. "Especially since the last two seem to be twins..." he stopped, his voice trailing off, golden-hazel eyes gone wide.

"Adam... love, what haven't you told me?" Jason's tone was wary, but since he was snuggling in on Damien's other side, it seemed like they *were* going to sort it out...

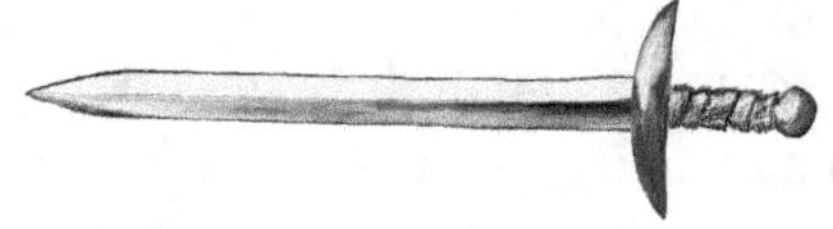

Chapter THIRTEEN

The End is Near

DAMIEN RE-CHECKED THE PART OF the parade-grounds that he had designated for this battle. He'd been out here several days ago to arrange things how he wanted them and now he was really just fidgeting. It was somewhat impossible *not* to fidget, though.

Twenty-four Royal Guards – Secret and Official – ranged around one side of the roughly circular space. Elaina had finally elected to stay back to look after Lord Aaron and insisted Marianna go to represent them both.

The timid young woman had been determined and emphatic enough that the King suspected her father was right – she might heal from the stresses of her childhood and the uncomfortable revelations of the previous Autumn, given time enough. And *space* enough. Space *away* from Brindlewell and her grandmother.

General Direlien had the Army arranged to back them up. The City Guard and Castle Guard had been left behind to do their regular jobs. There was no guarantee, after all, that there couldn't be some sort of two-pronged attack as there had been in the Fall. Pirates seemed unlikely – Azella had likely burned her bridges there, abandoning her sometime allies in the middle of the fight – but they still had no idea how much support Tomas Elsevier had from other parts of the Realm.

Between Lost Provinces and Rebellious Provinces, a good two thirds of the Realm had an iffy recent history with accepting the rule of the king in Emeralsee.

After Damien's nap, he and Adam had shown Jason the draft of the revised Vassal's Oath that they were planning the King should take on tour around the Realm. They had all agreed Damien needed to get out and about more, and Binding his vassals to the Land while they were actually physically present on it felt... right.

That hadn't been possible with all the insanity and unrest of the first few years. Damien had gone out when he could, most especially on visits to Elaarwen, but the bureaucracy needed his constant hand and he had needed the Power concentrating effects of the Castle and Throne-room to be able to do the other half of his work. Not to mention his own, unthinking reluctance to leave the Castle.

Taking the more expedient avenue had proven to be the wrong one, however. *This* time he would do it *right*.

The new version of the Oath would not leave as much leeway as his original.

He and Adam had still not come to an agreement about who would be fighting whom this evening.

"You need to save yourself for the magickal battle," Adam insisted. "And the whole point of *having* a King's Champion is that the king isn't *supposed* to fight his own battles. *Jason* would agree," he said a little sourly.

While that was certainly true, the Heir was not there to make the point himself.

He had been prevailed upon – by Adam and Damien both – to stay back in the Castle for his safety and in his place as Heir to the Realm... and had refused.

He had been prevailed upon – by Tim, Lord David, any number of others – to stay back in the Castle to defend it in his capacity as a Knight of the Realm... and had refused.

He had been prevailed upon – by Count Antonin who was Bound to Emeralsee City as Jason was now Bound to the province – to at least stay within the city walls so as to defend the city... and had refused.

When at last they had all made it down to the parade-grounds, General Direlien had seen the Crown Prince at the King's side. The powerful old man had cursed fluently, called them all damn fools in a half-dozen languages, and *ordered* the startled younger man to stay behind their lines if he wouldn't see sense and go back up to the thrice-bedamned Castle where he *belonged*.

Jason hadn't *dared* refuse.

Not that he'd gone farther back than behind their lines of men-at-arms.

"I'm not disagreeing in theory, Adam," the King said absently. "But I have some strong suspicions..."

He let his voice trail off as he kicked dust around seemingly at random, wandering around the acres-wide open space of the parade-ground. At least Adam didn't object to this activity, perhaps aware that it was preventing him from focusing on his nerves and perhaps serving to reassure him that nothing had changed since they'd come down here to prepare the place three days ago.

"*Suspicions.*" Adam stopped where he was, and folded his arms. "Suspicions that you won't *share* with us. It's impossible to develop a coherent strategy without knowing as many of the variables as are available, Damien. You know what Genevieve would say to that. *Or the good general.*"

The King winced. "Yes. I do." He squinted through the clouds of quickly-settling dust that he'd kicked up and gave his... *friend* a small grin. "Parade-rest stance on a parade-ground, Adam?"

Adam snorted, though whether it was from humor or dust might have been debatable. "Don't change the subject."

Damien sighed. "Worth a try." He looked around. "Kandy got her start here."

His Champion visibly startled. Damien never talked about his long-deceased sister – except to Genevieve. He *thought* about her rather more often than that. Twelve years between their births, but their parents had never given him any reason to suspect that he was an unintended 'Autumn child.' He had always felt completely secure in their love and protection.

Until the day he'd seen them murdered.

Kandy, on the other hand, had always treated him like a bit of a pet.

He hadn't minded, much. She had let him trail her around like a puppy dog, entertaining herself with him while she enjoyed the company of their older cousins. Until he was six, when she'd gone off with their parents' blessings to enroll as an anonymous recruit in the Army.

Right here.

Damien didn't need to say aloud that it was Kandy's moxy in having done so – and the stories of how good she was at it – that had put the Army in his pocket. He was no soldier himself, nor a knight, despite the training his... his *loves* had given him.

General Direlien had marked her rise – himself just a mid-career officer at the time – not knowing who she was, her false name and her dark, Eldridge-family appearance concealing her Alsterling heritage. She'd been loved by the first squad she'd been given, revered by each larger command, appreciated by her peers, and helped along by superiors who had quickly seen her for officer potential.

She'd served two tours on the front with the Rebellion – though she would never have faced Genevieve, since she was first an unmounted and then a mounted officer commanding infantry, not a knight, as well as being significantly older. She'd served another tour on the much-less serious front in Alpinsward where their grandfather had sent troops to try to reclaim the Lost Province only because it pacified those few nobles whom he felt still needed to be pacified rather than terrorized.

Kandy had come back home with tales of the despondency of the troops who knew their mission wasn't serious and the wishes she had heard that the people – and even the nobility – of Alpinsward wanted to rejoin Ilseador. She had said that it was Mercasia that wouldn't let them leave.

Damien had sat at her feet as she told their parents about her experiences, too old at nine to sit on her lap she'd said, but he'd listened as she finger-combed his dark-hair that matched her own... listened as he listened to everything Kandy every said.

Anything *anyone* ever said, really, but Kandy's words had always been the most important. Perhaps because he'd had so little of her time. Less, even, than he'd had of their parents.

Kandy had helped him learn to walk, taught him to read... and still watched over him in this way.

"You... don't mention Princess Kandra much," Adam commented warily.

The King gave him a half-smile. "No. But she's in my thoughts a lot. Fair, I suppose, since she taught me to think in the first place."

He paused. "She was a warrior and a strategist, like Genevieve. But she was never impetuous. She lived life like a chess game. Everything was always planned out well in advance, double- and triple-checked, and contingencies for every possible event. Father... always said she had Mother's mind. Mother said she had Father's heart."

"That explains a lot – about *you*," Adam told him. A gentle smile played around his mouth.

Damien sighed. "I've always wondered if she and Raphael Anvliyar were actually in love, or if their betrothal was a strategy to extract my family from Emeralsee. I've... never dared to ask him. He always seems so dour and laconic."

"That may be your answer right there," Adam pointed out.

A shrug. "I haven't had the chance to talk to anyone who knew him particularly well *before*. I don't even know how he and Kandy met."

Damien raised his eyes to the western horizon, where the sun was still a finger's-width away from beginning to disappear. "He's over *there*, Adam. And the Army is *here*. In many ways, it's Kandy watching over me now."

Adam regarded him for a long moment. "You carry a lot of ghosts, don't you?"

Damien turned, and by the way even Adam – who *glowed*, for pity's sake, brighter than the setting sun – winced away slightly, the King guessed that he had that *intense* look that so seemed to bother people.

"Yes. Queen Marian is just the only one of them who talks back to me. And I don't want you to be another one, Adam. You're the person holding this strangely shaped family of ours together."

He'd surfaced slowly from his nap to the familiar, soothing sound of the pair of them talking while they sheltered him from the world.

As they'd done for so very long.

As he hadn't realized how badly he'd missed them doing that these last several years.

Jason... was easier with things now. But he was still not exactly *easy* about how things had changed in his absence.

Not that Damien was exactly *easy* about all of it either, but he was sort of becoming resigned. Or... something.

Adam snorted. "Jase was perfectly fine with the idea of him having *you* in his bed. Or *Genevieve*. It's the idea of *me* having that kind of freedom that he objects to."

Damien shrugged a little. "He always needs time to get used to things. We all know that. At least he didn't shut down entirely."

"All the changes last Fall made him stretch and gain some mental flexibility perhaps," Adam said with a sigh. "Alexa... raised him to break before he'd bend. A pity David didn't join their family when Jason was younger. *That* man is incredibly flexible-minded."

He favored his King with a wry look. "Rather like you."

Damien refused to be drawn off-topic. "Jason needs you to be safe, Adam. *I* need you to be safe. *Genevieve* needs you to be safe, though I don't know if she knows that yet."

"My visions..."

The King shook his head. "Be that as it may. I don't want to put too much faith in Foreseeings and thereby miss something we should have *actually* seen."

"Which is why you waited so long on Lord Prydeen's Foreseeing," Adam reminded him. "And risked both your lives."

Damien knew his eyes were filled with the remembered pain and fear – the feeling that they'd waited *too* long and he'd lose not only his soul-bonded beloved, his hoped-for family... but all the Healing he had sworn to bring to the Realm.

"Adam..."

"You chose me your Champion, Damien. If you wanted to *protect* me, you should have chosen someone else."

Damien looked at him helplessly. "There's no one else who could have deserved it. You – and Jason – have been my Champions since you found me in the Library."

Adam tilted his head and gave him a sardonic smile. "And you'd be having quite nearly the same problem with anyone you put this choke-chain around."

He fingered it, the symbol of his office. "Face it, my King, you just don't want to put anyone you care about – and that seems to be everyone down to the grubbiest urchin in the streets or the crookedest official – in harm's way."

The King blinked. "Well, no, of course not..."

"But it's your *job* to do so, Damien. It's the job of a king to send people out to fight – and sometimes to die." Adam's eyes were full of compassion. "It's the duty you were born to, my friend, and you are better at it than anyone else precisely *because* you find it so abhorrent. King Reginald sent me out – and maybe to die – and I went because that *was* my place as a trained knight. I had to trust that the king had spent whatever efforts were possible to prevent that bloodshed and was doing it for reasons that were good, even if I couldn't see them."

He waved at the Royal Guards and Army ranged around the eastern half of the parade-ground. "All of us who have given our lives to the way of the sword make that choice. To trust our leaders not to spend our lives cheaply. Just as we trust our mothers and fathers to strive to care for us as children and do the same for our own children. Just as we trust the priestesses to pray for us and the architects to build safe buildings and the shipwrights to build boats that will not leak.

"Each of us has our duty, and each one has moments of difficulty in carrying it out at times. I don't pretend to know the insides of the constraints that architects and shipwrights find themselves under – perhaps their beloved child will sail away on that boat? – but I can imagine some of the difficulties of being a parent... or a king."

Adam gave him a wry look. "You gave me ten days of a taste of that, after all. And I've no desire to switch with you, so I want *you* to live a long, healthy life, my King.

"But my larger point is that we knights and soldiers went out to fight and die for King Reginald. And it's our duty – and our privilege to do so for you.

"And between the two of you – there is not a one of us out here who wouldn't rather have you be the king who decides when to spend our lives, because we *trust* you to spend us wisely."

A long speech... they both stared at each other for a moment.

At last Damien felt his lips curl up. "Reading Pardasian philosophy again, Adam?"

The knight shrugged a little self-consciously. "How often does a person *actually* get a chance to give a lecture on duty and trust to the leader of a nation just before an *actual* battle? I couldn't resist."

"But in the Pardasian legend it was one of the Gods lecturing their battle leader because he was hesitant to fight his cousins and countrymen. It was a civil war they were fighting. You're trying to convince me to let *you* do my fighting for me."

Adam snorted. "I'm also not a God. And you're just as hesitant to fight our countrymen as the Archer. The point, Damien, is that we each have our own duty and we each have our own battles to fight. Mine is with Tomas – or whomever he puts forth – as your Champion. Yours is to make yourself decide when to spend our lives to prevent a worse war."

He looked wry. "And also to fight the magickal battles. We really *need* Genevieve back. You're better spent on other hard things than making battle decisions."

Damien winced. "So, I should give that over to my lady-*wife* when it breaks *me*?"

"To your *warrior-queen*. She was born to do it. Just as *you* were born to be a king, Damien." Adam regarded him calmly. "And Jason and I were born to be warriors."

The King gave him a helpless look. "There's so much *more* to you both."

"I'd wop you on the head for that if we were in private," Adam told him with a snort. "I didn't say *only* warriors, you dolt."

His eyes flickered to the west and the last beams of the setting sun. "That's Tomas. And he isn't alone."

Damien turned to look also. The sun had set, but the sky was still full of light. It would be another hour and a half before it was truly dark. Probably at least that long before the demon manifested itself. Time enough for a proper single-combat and a short reprieve.

It was still his fear that despite defining the battlefield as this place, Azella would send her demon to terrorize his city. Or the countryside, where he'd sent as many families as were willing to go.

To Lynncrag, where Adam's family had all but adopted him.

To Elderwyld and Ravenscroft, where his cousins lived, the home of his childhood.

To Elmirscroft, where two women and one little boy who were all dear to his heart sheltered.

Or... outside of Emeralsee entirely. While the details of Damien's life were mostly public knowledge, he didn't think he'd given Azella enough of a look inside his soul to know where there were places and people dear to him. She might assume that he had no fond memories in Emeralsee at all – but there was no way she could not suspect his attachment to Elaarwen.

Demons were inimical not merely to *human* populations either.

At least he was fully connected to his Realm now. Ilseador Itself would tell the King where it was being attacked.

Damien had told Adam – and Tim and Lord David, though not General Direlien – that he could and would vanish himself to wherever in the Realm he needed to be to fight the demon and they were not to worry. Not that he could stop them from worrying, but at least they could hope he had a plan.

So could he.

The *best* plan was still here.

Tomas Elsevier strode up and stopped a good ten feet away, a slightly shorter, cloaked and cowled figure beside him. Adam regarded them calmly. Damien's heart wrenched.

"So, I see that you brought your *Champion* for all your brave words of facing me directly," Tomas sneered.

"I see you brought one as well," Damien responded. "Will you satisfy my curiosity, Tomas? Why are we going through all of this?"

"Because I want your throne, Damien," the Duke of Siovale said somewhat impatiently. "I would have thought that obvious by now."

The King felt obscurely disappointed. "So, simple ambition, no grand purpose?"

Tomas looked at him, his face wearing that expression that had always seemed so caring, so thoughtful, so reasonable. "You'd feel better if it was about wanting revenge on Reginald and his line, wouldn't you? Some lovely rhetoric about how the Alsterling line has sat the throne for too long and the last century has proven it. It worked well for the Rebellion, I must admit."

Damien sighed. "And Sildra? How did she buy into this?"

The Duke laughed. "What you *really* want to know is if Zachary Miramar is part of our... movement. And doubtless you've remembered that Tariana Eledor is my niece as well. You're well-known to have memorized the entire Royal Archives, Damien. I doubt your concerns end there. There's no reason not to tell you, I suppose. You cannot win, despite having turned over our little drama this afternoon. But... I think I'll leave it to your own fevered imaginings."

He glanced over to his shadow as Damien tried not to grind his teeth in frustration.

"Sunset, cowardly King. My Champion to face yours."

He stepped behind his Champion and lifted cloak and hood away...

Adam gasped, but Damien had known all along.

How could he not, when the Realm and his own blood were singing it?

Genevieve.

A Genevieve who seemed more alert than she had this afternoon, but whose eyes still glittered with *wrongness.*

A Genevieve who wore fighting leathers rather than the elegant riding habit she'd been in this afternoon.

A Genevieve who bore the Monarch's Blade.

Adam – and Damien, and the Duke of Siovale, for that matter – wore light armor for fencing. Light plate over long chainmail shirts. Genevieve wore nothing but soft leather and her long, red-gold hair was unbound.

Tomas laughed again. "See you what I mean, Damien? I cannot lose."

"A moment, I pray you." Damien tugged his Champion back a further ten feet and spoke in a low voice. "Adam. You can't do this."

Adam looked him straight in the eyes. "And *you* can? I've fenced her before, Damien. I can disarm her."

That was, perhaps a bold statement to make. She and Adam were evenly matched, with Jason a hair better than either. The King trailed all three, but only slightly.

On the other hand, Genevieve had spent the entire Autumn on bed-rest and most of the Winter sick with her pregnancy. If she had managed to fit in some training in the short intervals when she had been hale and whole, her husband would not have been surprised... but that would not compensate for coming up on a year without. She hadn't exactly been *well* when she and Jason had gone to negotiate for Elendria with the Army at their backs after all.

"It's not that," the King told his friend urgently. "If anyone can fence her safely it would be you – or Jason. And right now, it's probably better you than Jason."

The soul-bond... the baby... the *soul-bond.*

"It's the Sword. In *my* hands, in a situation of real danger, I'd be nearly invincible. I don't know what it will do in hers."

Because the Sword had 'spoken' for Genevieve *and* she carried a potential Heir to the Realm. At least, praise all the Gods, she was done with her nausea and her abdomen had not yet even begun to round.

Would Tomas have dared this drama later in her pregnancy? Damien was just as glad he would never know the answer.

"There's something else," Adam told him grimly. "*You* absolutely *cannot* fight her, no matter *what* happens to me. That damned Sword will probably interpret it as her attempting to usurp the Throne and cut her head off instantly."

Damien felt his jaw fall open in shock. He forced it closed, and nodded sharply. That was what the Monarch's Blade was supposed to do to usurpers who tried to wield it after all. Not that it had done so in living memory... though the Sword's disappearance and King Reginald's eighty-three-year reign might have had something to do with that.

All that was likely protecting Genevieve right now from that metallic retribution was that it was *Tomas* who was the potential usurper, not she. And doubtless *he* wasn't such a fool as to take the thing into his hands.

"Glad *now* that I came with you?" Adam said sardonically.

Damien gripped his arm. "Always, love." As Adam's eyes softened, he couldn't help adding, "Be careful."

Although of *whom* he couldn't make a distinction.

Adam snorted, and the ironic look was back in his eyes.

The Champion crossed half the distance between them and swept his Queen a florid bow. "Your Majesty. I believe I have this dance."

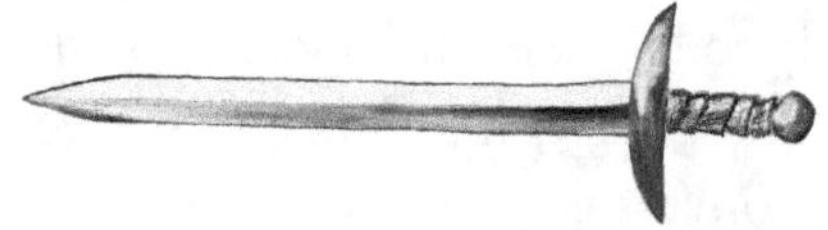

Chapter FOURTEEN

Duel to the... Death?

Traditionally the King's Champion was the best fencer in the Realm not also of royal blood. And the Heir's Champion would be the next best. Once upon a time, it had been an honor fiercely contended for among the ranks of the knights sworn to the monarch, though any fighter might present themselves to test the Champion's blades and win their place.

King Reginald had bastardized the office, awarding it as a plum to his favorites. Though he might not have been the first – Queen Marian's ghost had admitted that she had stocked the position with her lovers during her own long, but entirely unmagickal, tenure as ruler. Although, perhaps, she had merely made lovers of the Champions who won the position fairly.

Jason – and then Adam, when Jason had been himself named Heir and then discovered to be of royal blood – had never formally fought for the position.

They had also never been challenged for it.

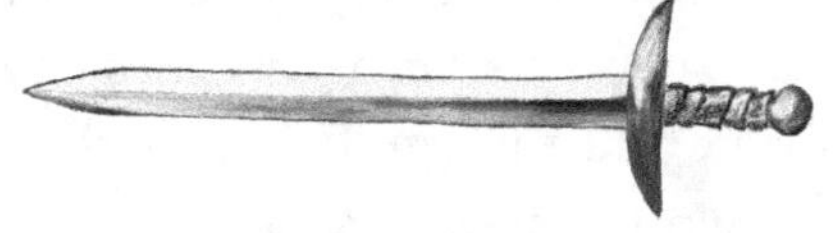

"It's a pleasure to watch two masters of their craft contend, is it not?"

Tomas Elsevier had edged around the ferocious battle to Damien's side. Or, not precisely to his side – not close enough for a knife in the ribs, too close for a flung dagger, and just out of reach of a sword – but close enough to converse.

Damien shot him a look of dislike, his heart in his mouth with every passage of blades.

Genevieve had, indeed, lost stamina and power, but her muscles remembered what to do and the Sword was clearly lending her... something. Adam was in perfect form, but was hampered by not actually wanting to hurt her... an effort impeded by her complete lack of armor.

"Why... Tomas I thought we were *friends!*" Damien couldn't quite stop himself from saying. "You supported me against Harald... if you wanted an Elsevier on the Throne, why not just support *him?*"

The Duke snorted a laugh. "I thought about it. Harald would have been a weak king, but I was his obvious Heir. Or Mark, if not me. I could have been the power behind the throne – and when I tired of that, claim it for myself in name as well. There was still Lord Prydeen, but I supposed my sorcerous friends to the south would deal with him on my behalf.

"But– *friends,* Damien? You had me swear the Vassal's Oath at swordpoint and placed magickal Bindings on me as even King Reginald had not dared to do with his vassals. And I know, since I'd sworn an oath to him as well. *Friends...* hah. At least you were fool enough to modify the language."

Damien winced at another terrifying clash of blades that imperiled both his loves – and his unborn child.

"I don't suppose you'd believe me if I explained that I have no control over the Bindings that the Realm includes with the Vassal's Oath – and that I'd decided to use the modified language before I ever had any idea magick would be involved?"

Modified language that harkened back to the original wording... to when the Alsterling line had been chosen as caretakers by the Land, and Bound by It, and then gifted the ability to do the same with others who were worthy stewards.

Tomas snorted. "Hardly."

Damien sighed, trying to watch the duke more than the battle and simply trust Adam, but unable to entirely tear his eyes away. "It's true, though."

A shrug. "We'd made our choices, we Elsevier Dukes, long before that. Although I suppose the next will be a duchess. 'Bella has the strength and Mark... is clearly too weak."

"Funny," Damien replied as Adam dug for a bind and twist that had worked to disarm Genevieve during any number of practice sessions. "I would have put it the other way around. Mark is strong enough to think for himself, and Arabella is motivated only by ambition. You might be raising an Heir you'll need to watch your back around. Did either of them know about your 'sorcerous friends' to the south? It sounds like Harald didn't."

The maneuver failed – the Sword was clearly helping her with more than merely stamina. Though it was possible Genevieve had sorted out how to handle that attack before her collapse last Summer. She'd had Jason to spar with after all, and while it wasn't a move that hardly anyone would be *capable* of trying, it *was* one she'd been working on for some time.

From both sides of the blade, unfortunately, because she was now trying it back on Adam. And he didn't find it much easier to defend against than she.

It was clear that Genevieve might well have been a contender for the Champion's chain. Though she, too, bore royal blood.

Tomas chuckled. "You think to trick me into giving you more information again, Damien? And I *always* watch my back. Even around such quisling creatures as you and your 'Royal Guard.'"

He paused. "I suppose I must thank you for returning three of the Lost Provinces, though. And restoring the economy of Emeralsee. The throne seems a more lucrative proposition now, after you've sat it for five years."

Damien gave him an expression that was a baring of teeth but definitely not a smile. "You're welcome."

Another pass. Sparks were actually flying from the energy with which the blades clashed. He could only imagine the state Jason must be in, back in the ranks of the Army... and without an upcoming battle with a demon to distract him.

"What... what will you do with her – and me – if Genevieve wins?" Damien found himself asking out of morbid fascination.

It couldn't happen, of course. He clung to Adam's happy vision of family and children... and *all four* of them. He wouldn't *let* anything else happen...

It occurred to him that Tomas had anticipated exactly this. He knew that Adam – and Jason – would never let the King fight his own single-combat. He knew that although Damien had the sorcerous ability to end the duel in whatever way he wished, that he *wouldn't*. Not merely out of chivalry, or even the knowledge that even his own warriors on the field would object to magickal interventions, but because he was hoarding his Power for use against the demon to come.

Except... Tomas was subtle but knew little of magick. And Azella was *not* subtle. Not at all.

"I'll use her and the child to lure Aldred out of those mountains," Tomas said easily. "I can learn from the lessons of history. Elaarwen can never be taken from without, but it will be a constant thorn in the side if it *isn't* taken. But Aldred is practical. He and I will understand each other. He'll be willing to work with me and be restored to his title – his *full* title and powers. And since he'll have his son to raise up as his Heir, he should be a bit more philosophical about Genevieve."

He caught Damien's startled look. "Oh, you hadn't heard that Ciriis delivered? A healthy boy. A pity the mother didn't survive the birth, but they say that's a problem at the higher altitudes. And Aldred will doubtless prefer not to have that snake of a woman setting policies for him and subverting his son."

They were too far apart for a knife in the gut.

Yet the Duke of Siovale had managed one anyways.

Ciriis... his first lover... elder sister, substitute mother, caregiver, Spymistress, architect of his reign... She couldn't be... *gone*... And if the birth had gone poorly because of Cloudcroft's high location... then it was *his* fault for banishing them there...

He tried to remind himself that the traitor duke was hardly the most reliable of news sources. Surely, he knew how close Damien had been with Ciriis. Surely, he knew how such news would devastate the King.

The Duke was still talking. "I'll keep Genevieve in my castle, of course. You said the child is a girl – I've thought about marrying her to one of my boys in due time. Raised properly, she should be pleased about it – they're all good boys, not like their bastard uncle."

He rolled his eyes. "Why my mother felt it necessary not only to let herself bear a cuckoo's chick, and then also spoil him rotten, I suppose I'll never know. I know that *she* knew of our longer plan. *I'll* be a much better king than Harald."

That was undoubtedly true... though not much of a bar for one's horse to hurdle.

Tomas sighed. "It was a better plan when Mark would be my Heir. It's a while to wait for a bride to grow up, but there will doubtless be those who will be pacified by having Alsterling blood coming back to the throne in a generation. For Arabella... the only option would be your catamite Crown Prince." He shuddered. "Well, we must all do what we must to reach our goals."

Probably not a time to remind him that Aldred's new son was as close to the throne as Genevieve's child by some accountings. Not when Tomas had just talked himself into keeping both Jason and Genevieve alive – and himself, because of the soul-bond. Though not *Adam*...

None of it was going to happen. *None.*

"And once the babe is born?" Damien asked, trying to insert a note of hopelessness. Tomas seemed to be responding to that better than to casual interest. He wasn't getting *everything* he wanted to know, but enough, perhaps...

"If his grandchild is enough of a lever on Aldred, I can dispose of Genevieve. Azella the Unpitying has assured me that she can complete the breaking of your soul-bond, given enough time, though it may not leave Genevieve much of a mind. A mad noblewoman is no threat and will make it that much easier to control the child."

He gave the King a vicious grin. "You, of course, return to Azella's tender care. She says she has plans for you. *And* some more-secure way to keep you where she intends."

He sounded a bit displeased.

"Hmmn," Damien kept his eyes on the bout. "I threw off your timing when I decided to leave her Keep, did I?"

Was Genevieve tiring just a hair beyond what the Sword could propel her muscles to accomplish? Adam had needed to stay nearly entirely on the defensive, taking the initiative to attempt a disarming only as the odd opportunity arose. Damien was well aware that his Champion could go on like this for *hours* without flagging... but the sky was darkening and torches had been lit all around the parade-ground, though they were far enough away not to actually shed much light out here.

Darkness meant it would be more likely for Adam to make a mistake.

Damien could create light. It wasn't even difficult. But it would take a bit more Power than he really wanted to spare.

The evening breeze, beginning to roll out to sea, gave him another idea.

Please... he cast the thought out. *Help...*

"A bit," the traitorous Duke was admitting. "I hadn't intended to leave my children long in that decadent castle of yours. But I would have been satisfied for 'Bella to ensure the Queen died in childbirth and thereby took you down as well. Everyone knows Jason Solway isn't fit to be a king. I doubt it would have been more than half a year before he gave it up and *invited* me to come in and take over. You told me you'd have chosen me your Heir over him anyways. By that point, Harald's perfidy would have been forgotten and I would be the Realm's savior. A perfect, bloodless coup."

"Not quite," Damien noted.

Tomas waved this off. "You would have survived if the sorceress succeeded. And if Genevieve went mad, we could have let her live as well."

Damien shivered, just as a pair of sylphs fluttered in before him. As with most Elemental spirits, they were invisible unless one knew how to *look* for them.

You asked for help, Bound King?

Aye, and my thanks. This man here would see me deposed and my Binding to the Realm ended by the sorceress to the south.

The sylphs seemed to think this a bad idea.

Could you possibly make my Bound Queen's hair fly into her face as if you were any other nighttime breeze? My Champion loves her and the babe she carries as much as I do and seeks only to disarm her... but he needs an opening before it gets so dark he errs and causes her harm.

The sylphs thought this sounded like fun.

Moments later, Genevieve's wild mane of unbound hair was being pushed into her face. For those who could actually see the sylphs, it was clear they had taken his instructions to heart and were actually hovering before her and holding her hair in front of her eyes no matter how she tried to bat it away.

Luckily, it was probably only Damien who could see the sylphs or someone would likely cry foul, though the Air Elementals had also taken care to send a surge of breezes to disguise their work.

It was the work of a moment for Adam to disarm Genevieve when she could no longer see. And but a moment more before he had her immobilized. He'd been training the Secret Cadre for years, after all, and the former Rebel Duchess had long since shared all her weaponsfree moves with them.

A half-dozen of her ladies-in-waiting came running out to help the Champion escort the Queen off the field of battle.

The King turned to Duke Tomas. "Do you concede your rebellion, my lord?"

The Duke snorted. "My Champion isn't *dead,* so it's hardly conclusive."

Damien stared at him. Then shook his head in reluctant admiration at the man's moxy. By the usual terms of such an engagement he was correct... though it was a forgone conclusion that no matter who had battled her, none of them would have attempted anything other than a disarmament of the Queen.

On the other hand, the Siovalese forces were now completely surrounded by the Army. While the Duke might not be entirely aware of that, he was a strategist *par excellence* and had to have been aware of the likelihood. His only leverage had been Genevieve's life and Damien's unwillingness to use magick. And now Genevieve was back in Damien's possession... or at least in the possession of his people.

"You really think you have the upper hand, don't you, Tomas."

"I do, cowardly King."

In a smooth move, the Duke unsheathed his sword and attacked.

While Damien hadn't exactly been taken by surprise, having little remaining faith in Tomas' gallantry and knowing this was the traitor's last chance to claim a victory, he was still a little slow on the draw. Part of it was intentional: all of his very extensive training with Jason and Adam – and later with Genevieve and his Royal Guards – had been based on the premise that it would be better for any potential opponent to underestimate him.

Drawing slowly enough that he appeared startled and just barely catching the Duke's sword on his own surely contributed to that impression.

But part of his slowness *was* his distraction.

Genevieve was fighting her 'captors' with tooth and nail – literally – and they were hampered by trying to subdue the pregnant Queen without injury to her.

Damien had almost managed to put aside his concern about the work that his Royal Guard and Army was going to in quietly capturing the Siovalese forces... But when Arabella Elsevier let out a high-pitched scream, he couldn't help but spend enough thought to categorize it as *outrage* not *mortal injury*.

And darkness was continuing to fall, and the likelihood of the demon showing up was increasing by the second... He could almost feel its footsteps, though for some reason he had thought it more likely to fly...

Nonetheless, Damien was ready for Tomas' *next* attack well before the traitor Duke began it.

The King knew that Tomas of Siovale had been considered a doughty warrior for the Rebellion, though his skills as a field-marshal had eclipsed his personal skills. Genevieve had been their strategist, Tomas had directed their battles, and Rosa had served as their negotiator – and never mind that the Countess of Zialest had begun her career by 'negotiating' with Prince Oskar by sticking a fire-poker through his belly.

Granted that the Duke was more than ten years his senior and Siovale hadn't seen any action since the Rebellion ended five years earlier...

But... it was almost like his sorcerous battle with Lord Prydeen, five years before when Damien had taken back his Throne from Tomas' bastard baby brother, Harald.

Disappointing.

Damien quickly found himself almost *toying* with the Duke. Not intentionally, either. Tomas' sword-skills simply weren't up to a level that challenged the King.

Nor were his dirty tricks, which amused Damien more than anything else. When Tomas attempted an unchivalrous strike to the back – and he *had* been knighted, long ago – the King was ready for it. And when he attempted a sweep of the foot, Damien was ready for that, too.

The Secret Cadre, after all, trained to *use* those tricks. And Damien had been training with *them* since he married Genevieve.

There was no real point in dragging this out. The King had better things to do.

"For shame, my lord," he chided Tomas as he disarmed the man and held him almost casually with the point of his sword at Tomas' throat. "Though I suppose following the Code of Knighthood is as meaningless to you as your Vassal's Oath."

The Duke gave him a frustrated look. "It really *is* true that nothing makes you angry, isn't it, Damien?"

The King winced slightly, thinking of all the Realm's glassware hovering three inches up from its places... "Not quite..."

"Mark and Arabella didn't know. Nor the younger children. Just Sildra. She hates Zachary for having become Count of Dalizell when their sister Elsa died, though she was older... and married to me." Tomas looked towards the west, where it was clear that several members of the royal forces surrounded each of his people. "My great-great-grandfather made the arrangement with the sorcerer of the south. The contact has been kept between father and son – and occasionally the duchess – while we laid our plans. The people of Siovale are blameless. My men-at-arms are... under mild *compulsion* spells. Enough to make their loyalty to *me* stronger than their loyalty to the *Crown.*"

The man was sweating... "Tari and Rob – my cousin never knew..."

"Tomas!" Duchess Sildra's voice screeched. *"No!"*

Damien's attention was just briefly distracted, but it was enough.

"I'm sorry, Sildra!" the traitorous Duke cried – and flung himself onto the point of Damien's sword.

The razor-sharp steel ripped through skin and muscle and cartilage – the Duke of Siovale's throat. Blood fountained up in a great gush, spurting forwards and slathering the startled King until he was coated with the hot, sticky blood of a man he had once thought of as one of his dearest friends.

If he'd held his sword lower, it would have been a gut- or chest-wound. Damien could have Healed those. But this... Tomas had almost severed his own head... hopeless...

It was Damien's automatic reaction to try anyways. He pulled back his Power almost instantly.

Why bother? All that awaited the man was to be nailed to the wall of the Castle – even if he *could* Heal him... surely this was a mercy he could allow...

He pulled his sword free and stumbled back...

Sildra had ripped herself away from the Royal Guards – or Secret Cadre – who had been holding her and threw herself, weeping, on her husband's body.

Mark and Arabella followed more slowly, unsurely, Royal Guards following them, but allowing some mercy for the young pair. The girl was clearly overcome, and fell to weeping beside her mother.

The young man... stood back. He lifted his hands and scrubbed his face several times, then undid his swordbelt and dropped it where he stood. He reached out blindly for one of his guards – it turned out to be Marianna Loveress – saying something, and then stumbled with Marianna's guidance towards Damien, falling to his knees at the King's feet.

"Please, Your Majesty. I didn't know what Father and Mother intended until he brought the Queen and Prince Jason in to Elsevier Castle after 'Bella and I brought the little ones home. I didn't know *why* he summoned us home. And I *know* the younger children had no idea. I don't think 'Bella did either..."

The young man's words stumbled almost as much as his feet had, and he looked back over his shoulder at his sister, then shuddered away, perhaps remembering her attempts to sever Jason's finger just hours earlier.

"I... don't know... Please don't... my little brothers and sisters... Have mercy for them, if not for me, I beg you. And for our people. I don't know how Father did this, but I would swear he had no conspirators besides..."

He couldn't stop himself from looking back at his mother, weeping over his father. Mark crumpled in on himself further.

Damien felt frozen to his core. Here he was, covered with the blood of this young man's father, his still-dripping sword in his hand. He had no choice but to complete their orphaning – Sildra had known, it was clear even without her husband's confession.

He swallowed hard, his mouth utterly dry.

"Your father absolved all of his children of conspiracy with his last breath, Mark," the King found the ability to say. "Though since Arabella... attempted..."

Mark nodded. "I would..." he swallowed. "I would beg clemency for... for my sister. If... if it is possible I would keep her as we kept my grandmother. In a tower, for the rest of her days."

Though Arabella was only seventeen. Duchess Lydia had been in her sixties.

And the boy hadn't asked about his mother.

Damien reached up to pull off his steel helm and gorget and resisted the urge to wipe sweat from his face. He'd only be replacing it with Tomas' blood.

"We'll talk about it tomorrow, Mark." He nodded wearily at Marianna. "Take him back to the Castle. Take them all back."

"You're coming, too, I hope," Adam's youngest sister said pointedly. "Your Majesty. Queen Genevieve needs you and..." Her eye traveled down his blood-splattered form.

"Soon, Mari," Adam strode up right then. "The King is *my* concern. Go on."

"Adam," she began argumentatively, but her brother ignored her.

The Champion took Damien's sword from him gently before cleaning and resheathing it. There was little he could do about the blood now drying on what had been pristine steel armor, but he put his arms around the younger man and held him tight.

"He made his choices, Damien," Adam said softly. "And this... was easier than it could have been. *Would* have been."

"He gave me a confession before... before he..." The King couldn't continue. "He said... his men are under *compulsions* – I can test the truth of that. And he said the children didn't know. Just... just *Sildra*."

He mustn't cry.

Kings did not cry in public.

Victors in single-combat did not cry.

No one with *sense* cried over killing the traitor who had threatened his wife and best friend (and love) and his throne.

"It's okay to cry," Adam said gently. "Just... maybe not now. It's getting awfully dark, love."

They must be well-alone for Adam to dare that word out in public.

Damien nodded, and heaved himself out of Adam's arms, vaguely noting that his Champion was now also covered in Tomas Elsevier's blood.

"Thank you…"

Adam nodded. "You've never killed someone like this before. It… takes most of us pretty hard."

A suggestion that the people around him who had seen him fall apart might not judge him too harshly for it. The soldiers, anyways, who had fought and if, by a miracle, they hadn't killed someone themselves, they had been with someone who had.

His Royal Guards – save Tim – were all practically babies now, not veterans of King Reginald's time… they might not be so understanding. But he could beat them all in the practice-ring so they were unlikely to say anything about it.

"Genevieve?" he asked.

"Up to the Castle." Adam's face was shadowed in the late dusk, but his sardonic grin was hard to miss. "Bound hand and foot. Jason went with her."

Damien nodded. "I'll break whatever *compulsions* she… and the Siovalese men-at-arms… are under… later. Marianna might be able to do it – but spells that affect the mind… I'd want to be there to guide her–"

"No sooner than *tomorrow*," Adam told him firmly. "Possibly not till the day after that." He grinned again. "Besides, Genevieve is teaching your Royal Guards all sorts of things about language."

The King gave him an incredulous look. "She's cursing?"

"Swearing up a storm," Adam confirmed with a chuckle. "Not as far-ranging as what you'd hear down on the docks, but then she's never spent time there, thanks to Jason. Those mountain-folk of hers can get pretty creative, too, it seems, if not quite so, um, *dirty*."

Damien gulped back an involuntary laugh. It seemed… inappropriate.

"Go ahead and laugh," Adam told him. "We're still alive. We stopped a war. We should take the time to appreciate it."

Damien shook his head. This had been more emotionally draining than he had anticipated and it had put him far too close to the edge of hysterics. *Again.*

Adam gave him a knowing look. "You're keeping that spiral under control. You'll be fine."

"I have to be. For what comes next." The King shivered. "So much for the idea of a respite in between..."

Adam snorted. "What do you think *this* is, my sweet prince? A few minutes of peace – and I made sure no one else was going to come up to check on you. I'd kiss you now, but there's still too many people about. *Later,* though..."

Surely it was too dark for his flush to be seen. *"Adam..."*

A small laugh. "Do you want to keep your armor on? Or do you want help removing it?"

Damien shook his head. "I don't think it matters. Leave it be. Just... get everyone off of the parade-grounds. You know where. Ten feet farther back at least."

Adam's look was probably tolerant... in light. "You marked it all out and everyone knows."

"Then you go, too. I'd... rather no one else was here at all–"

"Because we'd leave our King unguarded at any time."

"I'm not objecting, am I? But you. I need *you* out of sight, Adam. I... I won't be able to focus if anyone I know *well* becomes a target."

He met those gentle golden-hazel eyes that so effectively picked up the dim light of faraway torches. "I love you."

"Don't do anything stupid," Adam said matter-of-factly.

"No." There was nothing else to be said. He'd come to terms with them needing him as King... and as himself, Damien.

Adam turned and started walking away.

He never saw what hit him.

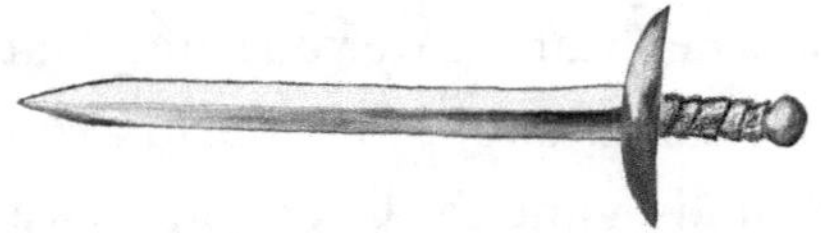

Chapter FIFTEEN

Deceit and Distrust

"A*DAM!*"

Damien started towards him, his heart clenching in cold fear, then realized that was the *worst* thing he could do. He turned back to face whatever was coming in.

Coming from the *west*, based on the orientation of Adam's prone form. Not from the *south,* where Azella was surely safely ensconced in her vile Keep. Why the *west?*

A lone figure stumbled down the road. The soldiers stationed around the parade-ground stopped him, but then escorted him in to their King, bringing a torch along to light their way.

"This lad says you told him to come to you, milord," said the sergeant in charge of the group.

It was... Mikhail – no, Jeremy.

He looked terrified, worn, exhausted, filthy, the many braids of his golden hair raveled and frizzing... and just as weirdly beautiful as when Damien had first met him. Just as the King had imagined him arriving.

It was also *entirely impossible* for him to have made it here in the eleven days since Damien had left Azella's keep.

"Thank you, Sergeant," he told the solid-looking woman. "I did indeed. You may leave him with me."

She hesitated, bless her heart. "Are you sure, Your Majesty? We've heard tell of untoward things about to happen, and you've told us all to stay out of the 'grounds... and the Champion...We should move Sir Loveress'... body." She gestured to Adam's body and Damien ached to ask her to remove him to a safer distance.

But he dared not.

If the sergeant and her troops didn't get back out of this area he'd have more people to defend.

"This lad is a special case, Sergeant. He was a fellow-captive in the sorceress' stronghold to the south, weren't you... Mikhail?" The King wrapped an arm around the youth's shoulders and Jeremy nodded energetically, the way a scared lad might do. And Damien's slight hesitation over what to call him might be put down to being unwilling to reveal the boy's new true-name.

"Adam will be fine in a few minutes," he added, "and he won't appreciate a fuss. He's been very close to the Queen – fencing her like that was harder on him than he expected."

Adam likely wouldn't appreciate the gossip that would follow from *that,* either, but time was of the essence. These soldiers had to get back behind the line of safety, and that surely couldn't happen if they were trying to carry Adam's heavily-muscled form, nor did Damien have time to come up with a better excuse.

"Back to where you belong, Sergeant. Take the torch with you," Damien added quickly before she could come up with any more reasons to not leave the King unattended, save by an unconscious man. "I won't need it."

Reluctantly, she led her troops back across the open ground.

Damien had to buy them time to make it to safety.

"You ran faster than I guessed you could, Jeremy," Damien said in an approving tone. "I wasn't expecting you to arrive for some time yet."

"There was much incentive," came the reply. "The sorceress dogged my path, but I stayed on the path you had marked for me."

Damien nodded, letting go of him and stepping slightly away... and not coincidentally, between the boy and Adam.

"Obedient of you. I wasn't sure if you would decide to strike out on your own." He paused. "So... why *did* you leave the path?"

"It was too *hard* to follow. It wiggled back and forth *all over* Farivera. I swear, it folded *back* on itself at least *eight times.*"

The boy he'd known would never have let such a whiny tone emerge. Would never have referred to Azella as anything but 'the Mistress.' Would never have referred to the land he crossed as 'Farivera.'

"It did," Damien confirmed a little sadly. "There was a reason for that."

And he would agree, it *was* hard to follow.

"How many folds did you make it past before you stepped off?"

It was hard to see in the darkness, but he thought the boy shrugged. "Four. Maybe five. I don't know."

"Ah," Damien wondered if this was fixable.

That... seemed to make sense if the spell he had wound around a piece of Pardasian philosophy as he ran meant anything.

That... would have been the place where he could see Jeremy needing some guidance.

If only he could have been there to give it... but there was the Realm. And Genevieve. And Jason. Adam. The baby. And so many others... His life was more full of *people* than he had ever imagined it could have been when Lady Theresa was his sole contact with the world...

Farivera had needed him to cover as much of its territory with his footprints as possible. Turning it into a lesson and a test for Jeremy had been an addition that he had added and built as he went.

Right view, right resolve, right speech, right conduct, right livelihood... Jeremy had no idea what sort of livelihood he might have outside Azella's purview.

The King sighed.

And called upon the air surrounding the parade-ground to speed up its tiny movements, but not its larger ones. A number of sylphs had gotten caught up with curiosity in his doings and they *loved* being called to twirl and dance in place.

Damien had suspected – the books Azella had given him hadn't specified, but he had *felt* the rightness of it – that Fire-sylphs and Air-sylphs were one and the same. Now he got to see the transformation for himself as he asked the air to essentially set itself on fire.

Light erupted in a dome around the parade-ground.

His people all around cried out in alarm and then in wonder.

The creature that had taken Jeremy's form – or, perhaps, taken *over* Jeremy's body – cringed away from the sudden brilliance. "What are you doing, Damien?"

"Using light to chase away the darkness," the King replied. "You were first named for a flower that loves sunshine, Jeremy. Surely this suits."

"Clever..." and the voice that came from the boy's throat no longer sounded like his. "But it isn't *light* that my kind fears. The light of your sun has certain qualities that we cannot abide – even reflected from your moon, it is too much for us. But there is none of *that* here."

Damien inclined his head. "I merely prefer being able to see what I am doing."

"A waste of your Power," the demon grated out... then paused. "How is this? None of it is your own Power! How are you compelling the sprites to do your work? You will have used up all the favors they have owed you in one fell swoop!"

"Perhaps it is still worth it," Damien smiled up at the Fire-Sylphs who – far from considering *him* to be in *their* debt seemed to be enjoying their transformation and entertaining themselves. The rest of the Air... was moving in accordance with the intention of the Realm. To the Realm it was similar to how Damien would feel to twitch a finger. It took some energy, but a completely inconsequential amount.

And the finger wouldn't be owed favors for its twitch.

"Leave the boy and go," Damien suggested to the demon. "Azella cannot have given you anything so valuable as to risk your existence."

The demon made Jeremy's body stand in a posture of ineffable arrogance and snort. "And what can *you* know of what is valuable to such as *I,* mortal man?"

Damien sighed. "To most creatures, continued existence is the most valuable thing of all. Unless, of course, there is a Greater Purpose. The survival of a mate, or children. Or others who depend on one. Perhaps there are other things as well. Have you a Greater Purpose, demon, or do you risk yourself for nothing more than greed?"

"What you call *greed* is the *key* to continued existence in my Plane," the demon informed him. "We either grow or we die. Being Called to this place and offered that which makes us grow is well worth what small risks you puny creatures might pose us."

"And what makes you grow is... Power." It wasn't really a question.

The demon stretched around to look at his form. "This creature was a good start. The one she has awaiting me is better still. It is *all* mine after I return this one and you to her."

The otherworldly blue eyes that had been unusual even when a demon didn't look out of them looked past Damien.

"She set no limits on what *else* I might do in pursuit of those goals. Perhaps I will feast on that creature lying there, first. It shines in a particularly delicious way."

Adam. Knocked unconscious by the – whatever it was. It had happened too quickly for Damien to identify it. Encased in his armor, it was impossible to even tell if he was still breathing – and unwise for the King to take so much of his attention away from this confrontation to really look to see, let alone send a whisper of his Healing-sense to check for the extent of Adam's injuries.

They'd both be dead if Damien's focus wavered.

And... no limits. That meant the entire Realm still stood at risk.

"No." Damien kept himself between them. "That *creature,* as you put it, is *mine.* You may not have him. You may not have *anything* from my Realm."

The demon focused Jeremy's eyes back on him. "You are an interesting creature yourself. If it were not for the woven Power with which Azella has laced me about, I would taste *your* Power. And that of this 'Realm' of yours."

The King looked at him steadily. "No. You wouldn't. And you won't now."

Dammit, this was going to be much trickier than he'd thought. In Damien's original plan he had only to ward himself and capture the demon. He had thought he might have to fight Azella at the same time, if she managed to get herself over here.

He had tried to arrange things so that he didn't have to defend people or animals, even plants or living soil or rock. The parade-ground was about as close to dead ground as could be found in his exuberantly *living* Realm.

Now he had to defend Adam... *and* Jeremy. It sounded like the demon was meant to return the boy to Azella, which suggested Jeremy himself was still in there. Somehow. And that the demon could be exorcised without fatal damage to the boy.

"Think you?" the demon laughed and Jeremy's body began to *expand*.

He grew in every dimension, becoming a larger version of himself. It looked like he was having to *pull* himself larger, however, one part expanding as he stretched it, then another. Every few rounds he grabbed his ears or his hair and chin and stretched his head into a larger size as well.

It looked... painful, though the demon didn't allow any expressions of pain to surface on Jeremy's now-oversized face.

But the difficulty of the expansion hardly mattered, because the demon was now taller than the main mast of one of Lord David's sailing ships.

Damien put a ward around Adam and called up the Binding Circle of stone that he had created here three days ago and then re-buried under layers and layers of packed dust. General Direlien had made his troops tramp up and down over it, and then Damien had packed in another layer.

It had been an entire day's work, but it was entirely worth it as the scrolled patterns blazed up, weaving Power in a hollow column that shot into the sky.

The demon glared at him with its giant eyes of that almost-unnatural blue and shot upwards.

The Air shot Damien upwards as well.

He had to weave the top of the column shut by hand, as it were, so it was a race.

And the demon clearly knew it as well.

But it was a race Damien was going to win, so long as he got there before the Air thinned too much to support him. There were other ways he could fly – using the Powers that shimmered between Earth and magnetic metals, for one.

But he had only been able to steal the smallest bits of time to experiment with this and his requests to the Realm had to be incredibly specific... or his results might be very unusual indeed. Over the last several years, Damien had tried giving the Realm his end-goal as an *intention*. And while the Realm *had* come through every time... the pathway it had taken to get there had sometimes been incredibly circuitous and the side-effects had sometimes completely overwhelmed the effect he was going for.

Damien had yet to meet a God, but those first couple years he had expected an angry one to show up practically every other day while he skirted the edges of drought and famine, flood and forest-fire for various parts of his Realm. Fixing his mistakes had taken far longer than fixing the original problem... once he had a handle on how to figure out how to do that. It seemed an almost frightening oversight that he *hadn't* been visited by any Gods.

The demon saw Damien pulling ahead and narrowed its huge eyes at him... then suddenly dove.

The King swore. Weave the column together and contain the demon – or rush back to protect Adam?

He knew what Adam would tell him to do.

Luckily, Adam didn't get a vote.

The woven Power of the column continued upwards beyond the very world itself. Even he wasn't sure how far it extended. He had no idea if the demon could survive in that airless space that he *knew* existed high above the mountain tops and clouds. He was fairly sure that Jeremy's body – no matter what crazy had been done to it already – could not.

Nor could his own.

At least... not for long...

The demon was going downwards as fast as it could push past the air... Great cracks of thunder were beginning to boom in its wake...

There was no way for Damien to go that fast – or faster. No way to cut through the air in time to get to Adam...

Air... Air was the problem in both directions...

Damien grabbed for the strands of power that stretched for the stars, cast a warding upon his own skin and filled his lungs... then begged the Air to get out of his way until he was twice his own height from the Earth.

And then, as he began to fall faster and faster... Damien reached out to the Earth. To those beautiful bands of Power that the Earth itself created and that were so very fond of metal... *steel* in particular, or rather the iron in the steel.

Damien was *covered* in steel.

He asked the Earth to call him home.

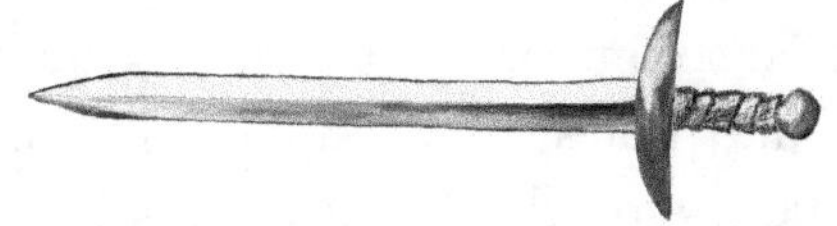

Chapter SIXTEEN

A Worsted Solution

No human was ever meant to move so fast.

Damien somehow managed to get himself twisting as he fell, pulling in the column of Power behind him and pulling it down behind him.

It was... like spinning wool. One of Genevieve's mountain-folk, a shepherd boy, had taught him how to do that on one of his early trips to Elaarwen. Damien had come home entirely enchanted with the concept and had spent hours upon hours spinning wool on a simple drop-spindle to the amusement of almost everyone around him. Genevieve had suggested a spinning wheel – curiosity had made him look at one, but it held his interest only briefly.

What had fascinated him was how the individual strands caught at each other, how losing the twist could make the whole thing fly apart into individual tufts of roving again, how to make the yarn come out smooth or slubby... and how a clutch of singly-twisted yarns might be twisted together in the *opposite* direction to form a thread that would *not* unwind. 'Worsted' yarn had utterly fascinated him.

Adam had been the only person who hadn't chuckled over his King's latest weird obsession. He'd also been the only other person who had actually tried spinning. The only one who had looked over Damien's drawings and notes, made some additions of his own... and then sent out queries to other lands for books on thread-magic, making explicit the connection that his King had only been toying with.

Now Damien himself was the spindle.

Twisting the threads of Power in two sets – three would have been better, but he only had two hands – while overtwisting them in the *other* direction... while falling (and being pulled down) at a ridiculous speed in order to beat the demon back to Adam... took both more concentration and greater gymnastics skills than he had thought he possessed.

At least it helped that his physical position while falling without Air was completely irrelevant. The twists and turns and flips he was executing made no difference to his speed of descent, neither slowing him down, nor speeding him up more than the collusion of Earth and Air was doing already.

But he *was* speeding up.

And it occurred to Damien that two man-heights of Air might not be *enough* to prevent him from being splattered in a thin layer across the ground.

At least, in that case, the threads of Power that he was spinning together *might* serve to contain the demon, but would do nothing to actually Banish it. Nor to protect Adam. Rather the reverse, in fact, since the Champion would be trapped in an even more confined space with the thing.

And Damien himself was running out of that breath he had begun with and beginning to go more than slightly light-headed with lack of air.

HELP!!! Damien had no idea what to do and just threw the *intention* out to the Realm and to every Elemental that might hear him. This had worked before, after all, though never in a way that he could have planned – which was all to his advantage right now, given that he was entirely out of his own ideas.

And out of *time* to figure anything else out.

All he could hope – *pray* – for was that the inevitable complications would be less problematic to manage than his and Adam's deaths. For themselves at least. Hopefully for everyone else as well.

Letting Adam die wasn't on his to-do-list for the day.

Or any day.

Ever.

PLEASE!!! he added, out of some obscure sense that politeness might be appreciated.

*Oh, I **do** like polite boys.*

A million hands caught him and slowed him down, each just by a hair, but there were so very *many* of them. It felt like falling deeper and deeper into a vat of feathers.

He had set the twist for the threads of Power. That was going to work. His new fear was that he was slowing too *much* and would not make it in time to save Adam from the demon.

Silly boy.

It was a woman's voice, he realized suddenly. Rich and amused and wispy and flirty all at the same time.

The 'vat of feathers' was getting much denser than he had guessed it could. Surely all those feathery touches were the hands of more Air-sylphs than inhabited his entire Realm... but Air-sylphs couldn't pack together like *this*... Surely not...

*They can. It's a close thing. A little more and I **would** have to turn you over to one of My Sisters. Or Nieces anyways. But we'll manage. Whyever didn't you set it up to ward the top the way you warded underneath? Nevermind. You're still new at this.*

The impossibly dense cushion of Air – that was not *quite* dense enough to be *liquid* – deposited him neatly on the ground next to Adam. Who was, praise all the Gods, stirring.

*Well, of course. He's one of Mine, after all. Though it was really just **Me** this time. Not all of Us.*

Damien tried to reclaim his wits as he released the ward on himself and took great gasping breaths. *My Lady. How can I thank You?*

He had no doubts at all that he had been rescued by a Goddess.

Bring Me your firstborn child and... There was a completely strange sensation of giggles as he panicked. *Not to **keep,** silly boy. Bring her out to visit Me occasionally. On the Cape, perhaps, though the tower tops of your Castle will do in a pinch as well. That one is meant to fly far, so she should get used to the sensation.*

Damien didn't dare ask questions. Not *now* anyways.

He barely had the breath to do more than kneel, gasping between Adam's barely-beginning-to-wake form and that of the demon who inhabited the body of a boy he'd once cared for. Kneel and gasp for air... and spool down the worsted Power, drawing it smaller and closer.

The demon settled down, normal human-sized again, and glowered upwards.

"Release it," the demon growled, "and I *may* let your minion live."

Damien ignored it and continued to spool the Power. He was catching his breath now, and the Power to do this had been gifted by the Realm – all of it so far, save the wards he had placed on his own skin when he came tumbling down, and on Adam.

Though he *had* done Adam's wards – against the irritated and offended protests of his Champion – in the brief interval after his nap and before they'd all had to dress for the evening confrontation. Damien hadn't been willing to allow his brave *friend* into yet another situation where he'd be at risk without such protections as he could offer.

During Adam's duel with Genevieve, the King's main worry for both of them had been what the *Sword* might be able to do to those wards. Had Genevieve wielded a *normal* sword – like the treacherous duke – there would have been no need for concern other than for *her* safety.

And right *now,* Damien was concerned about what the demon might be able to do to his carefully set wards – both on himself and on Adam.

Damien's understanding, after all, was that the Power of a mortal Elemental mage could not stand against that of a demon when the two were matched, hand to fist as it were.

That was apparently the *demon's* understanding as well, because it reached out for Adam, elongating Jeremy's arm and hand and turning the boy's slender brown fingers into spindly claws. Reaching, reaching, for Damien's friend, his love, his teacher...

And then it jerked back as if burned.

And glared at Damien.

"How did you do that?"

The Sorcerer-King of Ilseador *(etc., etc.)* looked at the demon calmly and continued to spool down his woven cage of Power. He wasn't about to explain, just in case the demon escaped in the end. Nor even to *think* about it too very hard, just in case the foul creature could somehow lift thoughts from his mind.

The demon looked at him thoughtfully.

"Tell me how you warded your minion like that and perhaps I shall not take you back to Azella."

So... the limits placed upon a demon in a Summoning were malleable. More malleable than Azella thought? Or was it simply that it was choosing to forego its benefits from the contract she had made with it? Denisa, presumably, was the demon's reward for retrieving Damien.

Or, more than possibly, it was lying in order to convince him to give up his secrets.

What support the demon was to have given Duke Tomas – or, indeed, what benefit Azella's master had expected to obtain by toppling the Alsterling line – Damien supposed he would never know.

The demon was starting to cringe down, away from the shrinking cage of Power.

"Stop, damn you! Are you going to pull that thing down on your own self? And on your minion that you love so well? Or on..." The demon's eyes in Jeremy's face grew crafty. "Or on *this* creature that I am using? You love *it* also, do you not? Shall we all die here together?"

"That would be unacceptable," Damien deigned to answer. "But as you can see–" the cage shrank further and... moved *through* Adam without any perceptible alteration to *him*. By mage-sight, Adam even still shone like a star fallen to Earth.

The demon gaped. "It cannot *be*. You are nothing but an *Earth-mage* with some understanding of the other States. So Azella told me, and I can sense truth from lie!"

Interesting information in and of itself, but...

"She wasn't lying to *you*. She is, however, very good at lying to *herself*." Damien felt that was enough to give the foul being.

Foul... by his standards. Presumably not by its own. Nor by the cutthroat paradigm from which it seemed to hail... It wasn't even here by choice, but *compelled* by Azella. Was it fair to destroy the thing for living as it was made to do, and following the *compulsions* that had been placed upon it?

Could one blame the mountain lion for devouring the elk? The cat for eating the rat – even one of the golden rats of Emeralsee of which he was so fond?

Or... Tomas Elsevier for attempting to devour the Realm?

Yes.

Yes, he could.

And the rats or elk should not just lie down and allow cats or lions to eat them.

Jeremy's body was cringing into the shrinking space. The cage passed through Damien, and all that was left was around the body of the boy who had been bred for such Power and beauty.

"Let me *free*," the demon shrieked, "And I will bring you all the wealth you could wish for!"

Damien continued his work.

"Love, beauty, strength – I can grant you any of these things!"

Lies, all of it. Even did he not already have all such things he wished, Damien would never have believed a demon.

And finally, as the cage began to pass *through* Jeremy's *own* body, *"Let me free and I will keep you alive for a thousand years so I can kill you every day in a different and more painful way!"*

Truth, at last.

And then it lost control of Jeremy's mind and mouth and throat and lungs. A different look came over the youth's face: pain and horror and... *presence*.

With a powerful wrench, Damien wrested the cage free of the boy's body entirely.

Jeremy gave him a look of unutterable gratitude and keeled over.

Not all was well with him, but Damien had no time to deal with anything yet, but the demon. He had to make a decision, *now,* about whether he was going to end the creature's existence. That, it turned out, was easier than Banishing it properly back to whence it had come.

But there was a moral question of whether he *should* do such a thing.

Doubtless Adam would tell him he was being an idiot to worry over such things.

Praise... well, one *particular* Goddess especially that Adam would have a chance to do so.

The Power had almost entirely spooled up. Damien shook his head. He could sort out what was to be done with the evil thing later on. For now... He saw a water-flask, discarded in the dust, by someone earlier, likely without intention. It would serve.

The sorcerer-king spun the small glass bottle in his hands to coat the inside thoroughly with what water remained, before pouring out the excess fluid. Then he stuffed the cage of Power, with its unhappy occupant, into the flask and used a touch of Fire to melt the leaden cap so that it could no longer be opened and to pinch off the trailing yarn of worsted Power. With all four 'Elements' thus involved in the creation of the prison cell – and the whole thing being the product of his mind, and thereby the Aether – it felt very secure.

Damien stashed the thing in his pocket and released the threads of Power back to the Realm to be un-spun and re-woven into the fabric that underlay everything.

And then – at *last* – he was able to turn his attention to the truly important things.

A hand on Adam's cheek told him everything he needed to know. Adam was coming around, and seemed to be completely unaffected by the ordeal. Whatever had knocked him out – and the King was beginning to suspect it of being one single gout of magickal energy from Azella intended entirely to prevent Adam from leaving the marked space – it appeared to have had only a physical effect.

The King had been fairly sure he was still alive. If that blast had killed Adam, after all, Damien would have had no reason to be torn between defending him and capturing the demon. Though it had been entirely possible that he could have been dreadfully injured... apparently Azella had spent as little effort in knocking the Champion out as possible.

Husbanding her Power against dealing with the demon? Damien could only pray it was so – or else he should need to be on the lookout for a further attack. Although he suspected Azella would take a long, long time to believe he really *had* defeated her demon...

A hand on Jeremy... gave a different result.

Pain – Damien could deal with that. As he did, the youth began to uncurl a little from the fetal position he had assumed in his collapse.

But for the rest... much of Jeremy's huge trove of magick had been ripped from him. The demon had fed upon it, presumably, or used it up in contorting and moving his body. Whether the Power would replenish in time, Damien had no idea. For now at least, the boy felt like a sieve – Power might settle in him but would pour right back out.

And the ache of that loss... was something the King could do nothing about.

"I... did not even know what I had until it was gone, Damien," Jeremy whimpered... but somehow his voice still wasn't whiny.

"I'm sorry, lad," the King said gently.

The boy shook his head. "I am free. Free of the Mistress. Free of her demon. It is... something I never hoped to have. Perhaps... perhaps the loss was the price of freedom."

But he looked up with bewilderment in those unnaturally bright blue eyes. "But... Damien... I do not know what is to be *done* with this 'freedom.' How to live. Who shall feed and shelter me."

The fifth fold of the path, just as Damien had suspected.

Damien put a gentle hand on his shoulder. "For now at least, I can take care of those last things. For the rest... you'll have to learn. But I wasn't much younger than you when *I* was freed to learn those things. It can be done."

In some ways Jeremy was much less prepared... but in others he was so much less innocent than Damien had been.

Perhaps Adam and Jason would be willing to help out with another 'stray.'

And speaking of whom...

"Damien? What the hell hit me? And why is the sky full of fire? And who, in the name of all the Gods is *that?*"

The King let a relieved smile take over his face and threw himself into Adam's arms. Eyes of the public be damned. "Not *all* the Gods, dearheart, but one of Them, *definitely.*"

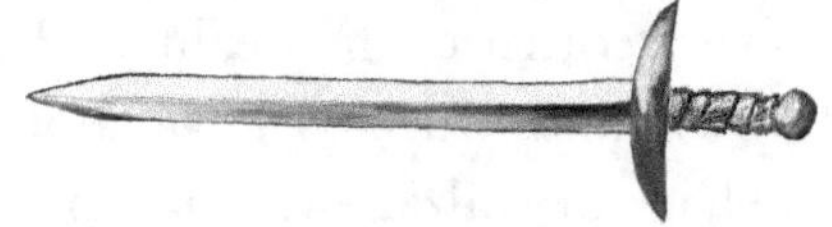

Chapter SEVENTEEN

Tying Up Loose Ends

CLEANING UP... ALWAYS TOOK MORE time than the battles themselves.

In this case, though, it appeared that while some aspects dealt with themselves almost instantly, and others would take a few days, some... would be the work of years.

Damien slept for two solid days – in Adam and Jason's rooms because Genevieve wasn't fit company for anyone. Jason stayed with her for awhile out of a sense of duty, but eventually even he fled, soul-bonded or not, leaving her to the patience – and short shifts – of her ladies-in-waiting.

When the King finally woke up, he went almost immediately to break the *compulsion* spells that had been rather too skillfully set on his wife. *Almost* because Adam insisted he eat breakfast first.

Genevieve fell asleep as soon as Damien finished breaking the spells. Later she would wake, exhausted, starving... and with no memory whatsoever of leaving the Castle nearly three weeks earlier.

While his Queen slept, Damien took care of other business.

His Peers of the Realm had arrived, both to greet their returned King and to re-pledge their Vassal's Oaths. There was no question but that they would do so, nor did anyone question the new wording that Bound them each a bit more tightly – nor Damien's decree that he would journey to every corner of the Realm and they would each swear *again,* on their own land. Duchess Tariana of Embervest wept a bit, as did Duke Zachary of Dalzialest... but no one took them to task for it.

Lord Aldred arrived, with his newborn son, escorted by a trio of rough-seeming mercenaries who were greeted with considerable joy and relief by the King. Two of the mercenaries seemed entirely overwhelmed by the experience, but the third was a thick-bearded mountain-man of Elaarwen and he took everything in stride.

Damien's meeting with his father-in-law was... first hesitant and then they fell into each other's arms. Aldred might not be a wise person to trust the future of the Realm to, but he *was* family and that much more precious for having so nearly been lost.

And when Damien asked to see his new brother-in-law... the cloaked and cowled wet-nurse showed him the baby and Damien cooed over it and said nothing about her identity. If Ciriis wanted to live anonymously, it was up to her and Aldred after all. Though he did have a discreet word with both of them to make sure they would tell their son the truth. The lad deserved to grow up knowing he had two parents who loved him, after all... and old as Aldred was, there was no guarantee he could see his son to adulthood.

He told Genevieve, Adam, Jason, Tim, and Aryllis of her survival – and choice – himself.

Ciriis' 'death' before Aldred had managed to wed her left the child as an acknowledged bastard... not another contender for either the Crown of Ilseador or the coronet of Elaarwen. Not unless Genevieve or Damien should name him as such.

Aldred was relieved to be allowed to visit... and he planned to be present when his daughter was expected to give birth. His enthusiasm for that, and his obvious gentleness with the baby, went far to mollify Damien's feelings about the old man's parenting of his wife.

Jeremy had somehow found his way to Lord Aaron's recovery room while Damien slept. With some help, of course. (*"I could see why you fell for him," Adam said dryly. "I thought he might need some distractions. Before he turned into one.")* With his Power – and his identity – all but gone, the boy was almost as much of an amputee as the cynical young assassin, and they spent much of their time together, at least part of it playing chess.

Arabella Elsevier had asked to see Aaron and he had refused her, to no one's particular surprise. Damien still wasn't sure what to do about the young woman. She was barely past girlhood, but her willingness to do Jason harm in the pursuit of power – or at least of her parents' approval – made it hard to look at her as such.

Duchess Sildra, however, met the usual end of a traitor and was nailed up beside the remains of her husband.

As always, Damien set the first nail.

Her son, Mark, looking ready to vomit, stood ready to set the second one to prove his loyalty and save himself and his siblings' lives. But the King's eyes challenged the gathered nobles – and the commoners watching from the streets across the moat – and he took the young man away instead.

Sildra's last request had been to hold her daughter – not her son, and not the four younger children who had been brought in from Elsevier Castle – once more... so Arabella was there on the battlements as well.

It was a last gift that was more of a punishment than a mercy. The reality of the situation clearly hadn't set in before; Arabella had been twelve when her unlamented uncle Harald was nailed to the walls for briefly usurping the Throne and her grandmother, the Dowager Duchess Lydia, had been locked up for the remainder of her life in Elsevier Castle. Her parents had not brought her to the capitol until Harald's remains had rotted away and been removed at last.

As their mother cried out in pain, Arabella stood frozen in shock. Mark broke away from the King's protective grasp and went to fold his sister into his arms. She tried to shake him off, but he held her close and let Damien guide them away.

To Damien's own chambers, as it turned out, where 'Aunt' Genevieve had kept the younger children. All of them orphaned now.

And then, cursing himself for cowardice, Damien stumbled down to Adam and Jason's rooms and drank himself drunk for the first time in his life.

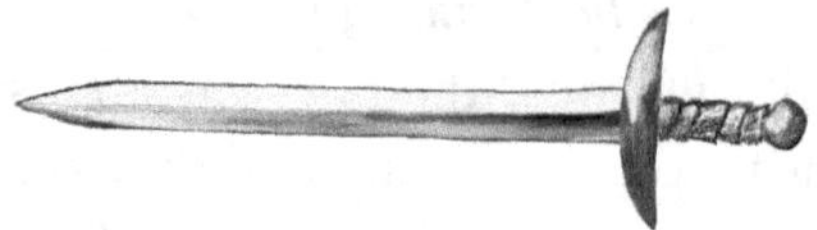

"Gods, Adam, what do I *do* with them?"

The Realm had not put up with Damien's insensibility and had proceeded to remedy it... *all* too soon in the King's opinion, though there would surely never be a time when he was ready to face the Elsevier children.

"There *has* to be some less-barbaric way to deal with traitors," he muttered, leaning his elbows on his knees and scrubbing his hands back and forth through his hair as he perched on the edge of their bed. "It's clearly not even effective as a deterrent, and surely that's the only possible justification for... for *this.*"

Seated beside him on the edge of the wide bed, Adam sighed and rubbed his back. Jason had been gone by the time Damien sobered up – to play the part of Crown Prince and deal with the rest of what his sovereign could not bear to do; adding another measure of guilt to Damien's overflowing cup.

"The word coming back from Siovale is that the people are furious with Tomas. But that they want Mark as their Duke."

"I have to go out there before we can even consider it and make sure there aren't hidden *compulsion* spells just waiting to spring on the boy like a trap." Damien scrubbed almost violently at his hair again, and Adam pulled his hands away from his head. "Assuming that it even makes *sense* to install Mark as duke. At least four generations of traitors in his family – and then Harald as well..."

"Stop that. You'll hurt yourself if you keep that up." Adam paused. "Can spells be left around like that? And no one will blame you if you give the province to someone else. I just wanted to let you know what the citizens of Siovale would prefer."

Damien looked up at him, his eyes red with weeping. "Spells left in waiting... If it can be imagined, it can probably be done. And likely has been, *some*where. Magick has few limits besides the imagination as far as I can tell. Once something is thought up, it's less a question of 'if' and more a question of 'how.'"

194

Adam made a disgruntled noise. "You'll have to setup a caretaker government for Siovale until you make a permanent decision. And you need to go out to Farivera anyways."

"And come back by way of Elaarwen," Damien added with a sigh. "I promised them I'd come out this Spring, whether or not Genevieve could travel. And then the *rest* of the Realm, to take everyone's oaths all over again."

"She seems fine, despite it all," Adam pointed out. "And a trip home might do well for her. She could meet us up there."

"Hmmn." After all the failed pregnancies, the last thing Damien wanted was for her to be trekking about the country.

But... she *was* nearly at the halfway point now. That was double the length of any previous attempt, and both his own Healing sense and whatever mysterious other-sense Queen Marian possessed had confirmed both mother and child as healthy.

Damien, himself, had noted the correlation between mental health and time spent far from Castle Alsterling here in Emeralsee, so he should be eager to get her out of here. Especially for developing young minds.

Not that Castle Elsevier seemed any healthier.

Perhaps it wasn't an effect of the *magick,* but of the poisonous atmosphere of Courts that were focused on treachery and ambition. Which suggested that Damien might be able to safely raise his own children in these halls. They would have *four* loving parents to protect them, after all, and the devoted care of the Royal Guards and Secret Cadre to keep them clear of the wiles of his courtiers.

That was a relief, though he would have to explore the concept carefully – and magickally – before taking the risk. He couldn't, as King, really spend most of his time elsewhere, after all, and the prospect of needing to insist on his beloved wife and adored children living faraway in Elaarwen most of the year for their own safety had been... unappealing in the extreme.

"It's really Arabella you don't know what to do with," Adam pointed out. "It seems unlikely that *one* of the others can't manage the Vassal's Oath, even in its new form. Likely even Mark."

Damien waved a hand at this. "I'm not actually worried about *that*. I'm willing to bet on Mark, as you say. But I do want to find a way to Bind all four of the younger ones. I don't want to raise yet another generation of angry, vengeful Elseviers."

And for their own protection, since such a Binding ran both ways. It would alert Damien if anyone threatened the children's wellbeing. He owed them that much, at least.

He sighed deeply. "Arabella... something is *wrong* with a girl who was willing to try to cut off someone's finger. It... seems immoral to punish someone for having something wrong in their head. We... haven't punished people for acting under the Power of *compulsion* spells before."

And a terrible precedent to set if he did. Genevieve had tried to kill Adam under *compulsion,* and the Champion could arguably have been charged with treason for fighting her. Though since Adam had been fighting in Damien's place and had been trying *not* to injure her...

It would be legally complex if they let Arabella's situation come to trial.

Not to mention all the *compulsions* Damien himself had labored under in Azella's keep and that he still didn't want to think about in any detail.

The Siovalese men-at-arms had definitely been under light *compulsions.* To strengthen their loyalty to Tomas, as the Duke had said, at the expense of their loyalty to the Realm, or even Siovale, but not enough to wipe their memories of the time as had been done with Genevieve by Azella's spell. And also to Tomas seven years earlier by Lord Prydeen.

Damien couldn't help wondering if the idea to so totally subsume Genevieve had been Azella's idea... or the Duke's, after his own experience. Jason had said it had been completely surreal – Genevieve had been entirely herself...until she wasn't.

Arabella Elsevier, unfortunately, had *not* been under a *compulsion* spell.

"Mark... says Sildra spent a lot of time with the girl," Adam said reluctantly.

Despite the rapport between the two of them, Adam's emotions were also so tangled over this that Damien could get nothing but a sense of unease. He couldn't tell if his Champion was reluctant to find some reason to absolve the girl – who had, after all, attempted to maim his wedded husband – or reluctant not to find a simple excuse to prevent hanging the child up on the Castle wall beside her parents.

"Sildra... may have messed with the girl's mind," Adam added. "We know for ourselves how *that* can be done. *Without* magick."

What Alexa Solway had done to Megan and Jason – and to a lesser degree her *other* grandchildren hung unspoken.

What Lady Theresa had done to Damien, persuading him to become emotionally dependent on her after betraying his family to their deaths, wasn't far from the King's mind either.

Genevieve's willingness to sacrifice herself for the Rebellion had surely been planted in her head by parental persuasion. Though, to be fair, Aldred had seemed nearly as willing to sacrifice himself from various stories Damien had heard.

And even Adam had taken years to wrench himself away from his parents' censure and expectations... though that story had ended better, of course.

Azella's personal horrors had turned her into the Evil Wizard who threatened his Realm. Still.

No. It was *hard* – Gods, but he knew for himself just *how* hard – to rise above what had been planted and tended inside one's own head. But it *could* be done. It *had* to be done, or there was no hope for a future for any of them and especially not for the Elsevier children.

Arabella could not be absolved.

But neither had it been her idea to do it. Nor had she succeeded.

"Perhaps... perhaps Zachary and Rosa could take her. For awhile," Damien said slowly. "Under guard, of course. Mark... is going to have enough to do to learn to be a duke. He shouldn't have to learn to be a parent at the same time. And a jailer." He paused. "I'd thought to ask them to take the younger children also, actually..."

Adam bit out a laugh at that. "According to Marianna, you're going to have a devil of a time convincing *him* of that. And you'll have to fight him to take the younger ones away from him. I think she said he'd rather take care of them than be duke."

Damien ran another hand through his hair. More gently this time. "Well. I don't think *I* could have done it. But–"

"But Mark has *one province,* not the *whole Realm.* And Tomas gave him responsibilities. He doesn't have as far to go as you did," Adam agreed. "When it comes down to it, those of us who were 'advising' you had as little experience with governing as you did."

"Except for Genevieve. And Aldred." Damien smiled briefly.

Adam nodded. "Except for Genevieve and Aldred. Whom you also forgave their treason."

"Treason against my grandfather," Damien pointed out. "Not against *me.*"

"Treason against the *Crown,*" Adam insisted. "And Aldred's *almost*-treason last Fall."

Fair enough. And this wasn't really a point the King wanted to argue *against,* after all.

Damien gave a shrug of acquiescence. "So, Mark wants to keep his brothers and sisters. Change as little as possible in their lives. I suppose that might be good for... all of them."

"I... gather he's been more of a parent to those younger four in some ways than Tomas. Or at least Sildra." Adam added.

"*That* wouldn't surprise me at all," Damien sighed. "Nor *you,* I would think. Until Kandy went to the Army, I never left her side. And I saw how your brothers and sisters are with you."

Adam looked away. "It's still hard with Martin and Marianna. They were only six and eight when I... stopped going home."

"Adam..." The King put his arm around the older man's shoulders. "I was six when Kandy left. And ten, when she was killed. It didn't make me love her any less. *You* have the chance to get to know them now, at least."

"I suppose."

"Why do you think they both decided to stay here? It was an excuse to stay near *you,*" Damien told him and Adam looked startled, as if that had never occurred to him.

"Desirée said *she'd* have stayed, too, if she could, but she has the boys and her own household to run... I told them all to come back whenever they could and for as long as possible," the King added with a smile. "And that you'd come visit when you could."

Adam blinked very quickly and leaned on Damien's shoulder.

"*We,*" he said firmly.

Damien's heart leaped, though he still wasn't sure how he felt about... all *this*. His couple of months at Lynncrag remained among some of his brightest memories – however tarnished by the unpleasant departure, with Adam swearing never to return, and the letter with Damien's grandparents' rejection. He wanted to go back and make more happy memories... and to bring their children to the only grandparents of any sort they were likely to get to know well, given Aldred's age and Lord David's intent to depart.

Even if Adam's parents could never *know* that the royal children were their grandchildren. Damien didn't doubt that his children would be treated just as if they were anyways.

"*We,*" he agreed softly.

After a moment, he added lightly, "And it's probably good for all of you that you're getting to know each other as *adults*. If Kandy were here, she'd doubtless be tousling my hair like I'm still six. Or nine. Of course, then *she'd* be Queen..."

Adam snorted. "I believe you when you say you aren't trying to give yourself up anymore, Damien. But you still don't believe you were meant to be king. The Sword would have Chosen you even if your 'perfect' older sister was around."

The King blinked in surprise. "Adam, you didn't know her," he began gently.

"I didn't have to," the Champion told him pointedly. "I know *you*. And since Queen Marian seems to enjoy having someone else's ear to bend," he added dryly, "we've spent quite an amount of time discussing the various deficiencies and benefits of the Sword. She's quite sure that it spoke for Aldred when he was a child. And that it *would* have spoken for Prince Eric. But no one else."

He paused. "And she's also fairly sure it's never spoken for *anyone* as enthusiastically as it has for you. *Ever.*"

Damien looked across the room at where the aforementioned hunk of steel hung in the sword rack. He'd felt a need to keep the thing closer than usual since he'd gotten it back, though he wasn't entirely sure why.

"It's... not *alive*," he said uncertainly. "Not in any way I can detect anyways."

Adam snorted. "Says the man who tells me *rocks* are alive."

Damien grinned at him, relieved at the shift of topic. "You can probably tell that for yourself now. Has Jason commented on how brightly you glow?"

Not to mention that a certain Goddess of Air had referred to Adam as 'one of Hers'... Not that Damien had mentioned that to anyone.

"You'd know if he had," Adam retorted, flushing a bit. "You've been with one or both of us every moment since he's been back."

"I spent most of that sleeping," the King reminded him, but with an apologetic tone. "And... I'll be gone tonight. And... *after* tonight."

He looked forward to waking up to Genevieve's glorious eyes again.

Though... he'd miss a certain pair of golden-hazel ones.

"Not *every* night." Adam's tone had a finality to it.

Damien sighed. "We need to... sort this out. The four of us, I suppose. And soon. Though I was rather hoping that all the... *extra* people would go home first."

"My sweet prince," Adam chuckled. "There will *always* be 'extra people' here or... other things to steal your attention from family matters."

Family... it was a word to cast greater enchantments than any sorcery Damien could draw on.

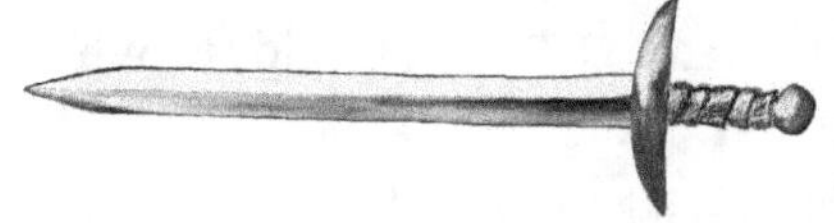

Spinning a Thread to the Future

"**S**HE'S BEAUTIFUL."

The woman had not been beside him a moment ago. Damien couldn't steal his eyes away from his newborn daughter to look. "As beautiful as her mother."

"And you fulfilled the promise I asked of you in return for My help. I thought you might have been a little too distracted to remember."

The King sighed. "I have another favor to ask of you, my Lady."

He nodded his chin at the warded and sealed flask he had set in the deep embrasure before him. No other hand than his had touched it, and he hadn't dared to carry the baby while he held the foul thing. Adam had carried her.

His Champion hovered nearby as always, but had elected to remain just out of sight. He'd just about come to terms with magery, he claimed, but dealing with deities was a step too far. Damien still hadn't found an opportunity to talk to Adam about his own magick.

"What would you?" The female voice was made of... sunshine on water. And sea-spray. And the urgent cries of gulls and the lonely calls of the albatross. It somehow was all those things and mingled them into a music that was wispy and cheerful and belied the seriousness of its sources... and held a feminine strength beyond even his own sweet Genevieve's capacity.

"It's a Powerful weapon," the Goddess who looked over his shoulder suggested.

"*Too* Powerful," the King agreed.

"You may yet need such a Powerful weapon in the future. Estelle of Deltheren still claims your sole remaining Lost Province and was willing to make her position clear by colluding with the sorceress who still sits athwart your southern border."

Damien shook his head. "Too Powerful *and* too dangerous, my Lady, to have lying about – or even in what I think to be some safely warded box in a hidden room. Should that demon escape and be anywhere in easy reach of my daughter... no. I have what Power I need to defend my Realm. But I do not know how to send that *thing* back whence it came without first releasing it from its confines. I suspect You do."

"Think carefully, Sorcerer-King. You may have the Power to *defend* your Realm, but not enough to rid yourself of Azella the Unpitying... and while the future is unwritten, the most likely path stands her to far outlive you. Would you keep such a weapon from your Heirs?"

"If they would use the Power of a being that is so inimical to all things of our world, they might be my *children*, but not my *Heirs.*" He dared a glance at Her. "You... aren't suggesting my little Marli here would..."

The Goddess looked almost ordinary, with short, pale, flyaway hair and eyes as clear as the sky about them. Her smile was whimsical.

"You've already heard what prophecies may be given you, Damien, even if they came from an unlikely source. If anyone can change that future, it will be the four of you." The other part of Prydeen's dying words. That the Sword would never speak for *this* child, and that his youngest would follow the evil old man's path.

The Goddess reached a hand to caress the baby's face.

Giendra Marlerite – they had decided to call her Marli for daily use – stirred enough to open eyes that were still the undefined shade of newborn blue. Damien had no doubt at all that those precious little eyes would settle into the same brilliant blue-green as her mother's. Her tiny mouth began to hunt, and he guided her thumb into it for a momentary pacifier. It wouldn't last long, though. She was ready to nurse.

"You said she'll fly far?" He couldn't bear the thought of this child being gone from him. It was hard enough to leave her to get his work done. Adam was quite nearly as enchanted... He suspected that once Genevieve was fully recovered it would be she and Jason who would do most of the governing of the Realm. Not that he didn't have his own tasks... but overseeing the continued Healing of the Realm didn't interfere with holding his daughter.

"When she's grown, Damien. And you'll miss her, but she'll be following her heart."

Was there really much more he could hope for?

"And she'll be happy?"

"That will be up to her, of course. But with four parents to teach her how, it seems likely she would choose that." A pause "Do thou continue on thy path as steward and parent and human and we are unlike to meet again. Neither thee – nor Ilseador under thy care – hath much need for Me and Mine made Manifest."

A compliment beyond all hope... but he had to ask.

"And when my grandfather ruled? Or... now, those poor souls in Azella's keep, and those born and bred and Bound into servitude to other Evil Wizards?"

A soft outbreath, a warm zephyr that curled past.

"What have you learned by asking the Realm to solve problems, Sorcerer-King? The *intention* alone is insufficient. There must also be guidance... but the most subtle pathways can yield the most profound results. Weather never hindered Metreedi ships bearing supplies for the Rebellion while troubles both great and small did encourage King Reginald to spend less and less time looking outwards until he missed even the signs of his own Apprentice's disaffection. Our Hand in all these things, but the Choice is always yours as mortals for what to make of what is Given."

She paused as Marli began to hunt for a nipple again. "I will take your 'inconvenient guest' off of your hands, Damien Alsterling. A wise Choice you have made and one I hope you will not regret. Take your lassie in for her feeding..."

The flask came up into Her Hand, and She drifted away as if merely another mote of mist in the warm, late Summer air.

Damien looked up into the sky after Her. "Thank you, Sifwisa of the Trade-Winds, Lady of Hurricanes and Gales."

You are welcome, young King.

Adam had come up and slid an arm around his waist so he, too, could look adoringly at tiny, perfect Marli. Damien leaned into his embrace... for a moment of peace.

Lord Aldred was inside, fussing over Genevieve.

Damien's Eldridge kin had sent word they would be here in a couple of weeks.

Adam's family was due to arrive today, and Lord David and his children kept finding reasons to 'check in' on the little princess. Damien didn't question what they might or might not know...

Duchess Rosa and Duke Zachary had sent their love and a promise to visit soon – Rosa was pregnant *again.*

Duke Mark and his newly-wedded bride, Duchess Marianna, were bringing the entire Elsevier family as soon as they could set their still-contorted province's needs aside for a few days.

From no family at all, Damien had almost more than he could believe.

"You're glowing, Damien," Adam chided gently.

The Sorcerer-King of Ilseador, Defender of the Realm, Father of Giendra Marlerite Stellarine Alsterling smiled.

Of course he was.

*Discover what happened between Damien's battle with
the demon and Princess Marli's birth in
The Heart of Ilseador
Available at all fine online retailers in time for
Valentine's Day 2025
Place your pre-order now!
https://books2read.com/Heart-Chronicles-of-Ilseador*

Alsterling Family Tree

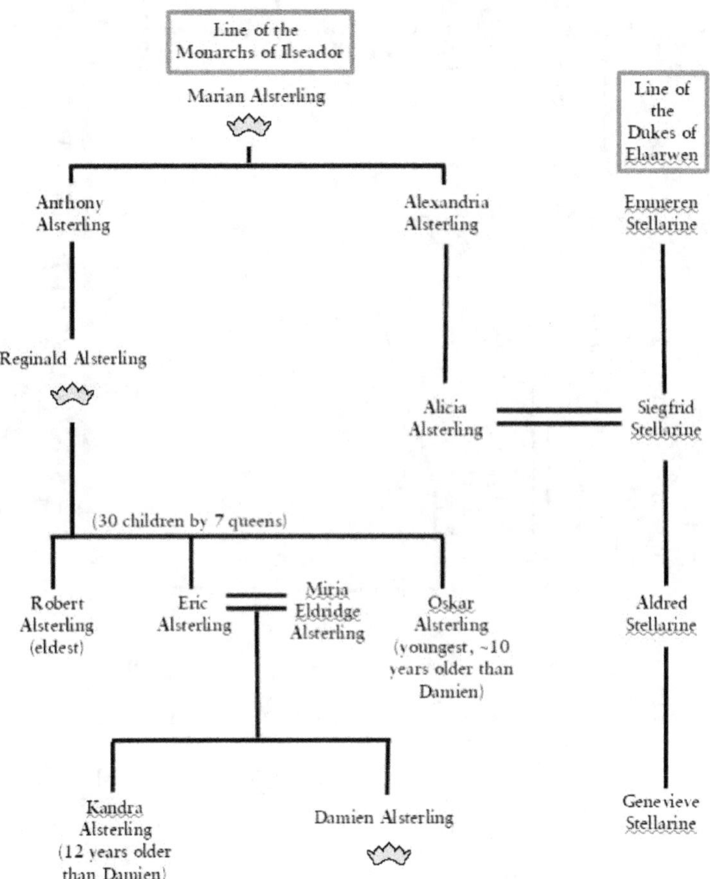

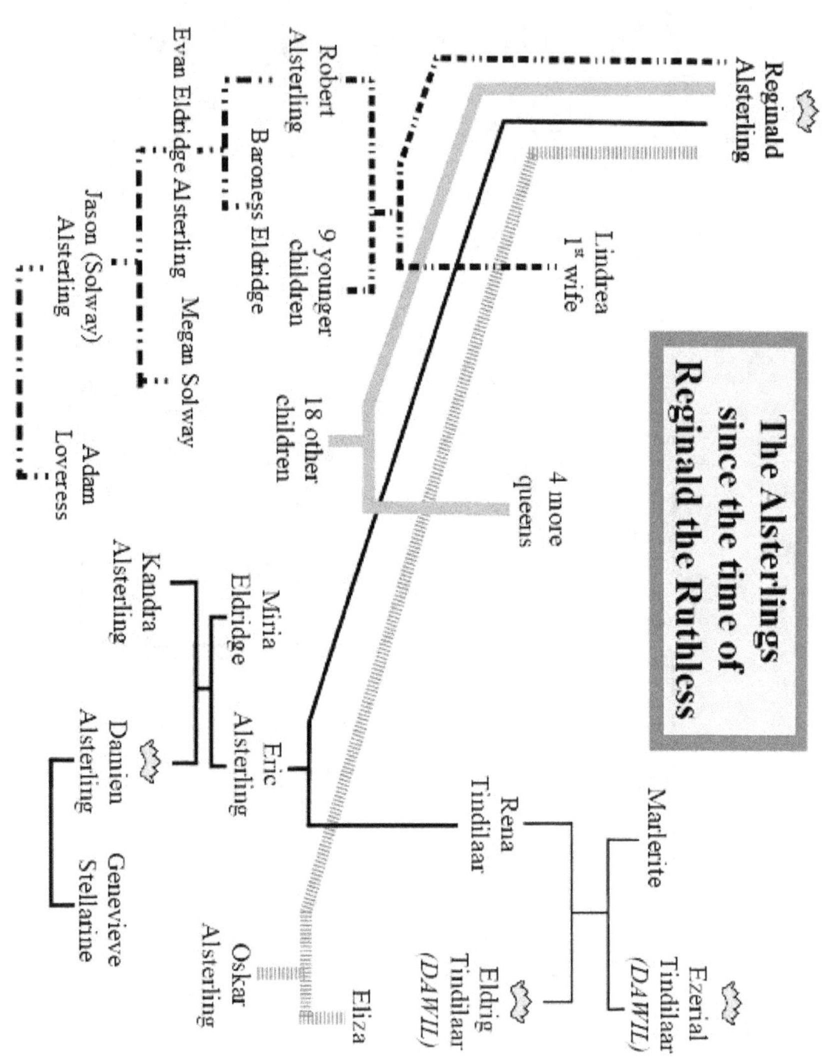
The Alsterlings
since the time of
Reginald the Ruthless
Reginald Alsterling
Robert Alsterling
Evan Eldridge Alsterling
Baroness Eldridge
9 younger children
Jason (Solway) Alsterling
Megan Solway
Adam Loveress
Lindrea 1st wife
18 other children
4 more queens
Kandra Alsterling
Miria Eldridge
Eric Alsterling
Damien Alsterling
Genevieve Stellarine
Oskar Alsterling
Eliza
Rena Tindilaar
Marlerite
Eldrig Tindilaar (DAWL)
Ezenial Tindilaar (DAWL)

Index of Characters

Characters that appear in this book are <u>underlined.</u>
Characters that are referenced, but do not actually appear are in plain type. Some additional characters are included who are not mentioned in this book to clarify relationships.
Deceased characters are in italics.
*Characters with speaking roles in this book are in **bold**.*

The grandchildren of a reigning king or queen are officially grand dukes and grand duchesses in Ilseador, but are also referred to as princes and princesses when the question of their position in the line of succession is not in question.
Damien was Crown Prince after Oskar died.

Contents of the Index:

- **Royal Family of Ilseador**
- **Provinces of Ilseador** in order of precedence and relevant ruling family members
    - » Emeralsee contains the following fiefs among others: *Seasbourne, Cedarwen, Eldyrwyld, Lynncrag, Elmirscroft, Ravenscroft*
    - » Elaarwen contains the following fiefs among others: *Brindlewell, Cloudcroft*
    - » Siovale
    - » Reyensweir contains the following fiefs among others: *Zialest*
    - » Embervest contains the following fiefs among others: *Minglemere, Everfields*
    - » Alpinsward contains the following fiefs among others: Dalizell
    - » Dalzialest, duchy (contains *Flowerdell*)
    - » The Lost Provinces: *Alpinsward, Minglemere, Elendria, Farivera, Everfields*
- *Others of Note*

Royal Family of Ilseador
(and noted individuals in the Royal City and Province)

- <u>**Damien Alsterling,**</u> King of Ilseador
  - <u>**Queen Genevieve (Stellarine) Alsterling**</u>, Duchess of Elaarwen (a.k.a. 'the Rebel Duchess'), King Damien's wife; soul-bonded to King Damien and secretly also soul-bonded to Prince Jason
  - <u>*Queen Marian Alsterling*</u> (a.k.a. 'Marian the merciful'), King Damien and Queen Genevieve's great-great-grandmother (common ancestress)... currently a ghost in Castle Alsterling.
  - <u>**Crown Prince Jason (Solway) Alsterling,**</u> son of Evan Eldridge Alsterling, secretly soul-bonded to Queen Genevieve, husband of Prince Adam
  - <u>**Prince Adam (Loveress) Alsterling,**</u> husband of Prince Jason
  - Others of the Royal Family
    - » *Eric Alsterling,* son of old king *Reginald Alsterling,* former Crown Prince, King Damien's father
    - » *Queen Rena (Tindilaar) Alsterling,* a princess from Dawil; mother of Prince Eric Alsterling; grandmother of King Damien; sister to *King Eldrig Tindilaar*
    - » *Miria (Eldridge) Alsterling,* King Damien's and *Princess Kandra's* mother; wife of *Prince Eric;* daughter of a minor noble family in the countryside of Emeralsee Province; oldest of seven children
      - * *Miria's father, David Eldridge,* was a failed squire, son of the former Baron of Elderwyld
      - * *Miria's mother, Alexa,* was a blacksmith's daughter
    - » *Grand Duchess (or Princess) Kandra 'Kandy' Alsterling,* King Damien's sister; Prince Eric and Lady Miria's daughter joined the army as a common foot- soldier at 18, worked her way up. Was to have married Lord Raphael Anvliyar of Cedarwen and helped her parents and brother escape to the Rebellion in Elaarwen

- *King Reginald Alsterling* (aka 'the old king' or 'Reginald the Ruthless'); King Damien's grandfather
    - » *'Lord' Prydeen*, his Apprentice Evil Wizard
    - » *7 wives*
        - * *1st Princess Lindrea Alsterling* (died before Reginald was crowned)
        - * *2nd*
        - * *3rd*
        - * *4th*
        - * *5th*
        - * *6th Queen Rena (Tindilaar) Alsterling* of Dawil, *Prince Eric's* mother, King Damien's grandmother
        - * *7th Eliza Alsterling* (Oskar's mother, married to *King Reginald* simultaneously with *Queen Rena*)
    - » 30 legitimate children (all dead), including the following:
        - * *Crown Prince Robert Alsterling* (son of Princess Lindrea); he quietly married the widowed Baroness Dara Eldridge of Eldywyld and sired her youngest child, Evan Eldridge AlsterlingPrincess Selda Alsterling
        - * *Crown Prince Eric Alsterling* (son of Queen Rena), father of Damien
        - * *Crown Prince Oskar Alsterling* (son of Queen Eliza), youngest son of King Reginald
            - ◊ **Sir Jason Solway**, *Prince Oskar's* bodyguard before Oskar was Heir, Oskar's Champion while Oskar was Heir
            - ◊ Sir Edmund Railston, *Prince Oskar's* Champion and bodyguard at the time Ring was taken from *Prince Oskar* (also Adam Loveress' first lover)
    - » Some 100 grandchildren (all dead besides Damien and Evan) including the following:
        - * *Alric Alsterling*
        - * *Grand Duke Salleen Alsterling*
        - * *Grand Duchess Kandra Alsterling*
        - * Grand Duke Evan Eldridge Alsterling (son of Prince Robert), sire of Jason Solway Alsterling; King of the Pirates of the Merutian Sea
        - * **King Damien Alsterling**
    - » 1 legitimate surviving great-grandchild
        - * **Crown Prince Sir Jason Solway Alsterling** (son of Grand Duke Evan, husband of Adam Loveress)

- # Others of Note in His Majesty's Government

- <u>General Direlien</u>, Commander-in-Chief (under the King) of the Ilseadoran military, Commander of the Home Guard

- **King Damien's Official Royal Guards**
    * **Champion: <u>Sir Adam Loveress</u>** (shield is puce with a rose, argent, crossed by a black sword), a close advisor of King Damien
    * **Captain and Knight Commander of the Royal Guard:** <u>Sir Timothy Ancellius</u> (a.k.a. 'Tim'), Second-in-Command of the Royal Guard when Damien is crowned, marries Secret Cadre member Aryllis after Damien is crowned, has son Enrico (a.k.a. Rico)
  » **Original Guards**
    * **Champion: <u>Sir Jason Solway</u>** (mother is Countess Alexa Solway), a close advisor of King Damien's.
    * **Captain and Knight Commander of the Royal Guard: <u>Sir Adam Loveress</u>**
    * <u>**Sir Timothy Ancellius**</u>
    * Sir Leverett Childress (a.k.a. 'Lev'), marries Secret Cadre member Terellie
    * Sir Otto
    * Sir Randolph
    * (plus seven others not named)
- **Newer Guards members** (five years into Damien's reign)
    * <u>**Sir Timothy Ancellius,**</u> **(Captain and Knight-Commander)**
    * <u>Sir Marcus</u> (Second-in-Command)
    * Sir Mikal 'Mik'
    * <u>Sir Rodney</u>
    * Sir Everett Ladler
    * Sir Drake Milbourne
    * <u>Sir Angelos Eldridge</u>
    * (and five others not named)

- **The Secret Cadre of Royal Guards**
  » **Original twelve King's Ladies:** the Secret Cadre of Royal

Guards (all but Lena and Ciriis marry one of Damien's
original Royal Guards following his coronation)

* Ciriis Celavell: Mistress of Protocol and Spymistress,
    Commander of the Secret Cadre under Adam Loveress,
    later King's Advisor and then Assistant to Duke Aldred

* Lena Devergnon: Poisoner/anti-poisoner,
    later Assistant Royal Librarian

* **Aryllis (Ieldore) Ancellius**: marries Royal Guardsman
    Tim Ancellius; mother of Enrico Ancellius (a.k.a. Rico);
    becomes Mistress of Protocol and Spymistress and
    commander of the Secret Cadre under Adam Loveress

* Felena

* Terellie: marries Royal Guardsman Leverett Childress

* Sasha

* Elsa

* Emerie

* Thielda

* Nalda

* Kamauri

* Licia

* Mirabelle

» **Newer Secret Cadre** (five years into Damien's reign)

* **Lady Alanna**

* Lady Lisa

* Lord Aaron

* Lord Devin

* Master Xavier

- **Castle Alsterling Personnel**
  - » <u>Elista</u>, senior maid, later Chatelaine. Began work the day *Prince Eric* and *Lady Miria* were killed, fed Damien until *Lady Theresa* discovered her. Widow of Robert, Captain of the Castle Guard during the Usurpation of Harald Elsevier; mother of three.
  - » *Captain Robert* of the Castle Guard, married to Elista, died during the Usurpation of Harald Elsevier
  - » Maree, knife sharpener for the kitchen, had a huge infatuation with Damien

Provinces of Ilseador
in order of precedence and relevant ruling family members

- *Emeralsee,* duchy – Alsterling family, gold and turquoise (guards wear dark blue and black)
  - <u>Duke Jason (Solway) Alsterling,</u> Crown Prince of the Realm
  - <u>Duke-Consort Adam (Loveress) Alsterling,</u> husband of Jason
  - <u>Damien Alsterling</u> former duke
  - <u>Genevieve (Stellarine) Alsterling,</u> wife of Damien
  - *<u>Ghost of Queen Marian Alsterling</u>*, great-grandmother of Damien and Genevieve and great-great-grandmother of Jason
  - *Dead-and-gone:*
    - *Prince Anthony Alsterling,* eldest child of Queen Marian
    - *King Reginald Alsterling,* eldest child of Prince Anthony (see 'King Damien Alsterling' at top for details of *King Reginald's* offspring)
    - *Other siblings of King Reginald* (and their families and Alsterling cousins)
    - *Other siblings and half-siblings of Prince Anthony*
    - *Princess Alexandria Alsterling,* youngest child of *Queen Marian* (fled Emeralsee with the Monarch's Blade shortly before *Queen Marian* was assassinated by Prince Reginald; played the role of 'Erawan the Kind Robber' while hiding out in the mountains of Elaarwen)
    - *Grand Duchess Alicia Alsterling,* only child of *Princess Alexandria;* married *Siegfrid Stellarine,* Heir to the Province of Elaarwen, had one child, Aldred Stellarine

- **Others of note within Emeralsee** (also see under 'King Damien Alsterling' at top)
  - <u>Captain Seldebard</u>, Commander of the City Guard

- *Fiefs within Emeralsee*
  - *Seasbourne,* county – family Laidly
    - *Cedarwen, barony* – Anvliyar family
      - » Baron Raphael Anvliyar (intended husband of King Damien's sister, Princess Kandra)
        - * *Dowager Baroness Theresa Anvliyar,* mother of Baron Raphael, former Royal Librarian and guardian of King Damien as a child after his parents were slain; died a traitor's death for having conspired to betray *Crown Prince Eric, Lady Miria,* and *Princess Kandra,* as well as for Conspiracy Against the Crown due to her role during the Usurpation of *Harald Elsevier*
    - *Elderwyld,* barony – Eldridge family
      (Note: names in the Eldridge family aside from *Miria, Alexa,* Angelos, Eugenio, and Evan have not been given in the story yet; they are included here to make the family connections clear)
      - » Baron Eugenio Eldridge
        - * Sir Angelos Eldridge, one of Baron Eugenio's sons
        - * *Previous Baron Eldridge,* grandfather of the current Baron (Eugenio), father of *Baroness Dara* and *David*
        - * *Baroness Dara Eldridge,* mother of Baron Eugenio and Evan; her second husband was Crown Prince Robert Alsterling
        - * *David Eldridge,* Lord of Ravenscroft (gifted to *Prince Eric* and *Lady Miria* and deeded to her parents), younger son of the *former Baron,* a failed squire, husband of Alexa, father of seven (*Lady Miria* was his eldest)
        - * *Alexa Eldridge, David's* wife; a blacksmith's daughter, mother of seven
        - * *Lady Miria (Eldridge) Alsterling,* Damien's mother, eldest child of *David* and *Alexa Eldridge*
        - * Evan Eldridge Alsterling, a cousin of Lady Miria's, son of Baroness Dara Eldridge and Crown Prince Robert Alsterling, half-brother of Baron Eugenio, sire of Crown Prince Jason Solway Alsterling

- **Lynncrag,** baronetcy – Loveress family
  - » **Baronetta Linda Loveress**
    - * **Lord George Loveress,** husband of Baronetta Linda
    - * Their children (ages given for the 5th
      year of King Damien's reign)
      - ◊ <u>**Sir Adam Loveress**</u> – 34yo, Captain of the Royal Guard
      - ◊ Charles (a.k.a. 'Charley') Loveress
        – 32yo – a forest ranger
      - ◊ Lorenzo (a.k.a. 'Lorry') Loveress – 30yo
        – married and divorced twice
      - ◊ **Desirée Loveress** – 28yo
      - ◊ Desirée's 2 little boys (8yo and 10y o)
      - ◊ Fontaine Loveress – 24yo – priestess
        novitiate (but left before final vows)
      - ◊ Martin Loveress – 20yo - healer
      - ◊ <u>**Marianna Loveress**</u> – 18yo – lady-
        in-waiting (Secret Cadre)
- *Elmirscroft,* property
- *Ravenscroft,* property
  - » *David Eldridge,* grandfather of King Damien
    - * *Alexa Eldridge,* grandmother of King
      Damien, wife of David

- *Elaarwen,* duchy – Stellarine family, violet and silver
  - <u>Duchess Genevieve (Stellarine) Alsterling</u>
    - <u>**Duke-Consort Damien Alsterling,**</u> husband of Genevieve
    - **Lord Aldred Stellarine,** widowed husband of Duchess-
      Consort *Giendra (Topasirre) Stellarine,* father of
      Duchess Genevieve, only child of Duke Siegfrid
      Stellarine and *Grand Duchess Alicia Alsterling*
    - **Ciriis Cellavel,** Lord Aldred's lover and
      nurse and mother of his child
    - *Duke Siegfrid Stellarine,* father of Duke Aldred, husband of
      Grand Duchess Alicia Alsterling, son of Duke Emmeren
    - *Grand Duchess Alicia Alsterling,* wife of Duke
      Siegfrid Stellarine, mother of Duke Aldred
    - *Duke Emmeren Stellarine,* father of *Duke Siegfrid*
    - *Duchess Shalla (Elemandros) Stelarine,* wife of Duke Emmeren,
      mother of Duke Siegfrid

    - **Others of note in the duchy:**
      - » Lord Adsel Topasirre, Chatelaine and Regent of Elaarwen,
        from Genevieve's mother's family

- *Fiefs within Elaarwen*
  - *Brindlewell,* county – Solway family
    - » Countess Alexa Solway, mother of Megan
      (banished from Court for life)
      - * <u>Lady Megan Solway</u>, only child of Countess
        Alexa, wife of David, currently a prisoner of
        Evan Eldridge Alsterling the Pirate-King
      - ◊ <u>Lord David Solway</u> (a.k.a. Captain Daffyd
        Metreedi), husband of Lady Megan
      - * their children (ages given for the 5th
        year of King Damien's reign)
        - ◊ <u>Elaina Solway</u> – 22yo– lady-in-waiting (Secret Cadre)
        - ◊ *Rudolph Solway* (deceased)(would have been 19yo)
        - ◊ <u>Roger Solway</u> – 13yo
        - ◊ <u>Esmerelda Solway</u> – 11yo
      - * <u>Sir Jason Solway</u>, eldest child of Lady Megan with
        Grand Duke/Pirate-King Evan Eldridge Alsterling
  - *Cloudcroft,* property – Stellarine family
    - » Lord Aldred Stellarine
      - * Lady Ciriis Celavell, Aldred's mistress and the mother of
        his child

- *Siovale,* duchy – Elsevier family, forest green and silver
  (guards wear dark green and black)
  - <u>Duke Tomas Elsevier</u>
    - » <u>Duchess-Consort Sildra (Miramar) Elsevier</u>
    - » Their six children (ages given for the 5th year
      of Damien's reign, not all of their names
      have been given in the story as of yet)
      - * <u>Mark Elsevier </u> - 20yo
      - * **Arabella Elsevier** – 17yo
      - * Lorinda – 14yo
      - * Denis Elsevier – 12yo
      - * Gemma Elsevier – 10yo
      - * Gary Elsevier – 7yo

> » *Duke Hector Elsevier,* father of Tomas, husband of *Lydia*
> » *Dowager Duchess-Consort Lydia Elsevier,* mother of *Harald* and Tomas, died a traitor's death for Conspiracy Against the Crown for her role in the Usurpation by her son *Harald*
> » *Harald Elsevier,* cuckoo's child of *Duchess Lydia* by *King Reginald,* died a traitor's death for Usurping the Throne after Damien was crowned... Genevieve Stellarine Alsterling's first husband

- *Reyensweir,* duchy – family Mirion
  - Duke Quillian Mirion

- *Fiefs within Reyensweir*
  - *Zialest,* county – Teraseel family (adjacent to Dalizell, across some challenging mountain passes from Elaarwen; HOWEVER see also DALZIALEST below)
    - » Countess Rosa Teraseel
      - * *Gavin Teraseel,* Rosa's brother; he was to marry Ciriis Celavell

- *Embervest* duchy – family Eledor
  - **Duchess Tariana Eledor**
    - *Duke Istvan Eledor,* father of Tariana
    - Lord Robard Eledor, Tariana's older brother

- *Fiefs within Embervest* The Lost Provinces of Minglemere (returned) and Everfields (still Lost to Vindalia) are part of Embervest
  - *Minglemere,* barony – family Krakenroost
    - » Lost to Vindalia some seventeen years before King Damien was Crowned
    - » Regained in the 4th year of King Damien's reign
  - *Everfields*
    - » Lost to Vindalia some fifty years before King Damien was crowned

- *Alpinsward*, duchy – family Marseill
  - The last of the Lost Provinces to defect (in their case to Mercasia after *Crown Prince Robert Alsterling's* negotiations failed following his murder by 'bandits')
  - The first of the Lost Provinces to return, following King Damien's coronation and negotiations with Queen Genevieve
  - Duchess Laura Marseill

  - *Fiefs within Alpinsward*
    - *Dalizell*, county – Miramar family; HOWEVER see also DALZIALEST below
      - » **Count Zachary Miramar**
        - * Sildra (Miramar) Elsevier, Zachary's next elder sister, was already married to Tomas Elsevier when *parents* and *Elsa* died
        - * Zachary's *parents* (died of flux)
        - * *Elsa,* eldest child and former Heir to Dallizell; Zachary and Sildra's older sister; died of the same flux as their parents

- *Dalzialest*, duchy,
  combined of Dalizell and Zialest when Rosa Teraseel and Zachary Miramar married just after King Damien's coronation – the Miramar family was granted the promotion to a Duchy in recognition of their loyalty to the new king (the counties had been asking for royal permission to merge for several generations)
  - Duchess Rosa (Teraseel) Miramar
  - **Duke Zachary Miramar**
    - 2 children in the 5th year of King Damien's reign
      - * Talia Miramar (a.k.a Tally), 3yo
      - * Betha Miramar, newborn

- The Lost Provinces
  1. Alpinsward, duchy – family Marseill
     Duchess Laura Marseill
     - Lost to Mercasia some five years before King Damien was crowned
     - Regained in the 3rd year of King Damien's reign
  2. Minglemere, barony – family Krakenroost
     Baron Densal
     - Returned to Duchy Embervest
     - Lost to Vindalia some seventeen years before King Damien was Crowned
     - Regained in the 4th year of King Damien's reign
  3. Elendria, county – formerly part of Duchy Alpinsward
     Countess Miraly
     - Lost to Deltheran some twenty-five years before King Damien was crowned
     - negotiations begun to Restore Elendria to Ilseador in the 5th year of King Damien's reign
  4. Farivera – formerly part of Duchy Siovale
     - Lost to… Sindalla? Some forty years before King Damien was crowned
  5. Everfields – formerly part of Duchy Embervest
     - Lost to Vindalia some fifty years before King Damien was crowned

- Others of Note
  - <u>**Azella the Unpitying**</u> (a.k.a. the White Witch of Farivera)
    - Her minions
      » <u>**Jeremy**</u> (a.k.a. Mikhail, Jerry, Jemmy, Dandelion)
      » <u>**Denisa**</u>

- Queen Estelle of Deltheren

- Evan Eldridge Alsterling, Pirate-King, Captain of the Red Sails, Scourge of the Merutian Sea (Ex-lover of Megan Solway, sire of Jason Solway Alsterling, son of Crown Prince Robert Alsterling and Baroness Dara Eldridge of Eldyrwyld)

MAPS

Ilseador

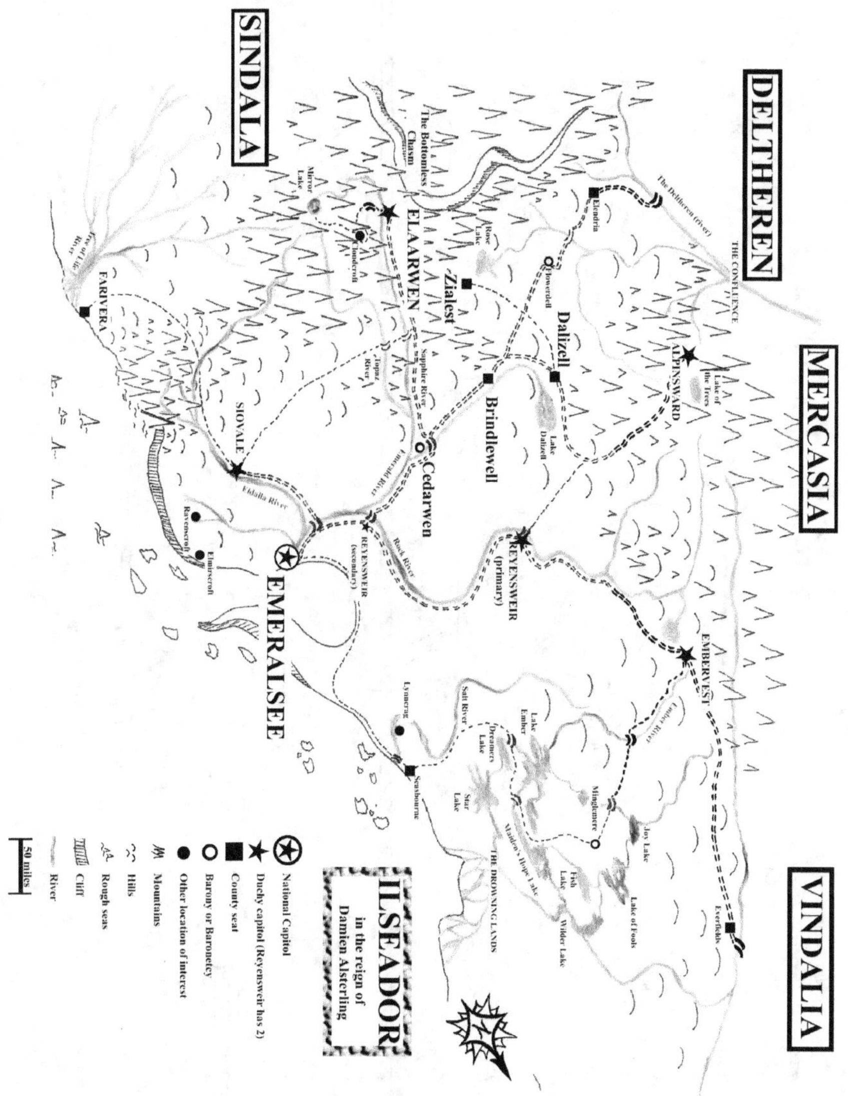

Mangala McNamara

LANDS Around the MERUTIAN SEA

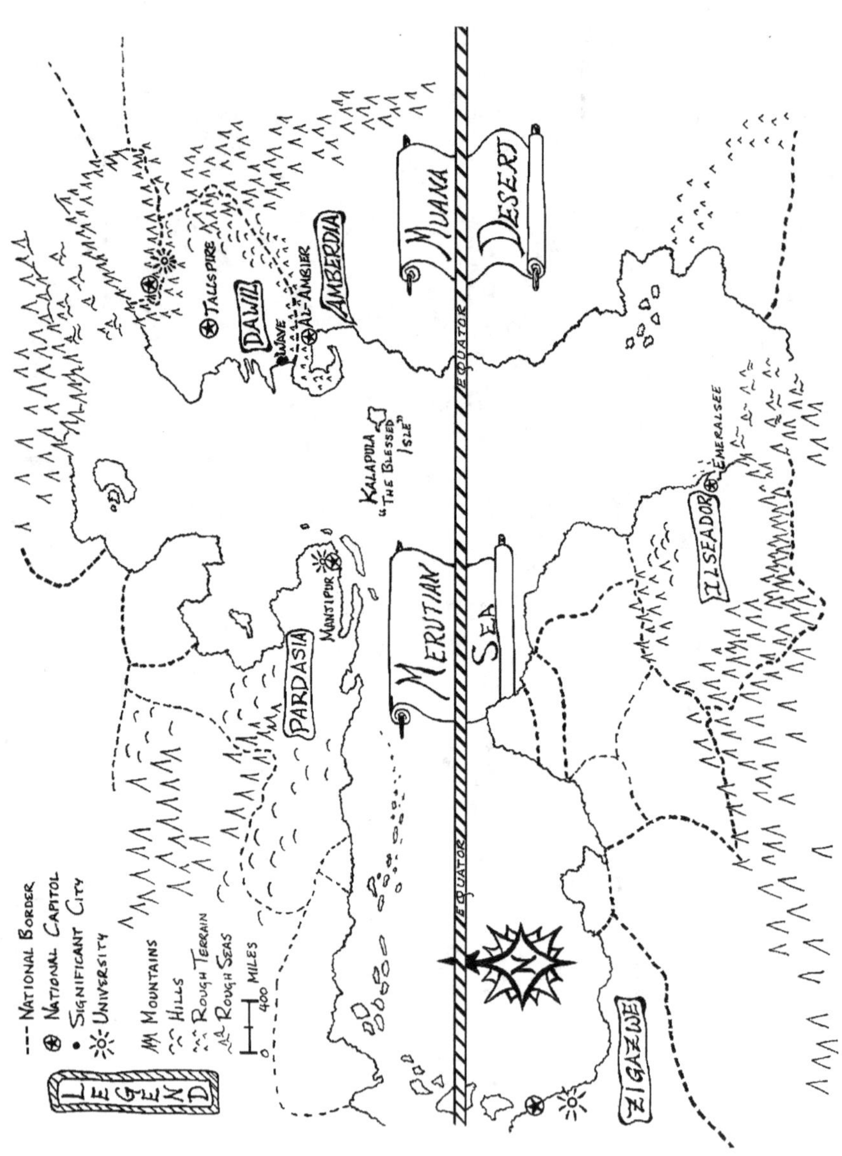

The REBEL
DUCHESS
Book One of the
Chronicles of Ilseador
KERRIDWEN MANGALA McNAMARA

224

Chapter ONE

Caught!

GENEVIEVE HAD NOT FORGOTTEN THE old king's pet sorcerer. She *had*, however, assumed he would not be a problem. This was clearly not the case.

She ducked into a rubbish-strewn alley and prayed that one of the doors leading off of it would open to somewhere that was not a dead-end. Unlike the alleyway itself. Genevieve really wasn't familiar enough with the layout of the capitol to be doing this sort of thing. As her advisors had repeatedly told her. Her chagrined memory replayed the scene of her tossing her head as she assured them that "the Rebel Duchess" could handle anything.

Not that she had *planned* to have to handle anything at all. She was just going to come in as part of the crowds hoping to get a glimpse of the new young king, on this last day of the coronation festivities. Just another gawker from the countryside. She still had no idea how Lord Prydeen had identified her.

The second door on the right opened at her frantic tug, and Genevieve hurried into darkness, pulling the door tightly shut behind her. She could hear people talking somewhere off to her right and the darkness seemed a little less dark in that direction. Perhaps there was a way through the building and back to the main street she had veered off of so abruptly. She needed to get back to the streets to complete her mission. The inhabitants of the room ahead would be startled, but if she could get past them quickly – before they decided to hold her for a thief – she might make it.

Just as the young woman started towards the sounds, the door behind her crashed open and the sorcerer stepped through.

Lord Prydeen was a master of dramatic effect, some odd corner of her mind noted absently. He stood framed in the doorway, too deeply cowled to see his face, his ankle-length black cloak flapping and curling about him in the sudden cross-currents of air between building and outside. The alley was brighter than the room – so perhaps he merely paused to let his eyes adjust – but in that moment he was more silhouette than shape, more demon than man.

Genevieve could not – *could not* – lead him towards those unsuspecting innocents in the room beyond. Perhaps the completely unexpected would gain her – well, *something*.

She took a deep breath, but carefully did not think too hard about what she was doing – though whether it was because Lord Prydeen was rumored to be able to pull one's thoughts from the air itself or because she wouldn't have the nerve if she did–

She spun on her heel and charged directly at the sorcerer, startling him sufficiently that she shoved past him and back out into the dead-end alley. Then to her left and back out to the main street – perhaps she could lose him in the crowd. She had to try.

In her haste, however, Genevieve's own hood was pushed back, exposing her signature red-gold hair – and confirming what had surely only been Lord Prydeen's guess about the identity of his quarry.

Fool that she was for not having dyed it.

Thrice a fool for deciding to skulk about the coronation festivities – like any small child playing "Erawan the Kind Robber" – instead of listening to the reports of her spies as the mature, careful, strategic leader of the rebellion should do. That stupid, romantic title – "Rebel Duchess" – really *had* gone to her head, as Rosa had accused her. She would do the Cause no good by being taken by the king's sorcerer. Even if the new young King Damien lived up to his month-old reputation for fairness, Lord Prydeen would never give her a chance to find out.

No time for this.

Genevieve jerked her hood back up and tried to blend into the crowded market square, trying to outguess Lord Prydeen. Which direction would the sorcerer be unlikely to go? – or which way would he be unlikely to follow? Surely the feared and hated Royal Sorcerer could not make his way through the crowd without causing an uproar that would let her dodge away... though he had before, when she first caught him following her. Could there be *any* safety for her here in the capitol, just six days after Damien's crowning? Surely the old guard was still in place and *no one* (not even the young king?) would dare to gainsay Lord Prydeen.

Abruptly, and entirely on instinct, not daring to look back to measure her pursuit, Genevieve swerved and tore for the royal viewing stand. Damien, if the stories were right – the stories that she had not believed and had come in person to verify – would merely have her executed for a traitor. Lord Prydeen – as she had reason to know – would sell her soul to demons and wring every last memory and secret from her shrieking heart.

The fine bright day taunted her travails, small poofy clouds ambling across a sky as blue as her own eyes. The market square – packed with a crowd of pleasantly frolicking merchants and peasants – impeded her swift progress. The swarms of children playing games of tag nearly tripped her up. The very *joy* of it all nearly derailed her thoughts, for such gaiety could never have been shown in the old king's rule, and part of her could not leave off trying to determine if there was still the undercurrent of desperation that she expected from her previous, and more successfully clandestine, visits to the capitol city.

But the Rebel Duchess knew exactly where the royal platform stood, both due to having marked it well when first she arrived and for the fact that it stood as tall any of the half-timbered two-story buildings surrounding the square. She had hoped to catch a glimpse of the young king from afar when first she arrived, and the royal platform had seemed like the right place to start. She had perhaps stayed still too long, staring too intently at the brilliantly bunting- and flower-clad structure, trying to discern which, if any, of the milling nobles on its three ornately decorated levels was the young king. Then, as now, the top level was empty, save for a matched pair of guards.

Part of her – the part that had insisted on this mad mission against all rational thought and advice – was certain that, if she could but look into his eyes, she would know if Damien was all that the reports claimed... or if he had been corrupted by his grandfather and Lord Prydeen.

Part of her – if she dared admit it – wanted to believe, even if it seemed beyond belief, that he could have been untouched. That the Cause was won, the need for a Rebel Duchess was done. That the Rebellion could quietly fold itself up and her folk could slip back to their homes, to their lives... though perhaps not the Rebel Duchess herself, recognizable as she was as a symbol...

Yet – how could those two old, evil men *not* have insured that the crown prince was a "fit successor" to the king who had controlled a creature such as Lord Prydeen?

Genevieve had met the prince once, when they were both children. He had barely been of an age for his first pony, and she – a few years older – had just graduated to a mild-mannered horse... and her father's half-tamed, firebreathing mare that Duke Aldred had no idea she would even attempt to ride. Her father had brought her to Court to make her curtsy to the old king and see her named his Heir. Damien had been but one of a pack of the old king's grandchildren – a nondescript royal child, good-looking as they all had been, but special in no particular way. They had spent perhaps minutes in each other's presence, on separate ends of the audience hall that had seemed miles-long to her then.

Now those other siblings and cousins, aunts and uncles, were all gone and Damien – unremarked offspring of an unremarkable parent – had been named Crown Prince, and now King. For him to have inherited would seem to signal that he had done something to earn the old king's approval – perhaps by being ruthless enough to have ensured no other contenders were available. Certainly, he had made no mark by protesting his grandfather's policies while the old king lived, no mark of any kind, in fact. Despite all the time Genevieve had spent at Court, she did not recall ever noticing him again.

Yet she could still remember a certain clear-eyed gaze from that long-ago child. A gaze that seemed to recognize and promise to right all the wrongs that existed in the world. A gaze that had haunted her dreams since she had heard he had been crowned, and had kept her skepticism from becoming outright denial when rumors of the new king's beneficence came to her. And so, she had come to see for herself...

She had reached the royal platform at last, and hunted for a spot to clamber up. Not an easy endeavor, as it was so heavily be-ribboned – in every color, not merely royal gold and turquoise – with bright buntings stretched between triple rosettes made of actual rose petals. An elegantly illuminated sign noted that these were the coronation gifts of the Weavers' and Florists' Guilds – but the small barrel that the sign rested upon was of more interest to her, as it gave her a leg up to the first level, which was filled with younger noblemen. These young men were here to satisfy fathers and mothers who wanted them close to the source of power. They eyed her with interest – her cloak had of necessity been pushed aside to climb and she was dressed in hunting leathers fit tight to her athletic frame – and she in turn ignored them, using the spigoted ale kegs at which they were amusing themselves to give her a step up to the recessed second level.

The older noblemen and -women – and their maiden daughters – on this level looked at her quite askance. Genevieve hoped her hood shadowed her face enough to keep any of them from recognizing her, for she knew no few of them, though she did not recognize the barely-grown girls, nor more than a handful of the hardly-older lads below. These nobles had toadied up to the old king while Genevieve – and her father before her – had sought to protect their people. She knew all too well that they would as soon sell her out to Lord Prydeen as look at her. Even now they were trying to toady up to King Damien, bringing their marriageable daughters to parade before him – an array of maidens scarcely past puberty, for their elder ones had been taken to serve the old king and Lord Prydeen in years gone by, many never to be seen again. They, too, must surely be hoping for better from Damien, yet she saw nothing but avarice in the faces of even the children.

A good-looking young man – unusual only for being the only *young* man on this level of the platform, did someone think the new king's taste ran to boys? – with very dark hair and clear grey eyes offered her a hand onto the level. Genevieve was not too proud to accept help, even from a scion of one of *these* families. They exchanged a startled look and nearly let go of each other as an electric spark seemed to jump between their hands. Surely it wasn't dry enough today for such things, and so close to the harbor besides.

Putting such irrelevant details aside, Genevieve brushed off her hands on her breeches as she looked up towards the highest level of the reviewing stand, but saw only the pair of Royal Guards – two blondely handsome men so perfectly matched as almost to be twins – decorating that august space. Knights chosen for their beauty, just as were the horses that pulled the royal carriage. She wondered who they were – might they have enough real skill at arms to have faced her in the Battle of Siovale seven years earlier? She'd caught no more than a glimpse of either of them so far, as they turned, watchfully, eyes raking the crowds. Perhaps they were more than merely decorative.

Hopefully the king himself was sitting down and merely out of view. Genevieve needed for him to be there, before Lord Prydeen caught up with her. It was a wild gambit – praise all the Gods at once that Rosa really could handle the Rebellion, since it looked like she was going to have to. Rosa – would never forgive her for getting herself captured and killed. The Rebel Countess – surely that sounded just as impressive. They had known it couldn't last – this would free Rosa to wed and produce the Heir that she needed. Genevieve's own proper title – Lady Stellarine, Duchess of Elaarwen (she dared not think "Princess of the Realm", though her bloodlines were as good as the king's) – would pass to a collateral line...

No matter. The issue at hand was to get up there to the top level and there was no obvious stair or ladder.

Genevieve dropped her useless disguise of a cloak before it could hinder her further in climbing higher, ignoring the massed gasp from the gathered nobles, and looked for a convenient way to boost herself to the king's level. The balustrade of the king's level – still festooned with those slippery buntings and banners – was more than head-high to her. It was higher than she could hoist herself on arm-strength alone.

That young man was still watching her – looking slightly amused, damn him. Or maybe that was *be*mused. Surely, he had little idea what to make of her and her sudden arrival. But he seemed to come to a decision and wrenched a ring with a large grey pearl on it off his finger, thrusting it towards her. It was the sort of thing a nobleman might offer a noblewoman to indicate interest – a sort of "let's get to know each other" offer, not quite a tryst, but more than an offer of acquaintance. The ring would have a house sigil on it, perhaps even a personal seal – enough information for her to find him again later on. A crazy thing to hand to the highly recognizable Rebel Duchess as she attempted to single-handedly besiege the new king's festival viewing platform. The young man must be completely daft.

And then he bent and cupped his hands as a stablehand might do to help someone into the saddle. The sparkle in his eyes suggested he was prepared to toss her high enough to pull herself up over that balustrade.

Again, the gathered nobles gasped, but this time there were also mutters and a fearful eagerness... and she guessed someone had spotted Lord Prydeen approaching.

There was no time for this. Genevieve stuffed the ring onto her finger – her beltpouch would take too long to open – put her foot in his hands and leapt up in concert with his toss.

And got the – third? fourth? – shock of the day as her reaching hands were grasped from above and an all too familiar voice gruffly said "Young miss, this is the king's place, you can't be climbing... up... her–" The voice cut off as and the hands fumbled and nearly dropped her back down, as their owner peered over the edge and then grabbed her more securely and helped her over the balustrade.

The Royal Guard was looking at her in exasperation and some of the same confusion Genevieve was feeling. It was the strangest and least appropriate timing on anything ever – but the touch of his hands had inflamed her with desire. *Not now, not now!* The Rebel Duchess thought frantically. She'd heard of this, but thought it a fairytale... Rosa, *Rosa* was her love...

"Jason Solway?" she managed to gasp out.

"Genny?" He was as flabbergasted as he was, and if the blush rising in those perfect cheeks was anything to judge, he was suffering from the same reaction. Suffering...

"Here now," said the other Royal Guard, coming forward from his ceremonial position. "Jase, what's this all about?"

She looked almost gratefully at the other man, just as gratefully *not* recognizing him as yet another childhood friend. But his familiar behavior towards Jason – were they lovers? Why did that thought make her heart – or something lower than her heart – do flips? And why, oh, why, *was this all happening at once?*

"Stand back, gentlemen," growled a low, cultured voice.

Lord Prydeen.

Apparently, she wouldn't have to sort any of this out after all.

The two Guards obediently stepped aside, though she rather thought that Jason only reluctantly let go of her hands, and she could see that the sorcerer had come up a set of stairs at the back of the reviewing stand. A brief surge of wind whipped the cowled hood from off Lord Prydeen's spotty, balding head, and tossed his long, drooping mustaches. He had not aged well since the old king's death; his hair had been thinning, but was still full when last she had gotten a good look at him, some months earlier, and the lines around his mouth were graven deeply, where once they had been entirely masked by his whiskers. Genevieve had heard tell that evil sorcerers cast vile spells to keep themselves young – by sacrificing true youths and maidens to demons, some said. She had scoffed, even as she wondered. The old king had lived long past his age, and Lord Prydeen, some said, had not aged at all, even as those noble daughters came to serve them both and were rarely seen again.

"Lady Genevieve." Lord Prydeen greeted her, coldly, but not correctly. He needed nothing besides himself to emphasize his authority, but he had brought a squad of his personal guards up with him. They fanned out behind him, blocking the path, even to headstrong young women who might push past a sorcerer.

She tilted her chin up – her nose was too snub to properly glare down it, but she was tall enough to try... and the arrogance might mask the tremble that the tumult in her stomach had settled into. "The proper title is *'Your Grace'*, messir." She was actually in line for the throne herself, with all of Damien's family gone, and 'Lord' Prydeen was, after all, a sorcerer of no particular breeding.

And if she told herself that a few more times, perhaps she could dare to face him.

A wintry smile passed over Lord Prydeen's lips – gone as quickly as snow in the Summer. "No longer, I fear. My former master stripped you of your titles for your treasonous activities."

Genevieve inclined her head. "So, I have heard. But even a Royal Decree does not make a thing reality. Even His – belated – Majesty never put it to the test in *Elaarwen.*"

Something sparked in the sorcerer's eyes. Anger, perhaps? Could such a one as he even feel something as tender as grief? He gestured to his men. "Bind her and bring her."

Jason bestirred himself to protest, "My lord–!" but the other Guard pulled him back and Genevieve found herself being roughly seized and turned around by hands that made no pretense of not enjoying their task. Even the king's own Royal Guards, it seemed, dared not speak against the sorcerer. Not yet anyways. If only she had waited to see if the young king could consolidate his power; if, indeed, he would continue in the way he had begun!

"My Lord Prydeen! What passes here?" The mild voice interrupted from the direction of the stairs, but was no one Genevieve recognized. She had been turned to face outwards towards the square whilst they bound her, and could not see the speaker.

Lord Prydeen's voice was a curious mix of ingratiating and dismissive. "Nothing you need trouble yourself over, my lord. Some rabble found her way up here, clearly to cause some trouble to you. It is my task and my privilege to safeguard Your Highness. We'll be away momentarily."

Gentle hands cleared away the thongs that had begun to lash her wrists. "Surely you are mistaken, my Lord Prydeen. This is no rabble, but Her Grace, the Duchess Genevieve Stellarine of Elaarwen."

"Yes, my Lord, the so-called 'Rebel Duchess'," Lord Prydeen's voice was growing impatient. "I am taking her to the castle dungeons to have out of her what she knows. You can make an example of her later on – you must not detract from your coronation festivities."

"Nonsense, Lord Prydeen," the mild voice replied. "That isn't how we treat visiting royalty... not to mention that the people would rise in protest and not even you could put them *all* down at once."

He came around to Genevieve's right side, and before she could register that this was the same young man who had cupped his hands for her boot like any stableboy, he gave her that same enigmatic smile, and faced the crowd – who had begun to turn as they saw their king. Damien lifted Genevieve's right hand in his left, holding them high above their heads and called out, "I give you Genevieve Stellarine, the Rebel Duchess!"

It was the sort of moment a Duke's Heir is trained for and – bemused as she was at the turn of events – Genevieve flattened her palm against the king's and stood tall before the crowds, the errant breeze tossing her red-gold curls like a mane. She smiled fiercely, trying to think if this would be taken as some sort of inadvertent admission of surrender.

Even as the people roared their approval – and Lord Prydeen fumed behind them – a sudden, strange crackling noise erupted and ribbons of white fire fountained up between their pressed fingers. It wreathed down to wrap their hands and curl around their arms.

For all that she was the reigning duchess of a province, the leader of a rebellion against an unjust king and an evil sorcerer, and had spent most of her life in that struggle... Genevieve was tempted to faint right then and there. This was absolutely the *last* thing she had expected. If she hadn't seen this happen before, she would have thought it was some new and clever attack by Lord Prydeen.

But she *had* seen this before. And, likely, so had every member of the crowd below.

At least young King Damien looked nearly as befuddled as she felt.

He, however, recovered more quickly than she.

"And your future Queen!" he announced in what sounded like a calm voice.

He pulled her in and kissed her.

And the crowds went absolutely wild.

Read the rest of this exciting story of rebellion and romance!
The Rebel Duchess
now at your favorite online ebookseller in print or ebook!

Also by Mangala McNamara

<u>The Chronicles of Ilseador</u>
    The Rebel Duchess: Book One

    The Prydeen Prophecy Cycle:
        The King's Champion: Book Two
        The Pirate-King: Book Three
        The Pale Sorceress: Book Four
        The UnCaptive King: Book Five

<u>The Prankster Prince</u>
    Thony and the Much-Anticipated Adventure

    The Raven War Saga (3 books)
        Thony Goes Astray! (in the Deep, Dark, and Dangerous Fairy Wood): Book Two
        So You Want to Be a Hero? Book Three
        How Thony Stopped a War (and Fixed a Friendship): Book Four

    The Pathremiri Problem
        Diary of a ~~Runaway Prince~~ Bold Questing Hero: Book Five

<u>Knightess of the Realm</u>
    A Not-So-Sacrificial Maiden

    Out of the Woods… Hopefully (a Prequel Novella)

    Turns of a Page (A Prequel Story Collection)

    The Heir's Journey mini-series (3 books)
        A Not-So-Simple Mission: Book One
        An Entirely-Unexpected Revelation: Book Two
        An All-Too-Surprising Homecoming: Book Three

    The Secrets of Dragon Mountain
        An Altogether-Curious Altercations: Book One

And more to come...

Author's Note

Hello dear Reader!
This may sound a little strange, but I have been looking forwards to writing this Author's Note for a really long time.

In a previous book in this series, I pointed out some connections with *L'Mort d'Artur* and Damien's story. I guess you could say that we finally met Morgan le Fay in the person of Azella the Unpitying. And I guess this would make Queen Marian the Lady of the Lake.

As I said before, none of this was 'planned' and 'plotted.' That's not really how I work. I feel like the stories I write are a Gift given to me – and since the *Chronicles of Ilseador* started with a recurring dream of Genevieve's escape from Lord Prydeen and first meeting with Damien (and, ah, renewed acquaintance with Jason), I really can't explain it any other way. While I read the occasional bit of Arthurian fantasy (who doesn't) it had been years since the last time I'd even thought about any of it!

In this book, however, some new things began to wriggle out of… somewhere.

I'm an Indian-American and raised Hindu with a great deal of exposure to other religions and the myths and legends of many cultures. (Thank you to my mom and dad for that!)

Damien and Adam's fascination with 'Pardasian philosophy' was another Gift. It certainly wasn't any plan of mine to sneak a bit of the Gita or the Buddhist Eight-fold Path into my rather-Northern-European flavored fantasy novel! But that's what the two of them wanted to do.

Arjuna, the Pandava king who was the greatest archer ever born, has always been one of my heroes. And Lord Krishna's lecture to him on duty (dharma) is one of the cornerstones of Hinduism. The version that I based Adam's lecture to Damien on is from *Amar Chitra Katha Vol. 505 The Gita*.

(If you aren't familiar with Indian myths, legends, and history in general, the Amar Chitra Katha series is a great place to start – each thin book is comic book style and a great starting point. I've been reading them since I learned to read – and exploring deeper when I needed to. Search on the company's name and then browse their collection – and I'll put a link on my webpage for this book.)

And using the Eight-fold Path to test the moral fiber of a nascent/recovering Evil Wizard was a bit of a stretch. The Eight-fold Path is a prescription for a good/worthwhile life, not a judgmental tool. But this was Damien's idea, and I can't really disagree with how he made it work. We all have to understand a thing before we can see where it can take us. Unfortunately, I didn't keep a copy of where I referenced the Eight-fold Path from… but it's not hard to find for yourself with a quick online search.

Not that Ilseador – or Dawil for that matter – are Northern European. You may have noticed that the World of the Living Gods (which is a fairly lame name, but I'm trying to figure out what it should be… finding the names of Ilseador and Emeralsee took me over a year after I started writing the stories…) has a number of cultures with different 'flavors' showing up. And if you've been following the *Prankster Prince* series, you'll be aware of a few more… and that Thony's world has its own mix.

The *Prankster Prince* series is delving into the question of why a little more, though there will be a fair bit of that showing up in the *Knightess of the Real*m books as we continue as well. And… eventually there will be some books about the origins of the whole thing. (Which aren't written yet – and I only have the edges of the explanation, so it'll be awhile.) The Ilseador books aren't really going that route, though when Damien eventually meets Karana that may change…

Oh, hmmn.

Yes.

Eventually.

Though she isn't even going to be born for some twenty more years, from Damien's perspective. So, it'll be awhile.

In the meantime, we have a LOT of stories.

A *Knightess* Prequel (3yo Karana is pretty cute) in December 2024, will be named *Scaredy Cat,* and will explore the challenges a parent faces when they're scared or unwilling to really let themselves fall for their child.

Then you get a regular *Knightess* novel (the next one in the *Secrets of Dragon Mountain* series), *An All-Too-Obvious Choice,* in January 2025. This is where you actually get to meet those dragons that kidnapped Karana and her Companions/betrotheds.

And then another *Prankster Prince* tale – *A Court of Mists and Misadventures* – where Thony gets in trouble for something that isn't really even his fault… while he rescues a handsome prince and… hmmmn. Wasn't it supposed to be a princess he was looking for?

And we lead it out with a contemporary romance story of mine *(Jack of Spades)* in a charity anthology that comes out the day after this book! (All proceeds from *Double Down on Love* will be go to the Pancreatic Cancer Network. The book will be available in eBook form on KU for a year, and also in print.)

But if it's more Ilseador you're waiting on…

Coming up next for Damien will be a little in-fill. The Heart of Ilseador – out in February – will cover some of the span of time that was sort of skipped over between the execution of Duchess Sildra and the birth of Princess Marli. Let's just say that Damien is still trying to stuff his life back into a more conventional box… and neither the Realm nor Adam is inclined to let him.

You can find info about any of my books at my website https://www.RisingDragonBooks.com

Please pre-order Heart as an eBook directly, using this link: https://books2read.com/Heart-Chronicles-of-Ilseador

Or this one: https://www.amazon.com/dp/B0DNNM7L35

After that… well, there is still Elendria and the sly Queen Estelle of Deltheran to be dealt with. And Damien is going to discover that Queen Marian isn't the only ghost he can see.

And we haven't heard the last of Azella the Unpitying, either.

Happy Holidays!

Mangala McNamara

About the Author

Mangala McNamara lives in Flyover Country (the far northern end of the US South) with her husband, The Professor, and four of her six children. The remaining children are in college – you can blame the oldest for the excessive amounts of math showing up in Mangala's fantasy novels, the second one for better attention to staging of scenes, the third for all the economics, and the fourth for great attention to history – and all of them for a focus on political science! Mangala is a former professional bellydance instructor, and used to enjoy knitting, crotchet and embroidering Temari balls but now is much more boring as she rarely does anything but write… although she also fences (the sport) and plays D&D with her kids. She owes her love of books and reading to her mother, who was a professional folklorist and could recite – from memory – stories from every nation in the United Nations.

Her Knightess of the Realm and Prankster Prince series occur in the same world as Damien and Genevieve's stories.

Learn about Mangala's upcoming projects (fiction and nonfiction both) and sign up for email updates at
https://www.RisingDragonBooks.com

More Fantasy coming soon...

Scaredy Cat:
  A Knightess of the Realm Holiday Prequel Novella
  (available December 2024)

An All-Too-Obvious Choice:
  Book TWO of the SECRET OF DRAGON MOUNTAIN
  (A Knightess of the Realm Novel)
  (available January 2025)

The Heart of Ilseador:
  A Chronicles of Ilseador Novel
  (available February 2025)

A Court of Mists and Misadventures
Book Six of the Prankster Prince
(available March 2024)

Visit https://www.RisingDragonBooks.com for more
upcoming books, maps, lore, art, and more!

9 781960 160652